THE GHOST

Highland Heroes
Book Six

by Maeve Greyson

ARE YOU SIGNED UP FOR DRAGONBLADE'S BLOG?

You'll get the latest news and information on exclusive giveaways, exclusive excerpts, coming releases, sales, free books, cover reveals and more.

Check out our complete list of authors, too!

No spam, no junk. That's a promise!

Sign Up Here

www.dragonbladepublishing.com

Dearest Reader;

Thank you for your support of a small press. At Dragonblade Publishing, we strive to bring you the highest quality Historical Romance from the some of the best authors in the business. Without your support, there is no 'us', so we sincerely hope you adore these stories and find some new favorite authors along the way.
Happy Reading!

CEO, Dragonblade Publishing

Additional Dragonblade books by Author Maeve Greyson

Highland Heroes Series
The Guardian
The Warrior
The Judge
The Dreamer
The Bard
The Ghost

CHAPTER ONE

Northeastern Scotland
July 1705

“I DINNA LIKE it either, ye ken? I know I said it before, but it bears sayin’ again. When Mama says go, I must go. And might be, she’s even right this time. Usually is. Besides, I didna see ye stepping forward to tell her nay.”

Magnus de Gray cut a dark look over at the entirely too talkative fifteen-year-old. Ever since leaving *Tor Ruadh*, he had managed civil responses to the youngling’s endless chatter. He had been curt with the boy but civil.

But Hell’s fire and all its demons, the days had been long. This leg of the journey should have been quiet. Time to reflect on what lay ahead. As it was, the only silence to be had was when the lad slept. It ended today. Magnus had tolerated all he could stand. "Evander! Shut it, aye?"

Evander Cameron, the eldest of Ian Cameron's adopted sons, shrugged away the scolding, then urged his horse into the lead. He obviously didn't care about the seriousness of this trip, nor the obvious insult his mother, Gretna, had dealt to them both before they left the keep. The woman had shamed them in front of half the clan, swearing the two of them needed a lesson in the proper treatment of females and that perhaps working together to find Magnus's newly discovered illegitimate son might teach them how actions always had consequences. How dare she say such a thing. In front of the clan, too. And damn if Alexander, the chieftain, hadn't agreed!

His guilt about the situation already weighed heavier than his enormous warhorse. Remorse for leaving the Lady Bree Maxwell alone and pregnant pricked his conscience just as great as if he had knowingly deserted the woman, which he hadn't. Or at least, he hadn't *meant* to leave her in such a state. She hadn't told him she carried his child.

And how had she gotten with the babe so easily? 'Twas but a single encounter. He had known at the time it was a foolhardy move, but the lovely lass had made it impossible to refuse. Her father's edict for her to marry a cruel man forced her to seek release from the betrothal in the most defiant way she knew. If she couldn't marry for love, she would at least lose her virginity to friendship. Lady Bree had hoped her deflowered state would free her from the despicable union, even if it meant imprisonment in a nunnery. She had been so desperate—and oh, so enticing. Especially after she plied him with her father's best whisky, and when he told her he didn't love her, she had laughed! Said it didn't matter. And now, even without that fickle emotion, look where his actions had landed him.

"Ye ken this wouldha been much easier if they had put where they were in that letter," Evander called back over his shoulder.

"The thing was faded, torn, and looked to have taken a good soaking. Some of the script washed away." Magnus still couldn't believe the missive had survived over five years before it found him.

"What was their clan's name again?" Evander asked. "Should we not have seen their keep by now? There's a village up ahead. See the white of the buildings against the blue of the sea? Is that not *Inbhir Theòrsa*? Ye said *Inbhir Theòrsa* was the last settlement before we reached the water's edge. Ye said if we made it there afore we found the keep, we had somehow missed the place and gone too far."

"I am well aware of what I said," Magnus snapped. As much as he hated to admit it, the boy was right. They should've reached the keep by now. How had they not?

Oblivious to his elder's sharp tone, Evander tilted his head and squinted up at the brilliance of the sunny sky. "Hear those birds a keenin'? Is that what terns sound like?"

"Aye. Those are terns." Magnus frowned as he turned his mount and scanned the landscape behind them. An eerie uneasiness stirred deep in his bones. "Their clan name is Nithdane," he added, more to keep the boy from repeating his original question and hopefully, delay him in coming up with any new ones. He needed silence to study the area. Something was sorely amiss.

"But I thought ye said her name was Lady Bree *Maxwell*?"

Dammit, would the boy never stop his chatter? "Aye, I said that because it was her name. Her fool of a father refused to share his surname with any of his daughters. Said only a son deserved the right to carry the clan name. The name Maxwell belonged to her mother." With a slow, steady pull on the reins, he turned his mount further, sweeping the landscape for clues.

"Ye said the keep was well before the village, aye? Said a good distance separated them, but they were still within view of each other?"

Ignoring Evander, Magnus urged his horse off the dirt path and backtracked. In the distance loomed an overgrown mound of charred stones he didn't remember. He headed for it at a dead gallop. An ominous sense of doom churned in the pit of his stomach.

Once he reached the ruin, he pulled up short. What once had been tall, imposing walls were now crumbling piles of rubble bleached white as old bones. A dark greening of moss stained the debris closest to the ground. Bits of charred wood and twisted remnants of rusting metal peeped out from clumps of sedge and thickets of nettle. Someone had reduced Nithdane Keep to nothing more than a memory.

"Is this…or was this it?" Evander asked, reining in beside him. The lad dismounted and poked around the tumbled-down shell of what had once been a decent-sized keep. Not a massive fortress, but large enough to make a small clan like Nithdane proud. When the lad came upon a rotting post with a skull at its base, he backed away, crossing himself with every step. "What do ye reckon happened here?"

"Back to yer horse." Magnus refused to dismount and disturb Nithdane's ghosts. He turned his beast toward the settlement, eyeing the peaceful stretch of white buildings rimming the bay and the fishing boats bobbing alongside the docks. "Hie wi' ye now," he said. "I'm sure someone from the village can tell us what happened." He snorted out a bitter huff as he waited for Evander. The place reeked with the stench of betrayal.

More likely than not, it wouldn't be difficult to discover what Nithdane's ruins refused to share. People loved retelling tales of carnage, suffering, and death. That was but one of the many reasons Magnus preferred solitude with no one other than his falcon, Merlin, for company. Regrettably, he had left the bird back at *Tor Ruadh* in the care of Evander's brothers since he had no idea what this trip might entail.

For the first time since leaving the keep, the boy did as he was asked without comment. They rode along in blessed silence. For that, Magnus was grateful. At least for a while. After tolerating Evander's constant chatter for days, the heavy blanket of quiet between them now was not only suffocating but filled Magnus with guilt for snarling at the lad. This hellish trip wasn't the youngling's fault. He clenched his teeth so hard it was a wonder they didn't shatter. By the gods, he would do better by this inquisitive young pup. The last thing he needed in this life was some-thing more to regret.

When they rode into *Inbhir Theòrsa*, the first thing Magnus noticed was that the folk of the small fishing hamlet seemed cautious—almost fearful. He didn't remember them behaving like that the last time he had been there. The men in front of the buildings turned away, avoiding his gaze. Most either sought shelter inside or hurried down toward the docks. Fisherwomen sewing nets and weaving baskets dropped their work, crossed themselves, then rushed into their dwellings and shuttered the doors and windows.

"What did ye do the last time ye were here?" Evander spoke in a hushed tone. "These folk act like ye're death's angel come to steal their souls." He bobbed his head from side to side when Magnus didn't answer. "'Course, with that white hair of yers. And them black clothes. Black horse, too. I canna say as I blame them." Squinting one eye shut, he studied Magnus, then nodded. "Aye, I can see it. All ye need is horns, black wings, and a pointy tail."

"Ye are not helping, boy."

"Sorry."

"The public house used to be down that way and to the right. We'll try there." Magnus urged his horse to a faster clip. Not only did the hairs on the back of his neck stand straight on end, but the scar between his shoulder blades tingled. A sure sign they needed to leave this place as quickly as they found the information they sought. This village possessed darkness he didn't like.

"Stay with the horses," Magnus said. The shutters for the windows on either side of the pub's bright red door banged shut. That hadn't happened the last time he was here unless a storm was about to hit. A louder thud hit the inside of the door, the sound of the bar being dropped across the threshold.

"Pub's closed!" shouted a voice from inside.

"In the middle of the day?" Evander taunted. "Are ye that afeared of the mighty Magnus de Gray?"

Magnus shot the boy a threatening look that surprisingly shut the lad's mouth. He made a note to remember that for future reference. Stepping closer to the door, he caught sight of a watery eye peering at him through a knothole. "Tell me what I seek, and the boy and I will leave."

"I got nothing to say to the likes of ye. Be gone now. I done spread salt across the threshold, and me wife's got a vial of holy water what came all the way from Inverness." The bloodshot eye blinked.

"What happened at Nithdane Keep?" Magnus widened his stance and fixed the eye with his grimmest stare. "What became of Lady Bree Maxwell's child?"

The window to his left creaked, and the barrel of a gun slid through the crack between the shutters. "Get out of here, ye devil. Ye've stirred all the evil here ye're gonna stir. We willna bear no more from ye! Be gone, or we'll see if ye bleed like the rest of us."

"Dinna shoot him," screeched a higher-pitched voice, a woman from somewhere inside. "He'll curse ye like he did Nithdane and the Maxwell women."

It was times like this that Magnus wished his mother had never instilled within him the belief that whatsoever you send out returns to you in thrice. Her warning had stayed his hand many a time—but not this one.

"Tell me what happened to Nithdane Keep and Lady Bree's child, or I'll curse the lot of ye to a slow death from the pox!" He added a thunderous stream of Latin to the threat, wondering if anyone within earshot understood the wicked-sounding words. His Latin was a mite rusty. If he remembered rightly, he had just threatened to awaken a dragon and feed their ships to it, but he wasn't sure. Wouldn't it be grand if he really could?

Apparently, Evander's education included Latin. His snicker changed to a coughing fit when Magnus jerked around and shot him a dark glare. If that boy ruined this ruse, he'd thrash his talkative arse for him.

To ensure the weapon's bearer heeded the woman's warning and didn't shoot, Magnus scooped up a clump of dirt and jammed it in the end of the barrel. "Now that yer weapon's fouled, ye best speak or die. Tell me of the keep and Lady Bree."

The gun slid out of view, but the crack between the shutters remained, held open by a thick, stubby finger. "Old Red Caunich razed the keep when his betrothed—yer precious Lady Bree cuckolded him."

Someone spit, making Magnus tighten his jaw. How dare that bastard spit after saying Lady Bree's name.

"His lairdship, the Caunich," the voice continued, "Didna take kindly to such disrespect. Killed all in the keep. Burned them alive. Leastways, the ones he didna hang from the cliffs or impale on the pikes." The voice wheezed in a deep breath, then coughed. "He hunted down many in the clan, too. Swore he wouldna leave a Nithdane alive to speak of this shame. 'Twas only by God's good grace that he spared this here village. Right as he was coming to attack us, a powerful ague came upon him. Left his sword arm paralyzed and turned him mute. The Caunich took it as a sign he had done enough to avenge the insult, so he returned to his keep and left us in peace."

Magnus scrubbed the stubble of his jaw, mulling over the man's words. The letter that had finally caught up with him at Sutherland MacCoinnich's keep had said the Lady Bree had died in childbirth. Said he had a son. When had Red Caunich attacked? "When?"

"When?"

"Aye. When did all this happen?" Magnus

shoved the shutters aside and reached through the open window, grabbing hold of the wide-eyed man by the throat. "When did Red Caunich destroy the Nithdanes?"

Clawing at Magnus's arm, the pub keeper made a futile attempt to wriggle free. "'Twas when his lairdship arrived to claim his bride and found they banished her for her whoring. Her and her sister both. The Nithdane thought the banishment might appease the raging laird, but it didna do so. Old Red Caunich said it was his right to punish the Lady Bree—not her father's. Said he wouldha cut the bairn from her belly and left'm both on the cliffs to feed the terns."

Magnus released the man with a shove. They had banished Lady Bree. And her sister, too. He turned and glanced back toward where Nithdane Keep had once stood. The heartless banishment had saved their lives. "Where did they go? Lady Bree and her sister?" For the life of him, he couldn't remember the sister at all. Before the pub keeper could close the shutters, Magnus slammed them both open wide and held them. "Tell me where they went or die."

"I dinna ken," the man said as he stumbled backward. He pointed a shaking finger at the floor. "That there's the salt. Ye canna cross it, ye wicked son of Satan." Then he jabbed a finger at Magnus. "The whore's maid ran from the keep afore old Red came. She told us ye were the one that put that bastard in her mistress's belly afore ye returned to yer throne beside the Earl o' Hell. Said we shouldha held her 'neath the waters 'til Satan's spawn left her soul in peace. But it was too late. The whore and her sister had done escaped."

Magnus launched himself through the window, shattering the glass as he slammed the sashes aside. He dropped to the floor, scooped up a handful of salt, then ground it into the sniveling man's face. "I've a revelation for ye, ye spineless son of a whore. I'm the most powerful demon of them all. Neither salt nor holy water stops me." He shoved the man back, bouncing his head against the wall. "What direction did Lady Bree and her sister take?" Tightening his hold on the fool's throat, he lifted him until his feet dangled above the floor. "And if ye value yer life, ye'll speak of her with respect, ye ken?"

"I swear I dinna ken where she went," the man rasped, his round face reddening.

"Follow the coast!" shouted a heavy woman from behind the bar. "East, I'd say. Along the coast." She shoved her disheveled mop of graying hair out of her eyes. "If'n it was me that got run off from here, I'd stay to the coast for food. Gull's eggs. Fish washed up and such. I'd keep movin' 'til I found folk who didna know 'bout me or 'bout what had happened. I'd go east 'cause towns are there that might have a kind soul who might help a woman breedin'. 'Specially if she lied and told them she was widowed. I'd bet the finest ale we got that's what her planned to do when she left here. East along the coast for certain, ye ken?" Her panicked gaze kept flitting to the chubby little man Magnus held aloft. "I swear it." She crossed herself, then clasped her hands and shook them. "Please dinna kill or curse us. We did her no harm. Surely, ye know we couldna give her shelter. If the Nithdane had found out, he wouldha run us out, too. We wouldha lost everything. Came close to losing it when Laird Red Caunich came through here." She crossed herself again. "Only God Almighty saved us."

Magnus released the pub keeper and stepped back as the man hit the floor. What the woman said made sense, and Lady Bree would have been canny enough to do just that. In fact, she had often told him of combing the beaches and cliff sides in search of *nature's treasures*, as she had called them. The memory made his heart hurt. Such a sweet lass. What had she endured because he had taken another mercenary campaign rather than wintered at Nithdane? The thought weighed heavy on him as he strode to the door, tossed aside the ridiculous bar, and exited. He despised those who would stand idly by and watch while an innocent woman was stripped of her kith and kin's protection. Out of the corner of his eye, he spotted Evander skittering back to their mounts. The nosy lad had been eavesdropping at the window.

"I thought I told ye to tend the horses?" Magnus said, gruff with the lad, but his heart wasn't in it. He settled into the saddle, struggling with the responsibility of all he had discovered. How had he managed to hurt so many with one foolish choice?

"I could see them from where I stood," Evander defended. "I canna believe ye didna kill that arse worm."

"I only kill when I must." He nudged his beast with his knee and headed east.

"So, we ride the coast 'til we come across someone who knew her?" Evander edged his pale gray horse up beside Magnus's black beast. "Reckon they traveled on foot?"

"I'm sure they did." The thought rankled him, stirring the rage simmering in his gut. He wondered if they had escaped with anything more than the clothes on their backs—if that. Bree's father had been an arrogant bastard, acting as though he ruled over the largest clan in all of Scotland rather than a wee cluster of folks he claimed were descended from Somerled himself.

Magnus had no doubt the man had made the banishing of his daughters into quite the spectacle. The fool had always lamented how his wife had failed the clan by not giving him sons.

Evander nudged his horse to a faster pace, keeping it abreast of Magnus's. "Would a chief really treat his daughter so harshly?"

The worry in the boy's tone warned Magnus this conversation had more to do with than just Clan Nithdane. "No *good* chief would treat his daughter so harshly. Most would just send them away. To a nunnery most likely."

"What about a lass whose father isna so high in the clan?" Evander waved away the words as though they were midges. "Say…like the smithy's daughter even."

"Did ye bed Ellen? Is that why yer mother was fit to be tied and sent ye on this trip?" Gretna's harsh lecture made sense now. While Evander might have the wants and needs of a man, he didn't have the ways or the means to take care of any consequences should they arise. "Is the lass with child?"

"Nay!" Evander stared at him as though he had just said they would eat their horses for dinner. "At least…I dinna think she is." He squirmed in the saddle. "I didna even get my willy all the way in her the first time we did it. When she pulled on it whilst I sucked on her teats, I couldna keep from spilling my seed." His horrified look plainly said how he felt about that. "It felt so good, I thought I had died." After a slow shake of his head, he added, "And the second time we done it, her da walked in on us. I thought I was dead then, for sure. That man's big as an ox."

Magnus bit the inside of his cheek to keep from laughing out loud.

"I went to chapel twice to thank God above that all the man did was drag my arse back to Mama." The boy made a face. "'Course, then I thought I was dead, too. She might not be big as the smithy, but God help ye if ye give her a case of the red arse." He gave Magnus an earnest look. "Ye think I'm gonna be a da? Will the chieftain make me wed Ellen? We only did it the two times, and the first shouldna even count."

"Do ye love Ellen?" Magnus decided to attack this delicate issue from that angle.

"Nay—leastways not enough to wed her." Evander frowned. "Did ye love yer Lady Bree?"

"That was a different situation."

"Different how?" The lad's eyes narrowed as though he smelled a lie.

"I was fond of her," Magnus lamely replied, wondering how the hell their talk had taken this turn. "When she asked for my help, I couldna refuse."

"Yer help with what?"

"The ridding of her maidenhead."

"Her what?" Evander stared at him in disbelief.

"Has neither Gretna nor Ian talked to ye about these things?" Magnus wasn't about to explain the joining of a man and a woman to the boy. It wasn't his place.

Evander grinned. "I was just funning with ye. I know about the getting of bairns. Mama's just afeared I'll be making her a grandmam sometime soon. As long as I pull my willy out before my seed spills. That should work at keeping them away, aye? What do ye do?"

"What I do is none of yer damned concern." If it wasn't for the fact he had sworn to take care of the boy, he would snap the little arse wipe's neck. "And ye would do well to remember it is a long walk back to *Tor Ruadh*."

"Ye think her sister's the one raising yer bairn?" Apparently, Evander preferred riding to traveling on foot and had decided to turn the conversation to a safer subject. "Ye think she's the one who sent that letter? Why ye reckon she waited so long? More than five years? Wonder what happened to make her decide ye needed to know now?"

"The date of the letter was just over five years ago. From the look of the parchment, that's when it was written." Magnus had asked himself those same questions. "Although, I canna imagine it being handed about and en route to me for all that time. How could it have survived? Maybe Lady Bree's sister helped her write it to give her peace before she died. Then it got set aside or lost. I dinna ken what couldha happened. All I know for certain is I must find the boy—if he still lives."

"Her sister couldha got too busy to send it. What with taking care of a newborn babe and finding shelter for them both, she probably didna have a minute to call her own." Evander looked thoughtful. "I know when it was just Mama and us bairns—it was hard for her to keep us all fed and safe. Many a night, her head didna touch her pillow."

When the lad talked like that, he sounded a great deal older than his fifteen years. Magnus knew life hadn't been easy for Evander and his brothers before their mother married Ian. "That's why we must find them," he said. "Lady Bree's sister and the boy."

"What's her name?"

Magnus frowned. What *was* the sister's name? For that matter, would he even know her if he saw her? No matter how hard he tried, he couldn't bring her to mind. Had he not met her during any of his visits to Nithdane keep? He finally shook his head. "If I ever knew it, I have forgotten."

"I wouldna tell her that," Evander advised in the tone of one who knew from experience. He squinted up at the sky. "At least this time of year, the days are long. Gives us more light to search."

Magnus agreed. "Aye, we'll only stop when the beasts need a rest. Ye've done well so far on little sleep, have ye not?" Or maybe it only seemed like the lad slept very little because that was the only time he was quiet.

The lad thumped his chest. "I can ride as long as it takes."

And so, they did. Hours along the coastline. Stopping at every sign of habitation, from the smallest croft to clusters of dwellings large enough to warrant the title of village. Many remembered Nithdane Keep's fall, but none knew what had become of the infamous woman blamed for it.

"Reckon we should change the way we ask about yer son and his auntie?" Evander suggested as they neared the last settlement they would reach before nightfall. "Maybe stop mentioning Nithdane and say ye're trying to find yer dead brother's bairn, after his wife died, too, and her sister wrote ye for help."

"Ye mean lie."

"Aye. When it serves a good enough purpose, a lie can be better than the truth sometimes."

The lad had a point. Although, Magnus doubted his mother would agree with her son's reasoning. "That shall be our story then. My dead brother's bairn. But will folk not think it strange and grow leery that I waited so long to find them? After all, it wouldha been two women traveling alone over five years ago."

"Tell'm ye been at sea and just got word." Evander gave a decisive nod. "Ye could pass for a smuggler, and might could even mention one of Master Duncan's ships if need be. Ye know at least one of their names, aye?"

This boy was a damned good liar. Duncan MacCoinnich, brother to the chieftain at *Tor Ruadh*, was also known as the smuggling lord, Devil Fraser Sullivan. After a run-in with the British whilst protecting his wife, Duncan and Tilda had settled on an island in the Archipelago of El Perdido, where they ran goods for Tilda's father, the chieftain of Clan Mackenzie.

"Perhaps, I should let ye do all the talking." Magnus winked at the boy.

Evander beamed with pride, reminding Magnus that he hadn't been as kind as he should have been to the youngling. "Forgive me, Evander. None of this is yer fault, and I should not have treated ye as if it was."

The boy shrugged. "I kent well enough ye didna mean it. Sometimes kin act that way when things go awry."

"Ye are wise beyond yer years, lad," Magnus said. "And I am proud ye consider me kin." He nodded at the upcoming settlement. "*Inbhir Ùige* up ahead. Alexander told me of it. Fair sized place for this far north."

"Reckon they'll have a place where we might get some supper?"

Magnus laughed. Evander was always hungry. He hadn't complained about anything during their travels but had been on the constant lookout for something to eat other than oatcakes. "As big as it is, I'm sure of it. We'll go there first. Maybe they'll even know something that will help us in our search."

They came upon an inn situated on the main thoroughfare. A decent-sized establishment busy with weary folk seeking a bit of food and drink to end the day. There was even a stable beside it, so Magnus decided both they and the horses deserved a night's rest with more comforts than a fireside camp offered.

As soon as they seated themselves, an older woman, tall and thin as a shadow, appeared at their table. With a weary smile, she tucked a wispy curl of gray back beneath her, kertch. "And what can I fetch for such fine gentlemen as yerselves?"

"Be that meat pie I smell?" Evander lifted his nose, sniffing at the air like a hound on the hunt.

"Aye, sir. That it is." After a polite nod, she shifted her smile to Magnus, obviously knowing he was the one with the coin. "Shall I bring ye both a hearty serving along with bread and ale?"

"That would do us both well," Magnus said. "We shall also be needing a room for the night. Can ye tell the innkeeper?" He tossed a pair of coins on the table. "This should cover the room and the meal, aye?"

The woman's weariness melted away as she plucked up the coinage and tucked it into her belt. "Two pounds sterling? It most certainly shall, fine sir. More than enough. I'll bring ye the key to our best room." She turned and snapped her fingers at the barmaid on the other side of the dining area. "Pies, bread, and ale, Maggie, as much as they want, ye ken?"

The young woman dipped a respectful curtsey, then hurried off toward the mouth-watering aromas.

Before she rushed off to see to another customer, Magnus tossed down another coin. "And this one is for yer time, mistress."

The matron's smile disappeared, replaced with a thunderous scowl. "I will have ye know this isna that type of establishment any longer."

"What does she mean?" Evander asked. "We still get to eat, aye?"

"Forgive me, mistress. Ye misunderstand my intent." Yet another reason Magnus preferred solitude. He had never chosen words well. "I merely wish ye to sit with us and answer some questions." He jerked a thumb toward the bustling room. "I can see ye're verra busy. I wouldna presume to take up yer time without compensating ye."

The bristling woman immediately calmed and lowered herself into a chair. "Then I must ask yer forgiveness, sir. I meant no insult to ye. Since my husband's death, some are still confused about the services offered here at Wickhaven." Her sharp chin thrust upward. Defiance and disgust flashed in her eyes. "Mr. Wicklow forced our maids to service our customers in any way they required. I thank the Lord Almighty every day for striking that man down." With a proud look, she continued. "I am innkeeper now, and Wickhaven is a respectable place."

Evander leaned close again. "What does she mean?"

"I will explain later," Magnus said in a tone he hoped would shut Evander's mouth until the boy could put it to use eating his supper.

"Ye may call me Mistress Wicklow," the woman said with a chuckle.

Magnus gave her a polite nod. "I am Magnus de Gray. Pleased to make yer acquaintance."

"Oh, dear God." The matron paled and clasped a hand to her chest as though unable to breathe.

"My name doesna usually cause such a reaction." Magnus noted all exits. The woman looked ready to bolt. She knew about Lady Bree. He could smell it. "Might I ask why my presence causes ye such distress, Mistress Wicklow?"

Working her mouth like a fish out of water, she clasped her hands and stared down at them. "It was I who sent for ye." Her mouth tightened, then she waved away the words. "Nay. That is wrong. I didna send for ye exactly. At least not when I was asked to do so." She swallowed hard, then looked up at him with tear-filled eyes. "But ye must understand, I couldna have any bairns of my own. And that…that precious babe brought me such joy. Please forgive me. I just couldna bear to part with him. For the longest time, he was this hellish place's only light."

Struggling to speak with a calm he didn't feel, Magnus glared at her. "Where is my son?"

Her tears spilled over as she gave a quick shrug. "I dinna ken. Brenna, poor Bree's sister, took him away when that beast of a man I married made her—" She cut herself off, angrily swiping at her tears. "Nay—I willna speak of it." After pulling in a deep breath, she sat taller in the chair and blew it out. "It was then that I finally sent the letter I shouldha dispatched at the lad's birth. I admit I held it a while longer, hoping she might return if she happened to hear the devil had finally died." Her shoulders slumped, and she shook her head. "But she never did, and I guess I canna blame her. Not after…" Dabbing a rag to the corners of her eyes, she pulled in another shuddering breath. "Anyway, it was I who sent for ye. Praying ye would come. She is out there. Alone. Her and wee Keigan. I pray they survived the winter. Surely, they did. Brenna's a canny one. But ye must still find them and see them safe for certain." With slow, stiff movements, as though she had aged a hundred years, she rose from the chair. She pointed a shaking finger at him. "But ye must hold her no ill will, ye ken? Brenna bade me send for ye the day after Bree died. But I didna do as she asked. I couldna bear to part with that precious wee mite." Her teary eyes didn't waver from him. "It was I who robbed ye of yer son. Not her."

Magnus sagged forward, fighting to breathe through a gut-wrenching punch of emotions. Keigan. His son's name was Keigan.

"Ye might search south along the coast. I know Brenna would never go north again. Not after all that happened." Mistress Wicklow shuffled a step away, then turned back. "I'll pack food a plenty for yer travels. And treats for my sweet lad." She slid her fingers under the cloth sash belted at her waist and pulled out the three coins he had given her. With a sad tilt of her head, she tossed them back to the table. "Room. Food. Drink. Stable. No charge. It is the least I can do after all I kept from ye."

CHAPTER TWO

"KEIGAN—FETCH ANOTHER BUCKET of water for the soaking pot. The rain barrel's almost empty, so ye'll have to go to the burn." Brenna stood in the open doorway, drying her hands on her apron. "And dinna be dawdling in the woods, aye? I need it now, mind ye."

The fair-haired child looked up from the strip of bark he had just peeled from a long green stick. "Want this one, Auntie?" He held it up and showed her. "It's tall as me!"

Brenna nodded. "Aye, that's a fine one. Add it to the pot with the others." She smiled as he placed the willow bark in the pot, then scooped up the bucket and scampered off into the trees. Her heart swelled at how tall he was getting. If only her sister could see him now.

A heavy sigh escaped her. How many times a day did she think those words? "Every time I look into those eyes that are just like hers," she answered aloud.

Keigan had inherited his pale blue eyes from both his parents—or at least her sister had always said that de Gray's eyes had been even lighter than hers. Like storm clouds split with lightning was how she had described them. Brenna had never met the man, so she wouldn't know. That was yet another way she had failed her sister. Maybe if she had stayed at the keep with her instead of living in the woods with old Ursala to learn herbal lore, she could have kept Bree from making the choice that had cost her life. With an impatient jerk of her head, she smoothed her apron back in place. "No sense fretting about that now. What's done is done, and canna be undone."

Checking the reeds and bark soaking in the pot, Brenna decided to let them go a little longer. The more they soaked, the more pliable they became and less likely to split or break when she started weaving. She and Keigan had gathered enough to make several baskets and maybe even a yair for the narrow spot in the river. The lad preferred guddling for trout in the streams farther inland, but when it came time for smoking and drying food for the winter, yairs or woven traps provided more fish with a great deal less effort.

Noise from the path in front of the wattle and daub hut it had taken her and Keigan weeks to construct made her draw the dagger she kept sheathed at her waist. She also pulled an oblong shard of stone from her pocket that she had ground to knife-like sharpness and the perfect weight for throwing. After their daily games of throwing them at targets etched on trees, she and Keigan had developed deadly aim. A woman and a child living alone could never let down their guard. The leafy bushes along the overgrown path trembled and swayed, marking someone's approach.

A hunched-over crone from the nearest village pushed through the last of the overgrowth and labored into the clearing. Brenna relaxed and put her weapons away.

"Greetings to ye, honorable Lady of the Wood," the elderly matron wheezed as she struggled to catch her breath. She kept her eyes averted. None of the villagers looked at Brenna whenever they visited. They feared her almost as much as they needed her.

"Greetings, Morag." She noted the woman's flushed cheeks with some concern. The village was a good stretch of the legs from here, especially for the aged. "Rest a moment 'til yer wind returns, aye?" None from the settlement tarried long whenever they came seeking help.

One had once confessed to her that the parish priest had warned them not to anger the strange, solitary woman with healing gifts so rare God Almighty Himself must have sent her.

"I dare not waste yer time, oh wise one," the old woman said with a shake of her head. Her gasping breaths slowed, settling into a normal rhythm.

Brenna wondered if Morag was one of the few who still followed the old ways and believed her to be the goddess Bride incarnate. Keigan had told her of overhearing that rumor from a pair of women who had brought their bairns to her. She didn't care who they thought she was as long as they left her in peace unless they needed healing. Their gifts of goat's milk, eggs, even tools, and furniture made her and Keigan's lives much easier. She did fear familiarity with the villagers. Too many risks came along with it. But her healing was the only way to keep her and Keigan sheltered and fed.

"I would ask for more herbs to ease my poor Alfric," Morag said in a reverent tone. "He breathes much easier and even sleeps some after taking in the smoke."

Brenna nodded and retreated inside the hut to fetch more thorn apple. She only gave the old woman enough for a few fillings of Alfric's special pipe. Too much, and the man would die. With the dried herbs secured inside a piece of scrap linen, she returned to the clearing, placed the small parcel atop a large boulder, then backed away. All who came to the wood feared her so much, they never allowed her closer than a few feet unless their ailment required her touch. "Remember, Morag, only one pipe a day. No more. And only in the shallow-bowled pipe I made for him. Any more than once a day, and ye'll find yerself a widow, ye ken? 'Tis important ye heed my warning."

"Aye, m'lady." The matron bowed, then shuffled over to the boulder and replaced the bundle of herbs with a folded cloth she pulled from the basket hanging from the crook of her arm. "Please accept this lovely shawl, m'lady. 'Tis woven from my finest threads and dyed green in yer honor."

"I thank ye, Morag." Brenna wouldn't pick up the gift until Morag left. It seemed to make folks nervous if she touched their offerings in front of them. "It looks most fine. I shall wear it with pride." At least, she could give the old woman those words so she could brag that the Lady of the Wood had complimented her handiwork.

Morag bobbed her bent head and gifted Brenna with a toothless smile. She seemed to stand a little straighter as she shuffled away.

Keigan appeared from behind the hut with a large gray and black striped cat trotting along beside him. "Auntie! Síth's back."

The child had a way with animals. Brenna had seen nothing like it. Only Keigan could befriend a wildcat of the Highlands.

Brenna waved him over. "Add the water to the pot, then I suppose ye might see if yer friend would like a taste of the fish left from breakfast."

The cat flattened its ears, easing forward in a low crouch with a growl rumbling at the back of its throat. With the end of its tail twitching, it locked its golden eyes on the spot through the bushes the old woman from the village had just taken.

"To yer bow, Keigan. Keep to the arrow slit in the door, mind ye. Watch me close to know when to shoot, aye?"

"Aye, Auntie!" The boy disappeared into the hut and closed the door behind him.

They had learned early on that the local wildlife's wisdom far surpassed their own. They watched the animals and followed their signals.

Brenna drew her dagger and throwing stones again. Rarely did over one soul from town visit in a sennight, much less twice in the same day. There had been no calls for help or to come running, so she doubted anyone had been injured or needed immediate help. Whatever or whoever had set the cat into battle readiness didn't belong here. The footfalls sounded heavy and purposeful. Male, if she guessed right. She hefted both weapons and resettled her stance.

A man as large as a Highland mountain loomed into view, his broad-shouldered massiveness made even more daunting by his black clothing. But it wasn't his muscular dominance that robbed her of the ability to breathe. It was his silvery-white mane that shot a sudden coldness through her. That hair wasn't the shade of old age but a shining crown he had borne since birth. The very same color as her Keigan's. And those eyes of his. The clearest blue-gray flecked with white—like storm clouds splintered by lightning. Just like her sister had described so many times.

"A step closer, and ye die."

The red-haired youth beside him halted, then inched back a step. "I think she means it. Ye go on ahead."

After a scowling cut of his eyes at the boy, he returned his attention to her. Lifting both hands with fingers outspread, he took another step closer. "We willna harm ye. I am in search of a child, and the villagers said ye were the finest healer—and mayhap even a seer who could help me find him."

Her first instinct was to lie so he would go away, but the rage she had nursed for years wouldn't allow it. Besides, Keigan needed to learn firsthand what an uncaring bastard his father was, so he wouldn't be tempted to search him out someday. She kept her weapons handy, itching to kill the heartless cur just like he had killed poor Bree. The only thing that stayed her hand was that his death would be so much easier than the one he had foisted upon her sister. "Ye're either the bravest or the most foolish man I have ever had the displeasure of meeting. The *child* needed ye years ago at his birth. My sister needed ye even before that. I canna believe ye've the gall to cast yer shadow across our threshold now." Years of angry suffering unleashed the fury within her. "She trusted ye. Cherished yer friendship. And how did ye repay her? By deserting her when she needed ye most."

His hands lowered to his sides while his icy stare stayed locked on her. "I know," he admitted quietly. "I wish I had never left Nithdane Keep and abandoned Lady Bree. But ye must believe me when I say, I only just found out about…everything. I never received yer letter until this month. Just weeks ago. I swear it."

He must think her an addlepated fool who would believe anything. She refused to grace such a ridiculous lie with a response. "Ye didna come when we needed ye. We have no need of ye now. Shake the dust of this place from yer boots and never return, aye?"

"I didna come all this way to turn tail and run when faced with yer hatred." He stepped into the clearing; his broad chest thrust out. "Ye can try to kill me but know this—I willna go easily."

Her clenched jaws tightened even more when the door behind her creaked. Keigan had always been the curious sort. What child of his age wasn't? "Come stand at my side, Keigan. Ye may meet yer father and then bid him farewell because he *will* be leaving."

"Should I bring my bow and daggers?" the boy asked.

"Aye, my precious one. Come out armed." She wished her loathing could turn the man in front of her into a pile of ash. But then again, she wouldn't wish him such a simple end. Nay. He needed to suffer as he had caused all of them to suffer.

The warrior's stance, dark and proud, softened when Keigan appeared at her side. His muscular throat flexed with a hard swallow, and he worked his mouth as though fighting to draw in air.

Brenna decided to yank the fool from his stupor so they might be rid of him sooner. With a dismissive flip of one hand, she rested the other on her nephew's shoulder. "I present to ye yer father, Keigan. The man who deserted yer mother and left her to suffer the wrath of a cruel clan. They tossed her out into the cold with no one to protect her. No one but me. His name is Magnus de Gray. But as ye know, I prefer to call him *the great and mighty deceiver*."

"Is it true what she says?" Keigan took another step toward the heartless rogue who had ruined their lives.

The muscles in Magnus's jaw flexed. "Aye, I left yer mother. I went to fight in a senseless war when I shouldha stayed at her side to protect her." After a shuffling of his feet, he lowered himself to one knee. "But I beg ye to believe me when I say, I didna ken ye were in her belly. I didna know when ye were born, nor that yer sweet mother had died while giving ye life." The man's pale brows knotted. Regret darkened his features. "I ask yer forgiveness, Keigan, and I also ask for the chance to make this right."

Brenna held her breath. Whilst she would give her last coin to see de Gray reduced to nothing more than a pile of ash, her sweet lad had a say in this matter, too. And she also owed it to Bree. For some reason, her sister had befriended this lying womanizer, and her dying wish had been for her son to know his father.

Keigan frowned, then placed his bow and throwing daggers on the ground. He marched forward until he stood mid-distance between Magnus and Brenna. His little head slowly tilted to one side. "Ye favor me. Just bigger." The boy pointed. "Our hair's the same. Granny Wick called the color of it *snow on the mountain.*"

A sad smile made Magnus appear almost wistful. "Aye, my mother called mine *frost on the heather.*"

A sudden vision of de Gray snatching up the boy and taking flight made Brenna step forward and stand next to her nephew. Let the bastard try it. She would stab him through the heart.

"Why did ye not come when I was born? I dinna believe it when ye say ye knew nothing about me." Keigan thrust out his little chin with the accusation. "Auntie gave Granny Wick the letter to send right off. It told about Mama going to heaven and how I needed a da right away. She told me so, and Auntie never lies."

"I met yer Granny Wick on the way here. She told me she didna send the letter until a few weeks ago because she loved ye and feared I would come and take ye away."

"Would ye have?"

"Aye." Magnus gave another solemn nod. "I wouldha come for ye quick as I could ride to *Inbhir Ùige,* and then I wouldha brought ye back to *Tor Ruadh.*"

"Then why did she send the letter for ye to find me now?"

Brenna smiled proudly. Her sweet lad was not a fool and had always been far wiser than his years.

"Because ye left yer Granny Wick, and she feared ye needed my protection." Magnus settled a hard stare on Brenna. "She knew yer auntie had suffered greatly and was afraid she would suffer more without me to care for the both of ye."

"Me and Auntie do just fine," Keigan said. "We protect each other."

"Of that, I have no doubt." Magnus blew out a heavy sigh. "But I am yer father, and I wish for the chance to be a good one to ye. If ye will allow it."

"Auntie says ye killed Mama," Keigan accused.

Brenna's heart swelled at the sight of her sweet bairn's hands fisted at his sides. Such a brave little man, her dear Keigan. This was so unfair to him. She wanted to grab him up and hold him but held herself back for his pride's sake.

Magnus stared down at the ground for a long while, then lifted his gaze. "I would never have hurt yer mother. But sometimes things happen. Things we canna foresee. Whether ye believe in fate or God, all of us are at the mercy of this world and what it does with us. I could not have saved her even if I had been at her side—as I shouldha been. All I couldha done was offer her what comfort I could as she passed through the veil to a better place."

"Would ye have?" the boy dared as Brenna struggled to swallow the emotions knotting in her throat. Her sister had suffered so very much, bringing this sweet lad into the world.

"Aye, lad. I wouldha done anything I could to ease her way." He clenched a hand atop his knee, flinching as though in pain. "What say ye, Keigan? Would ye at least be willing to grant me some of yer time? Time to get to know me?" After another glance at Brenna, he continued. "Then if ye tell me to go, I will go and trouble the two of ye no more."

The child frowned at him, studying Magnus with repeated up and down looks. The only sound in the clearing was the wind shushing through the trees. The boy sidled a glance up at Brenna. "What should I do, Auntie?"

The trust and confusion flashing in her precious one's eyes stopped her from blurting out that he should tell de Gray to go straight to Hell by the quickest route possible. Nay—she saw her sister in those trusting eyes. Again, she heard her sibling's dying wish that Keigan know his father. She gritted her teeth, knowing what she needed to say. But, damn it all, she didn't want to say it. With the lightest touch, she tapped the center of the child's chest. "What does yer heart tell ye, my brave little warrior?"

He looked back at the kneeling man and frowned. "I dinna ken for sure, but I kind of would like to talk to him a while since he knew Mama, and his blood flows in my veins, too." He drew up a shoulder and rubbed his cheek like he always did when thinking hard. "Do ye think she would want me to know him?" he asked in a reverent whisper.

No matter how much she hated Magnus de Gray, she could never lie to Keigan. She forced a smile and blinked away the threat of tears. "Aye, my dear one. When yer Mama held ye and kissed ye farewell before she went to Heaven, she said just that."

After a solemn nod, little Keigan squared his shoulders and faced Magnus. "I shall grant ye a wee bit of my time."

Magnus bowed his head. "Thank ye, Keigan."

"In my presence only," Brenna interjected. She would adhere to her sister's dying wish, but that didn't mean she would toss all caution to the wind. His tale of just receiving the letter and the why of it was too neat and tidy to be trusted.

Magnus stood and motioned for the young man behind him to step forward. "This is Evander Cameron. His father is cousin to the chieftain of Clan MacCoinnich."

Evander bobbed his head at Brenna. "Mistress." He grinned down at Keigan. "I'm glad we found ye, lad."

Keigan didn't respond, just stared up at him with a look that said he wasn't sure if he trusted Evander or not.

"Get the horses, Evander. Perhaps, the Lady Brenna could tell us where ye might water them." Magnus shifted in place, his unease apparent.

"Dinna call me that." The title struck her

sour. The fool thing had brought her nothing but pain. "Ye may call me Brenna." She paused and held up a finger. "Unless folk are here from the village, and then I am the Lady of the Wood, understand?"

"The Lady of the Wood?" Magnus repeated, both brows arching higher.

"Aye. I found it useful to instill a bit of superstitious fear into the locals when they found my way with herbs and healing a thing of wonder." She pointed toward the side of the hut. "Round that way. A few paces beyond the felled tree. A good-sized burn twists into a shallow pool that should do well enough for yer horses."

"I can show him," Keigan volunteered. "Horses like me." The boy watched her. In fact, they all watched her to see if she would grant him permission to accompany Evander.

Magnus moved to stand beside the pot soaking the reeds. "I shall wait right here until they return, aye?"

She didn't appreciate how easily he read her distrust. "Ye may go," she told Keigan, her heart clutching when he took off like an arrow shot.

"I didna come here to steal him from ye," Magnus said quietly. "I came here to set things right, but only if he allows it."

"*Things* will never be right," she said, pouring every ounce of hatred into her tone. Now that Keigan was out of earshot, she could speak her mind. "Because of ye, she's dead. And Keigan is just as banished from Nithdane land as I am. Land that wouldha rightfully belonged to him one day."

He looked at her with an expression she didn't understand. "Ye never heard whilst ye lived in *Inbhir Ùige*? How long have ye been out here in these woods?"

"Heard what? And we've been here a little over a year. What has that to do with anything?" What game of deceit did this fool attempt now? Even though instinct bade her keep them ready, she put away her throwing stones and dagger.

Keigan and Evander reappeared, leading a pair of horses that struck fear into her heart. The beasts were huge. "Keigan! Step away. Those animals will surely crush ye."

Keigan frowned. "Please, Auntie, no. They willna hurt me. Look—they like me." He tugged on the reins of the dark, shaggy-footed warhorse, and the animal followed, docile as a lamb.

"The horses willna hurt him," Magnus agreed. "They're accustomed to bairns. *Tor Ruadh* has many."

At war with the urge to grab the child up and protect him, she gave a curt nod and waved him on. "Fine, then. I guess I'll allow it. But mind the hooves, aye? They're big as yer head." She sidled a glare at Magnus. "If he gets hurt doing this, I will kill ye. Slowly."

Keigan beamed like the sun and continued leading the horses to the spring.

Remembering the interrupted conversation, she motioned at the surrounding wood. "Why did ye ask how long we had been here? What did I not hear while in *Inbhir Ùige*?"

He stared at her entirely too long before answering. "Nithdane is no more. Neither keep nor clan."

"Ye lie." His words pushed her back a step, but his eyes reflected nothing but the truth.

"Red Caunich destroyed the keep and murdered most in the clan. I was told he did so to clear the land of those who had shamed him." His expression hardened as his chin lifted. "Yer sister had hoped to gain release from the betrothal when he found her no longer a virgin. Even prepared herself to spend the rest of her life in a nunnery as punishment. But if she hadna been banished, he wouldha killed her. Both her and the unborn child. So said the townsfolk of *Inbhir Theòrsa*."

She huffed out a bitter snort. "So, my father actually saved the lives of the daughters he never had a use for. I'd wager he's spinning in Hell about that."

"Why did he banish ye with her?"

"Because I dared to defend her when no one else would." Brenna moved to the edge of the clearing and stared off into the woods in the direction the boys had gone with those monstrous beasts. She relaxed as the sounds of splashing and Keigan's endless chatter reached her. The day's revelations had threatened to knock her to her knees. They had revisited the past as much as she could stand. "If ye hurt him by coming here, I willna rest until I have killed ye." She turned and fixed Magnus with a look he would do well to heed. "Dinna underestimate me just because I am a woman."

"I have no intention of hurting him." A mournful note shadowed the rich, deep voice of the man she had despised for what felt like forever. "I also have no intention of hurting ye."

"I can take care of myself."

"Of that, I have no doubt." He strolled over to the hut, examining its construction with a critical eye. "If Keigan decides to be my son and returns with me to *Tor Ruadh*, I would have ye know that ye are welcome to come with us."

"My, my are ye not a self-assured bastard." How dare he think he could sweep in here with his warhorses and manly ways to win the favor of her nephew with no problem. Keigan might be entranced for a little while, but the boy loved her and enjoyed their life here in the woods. Keigan understood they were safe here. The fewer the people, the less chance of betrayal and pain. "Ye truly think ye can win him away from me so easily?"

"It is not my intent to 'win him away.'" One hand still resting on the side of the structure, he turned and frowned at her. "If he fosters an attachment to me, that willna change his love for ye. Ye're nay just an *Auntie*. Ye're the only mother he has ever known. He needs ye in his life more than ye will ever know." His scowl deepened. "I would never attempt to take that from him."

The man had all the right words. Said the things he thought she needed to hear. No wonder her trusting sister had so easily fallen under his spell. "Our home is too small for any other than us." She motioned toward the pile of sticks and branches she and Keigan had gathered during their walks. "Ye're welcome to sleep here in the clearing. If the night gets brisk, ye can build a fire with that wood."

"Thank ye. That is most generous."

It wasn't, but she didn't care. There was room enough inside, and she felt sure he could tell that. He might be a callous womanizer, but she had decided he was far from stupid. The rising wind held the smell of rain to it. Magnus and Evander would soon be soaked, but that was their problem, not hers.

A horse's loud snort announced the return of the lads. Magnus directed the boys to the left of the dwelling. "Tie them off over there. I dinna see any grasses or plants that'll cause them harm should they eat them, and those trees should give them safe enough shelter from the weather."

"Ye know about plants?" Keigan asked. He looked at Brenna with pride. "My auntie knows everything about plants and how to make folk better with them."

"Does she now?" Magnus looked suitably impressed, irritating Brenna even more. "Perhaps yer auntie would be kind enough to teach me what she knows," he added.

"It would take a long time," the boy warned. "She knows everything."

"Keigan—"

Thunder interrupted, rumbling long and low. The wind stirred the trees, growing stronger with every gust.

"Fixin' to storm," Keigan announced. He waved Evander and Magnus toward the door of the hut. "Best get inside. We got some fish left over from breakfast if'n ye're hungry. Auntie made some honey water, too. We found a hive and didna get stung a single time 'cause Auntie blew smoke on them. It made them all sleepy."

Unfortunately, Keigan had inherited a most exhausting trait from his mother. The boy was never at a loss for words with anyone.

"We'll be fine out here," Magnus said with a pointed look in Brenna's direction. Evander opened his mouth as if to speak, then snapped it shut and cast a disgruntled look up at the sky.

Without a word, he shrugged a fold of his kilt up over his head and peered out from it.

"But ye'll get soaked as waterweed," Keigan argued, holding open the door. "Tell'm, Auntie."

As if to make the boy's case, it thundered again, and large droplets of rain plopped across the ground, warning of the deluge to come.

"Ye can come inside until the rain stops, aye?" Brenna pointed at the door, refusing to look Magnus in the eyes. He would surely think her easy to manipulate if this kept up. But she knew in her heart if she behaved like a quarrelsome banshee in front of Keigan, she would lose him to the man for certain. This was a dangerous game that had to be played with care. "I am certain 'tis just a passing storm."

"I'm sure it is," Magnus said. "We shall be back outside in no time."

She could tell the fool was doing his best not to smile. He had better not, or she'd slip enough agrimony into his honey water to make him piss himself to death. Good for staunching wounds and making them clot, the herb also worked well at flushing a body's waters.

While the confines of the small dwelling were tight, at least they were dry as the sky held true to its promise and released a driving rain. She covered the lone window with a shutter she had made from a broken tabletop and lit the precious lantern one of the townsmen had given her after she had set his son's broken arm.

"Did the two of ye build this?" Evander asked, looking upward where they had lashed the branches together as the bones for the structure, creating a cone that coaxed the smoke from the center fire upward.

"Aye, we did. Auntie even climbed a tree and dangled down by her knees to tie the rope around the beams before we layered the mud and thatch on the roof," Keigan said with pride. He slapped his knee and laughed. "Ye shouldha seen her wearing them trews!"

Both Evander and Magnus turned and looked at her as though she had just sprouted horns.

"Keigan, I thought ye were going to share the fish and bread?" Brenna stirred the fire and hung a small pot across the edge of the coals. She had to get the child side-tracked before he divulged any more indelicate secrets.

"Evander," Magnus pointed at the door. "Run fetch the food from Mistress Wicklow before it's ruined." He gave Brenna an apologetic bob of his head. "I shouldha had him bring the goods inside before now. Forgive me." His gaze slid to Keigan. "But it slipped my mind," he added with a thoughtful quietness that made her heart hurt.

Before she could reply, Evander blew back inside with his arms overloaded with bundles.

As Keigan rushed to join the lad at the small

table in front of the window, Brenna stepped back out of their way and found herself shoulder to shoulder with Magnus. Well, they would have been shoulder to shoulder if she were quite a bit taller. As it was, even being a tall woman, the top of her head barely reached his chin.

"Thank ye for this, Brenna," he said softly for her ears alone. "I know I dinna deserve it, but I am forever indebted to yer kindness. Ye have no idea how much yer understanding means to me."

"Dinna thank me," she replied in a curt whisper. Frustration churned through her, made even worse by the feeling she had betrayed the need for vengeance she had nurtured all these years. His heartfelt whisper touched her more than she cared to admit, and she hated herself for it. "This was my sister's dying wish. For the child to know ye. No more. No less."

"Be that as it may," Magnus countered, "I shall owe ye the rest of my days. Whatever ye may need—all ye must do is ask it of me, ye ken?"

CHAPTER THREE

S HE HAD ALWAYS thought Keigan favored his mother. Little did she know how wrong she had been. The child's likeness was a reflection of his father. Disturbingly so. Same eyes. The slant of their smiles displaying the same dimple planted in their right cheek. With their heads bent close over the game they had scratched out on the dirt floor, barely a shade's difference could be seen between their hair.

"I have ye now," Evander crowed as he slid a rock toward another pile of pebbles within the circle.

"Nay!" Magnus and Keigan shouted in unison as they retaliated by moving their stones.

Brenna didn't understand their play and

couldn't care less. All she knew was that it gave her the advantage of observing Magnus. She was determined to reveal the genuinely selfish man that he was, the one he so craftily hid beneath a quiet, mannerly exterior.

The muscular man, a massive warrior, built for fighting battles and not crouching on the floor, changed positions and covertly massaged a knee. A moment of pity flitted through her. With the endless rains confining them, the three had been at the game a long while. Poor fool would be so stiff he'd be unable to walk by the time they finished. Good. Served him right for showing up to steal her dear lad away. She slammed a freshly washed plate down on the shelf so hard it was a wonder it didn't shatter.

Her conscience pricked at her, sounding a great deal like her sister's voice. The distant memory of Bree begging her to swear that the child would know his father. Brenna tossed down the rag she had used to wipe the dishes, fetched a three-legged stool out of the shadows, and thumped it down beside Magnus. "Here. Before ye cripple yerself."

"I thank ye, lass," he said as he hoisted himself onto the stool. "And my poor knee thanks ye even more."

She replied with nothing more than a dip of her chin. Curse the rains. Would they never cease and free her of this forced companionship?

"What's wrong with yer knee?" Keigan asked. "Was it a fierce battle? Did ye kill them after they wounded ye?"

Brenna rolled her eyes. What was it about males that made them glorify such things? She braced herself, half tempted to stuff rags in her ears to keep from hearing what would surely be a murderous lie of honor and glory.

Evander laughed out loud, then snapped his mouth shut. "Sorry," he snickered in response to Magnus's chilling glare.

"I hurt it saving a pup," Magnus said, leaning forward to slide a pebble to a different square within the circle.

"Ye mean when ye tried," Evander interrupted. "We had to save him and the pup both."

"Go check on the horses," Magnus ordered, jabbing a finger at the door. "Now."

"It's pouring buckets even harder," Evander argued. "I'm just now dried out from last time." Thunder rumbled in the distance.

"Yer ill manners just earned ye another good soaking and more chores. Now, go." Magnus rose to his full height and pointed at the door again. "And dinna come back inside until ye've moved the beasts closer to the shelter and seen that they're safe and calm. Understand?"

The sullen lad ducked his head and stomped out the door.

"Why did ye send him out in the rain again?"

Keigan asked.

"Because he needed a lesson in respecting his elders," Brenna explained before she could stop herself. She bit the inside of her cheek. What was wrong with her? Defending the fool man? And was that a hint of a smile tugging at his lips? By goodness, if he finished that smirk, she would throw a pot at him.

Magnus must have sensed her irritation because he cleared his throat and lowered himself back to the stool. "Ye asked how I hurt my knee. Remember?"

"Aye." Keigan scooted closer, his face alight with interest. "What happened to the puppy? Was a bad man trying to hurt it, and ye had to fight him off?"

It was Magnus who ducked his head this time, but he looked embarrassed rather than sullen. "Nay, lad. Nothing like that." He leaned forward, resting his forearms on his knees. "*Tor Ruadh* is built into the side of the mighty Ben Nevis. There are caves aplenty that run deep into the mountain. Some connect to the main stable and some to other parts of the keep." He stretched out his leg and rubbed the knee in question as if telling the story renewed the old injury. "The nosy wee dog went exploring and trapped himself down in a pit in one of the caves." He grinned, still staring down at his knee. "Luckily, the tiny scamp's crying alerted its mother. One of our best dogs at herding cows, horses, or children. She saw to it that we found her pup."

"It wouldha died if ye hadna found it." Keigan's wide eyes showed his heart and soul invested in the story. But then his fair brows drew together. "Did the dog bite ye? Is that what happened to yer knee? Surely, a pup couldna do that much damage."

Magnus's jaw tightened. When he lifted his gaze to Keigan's, he gave a sheepish shrug. "When I jumped down into the pit to fetch the wee mongrel, a rock I didna see foiled my landing. Twisted my knee something fierce and knocked me on me arse." He shrugged again. "Then we both had to be saved."

Keigan laughed out loud, then clapped a hand over his mouth. "Sorry," he said. "I'm certain that hurt verra much." He granted Magnus a braw smile. "But I am proud ye *tried* to save the puppy."

Brenna turned away and stared out the window. What sort of man told such a thing on himself when he couldha just as easily made up a story to save his pride and claimed Evander to be a liar?

"Aye, well...I couldna verra well leave the poor thing there to die, now could I?" Magnus once more stood, stretching to his full height. He opened the door and shouted at Evander, "Fetch wood and some water from the burn. Then ye can come inside."

"There's still plenty in the keg. I filled it from the rainwater barrel," Brenna said. Did the man not see the wooden cup floating so near the top? "And the wood ye brought in earlier is just now dry enough for the fire. If he brings in more, it'll be soaked all over again."

Magnus closed the door with a decisive thud. "Evander needs a wet walk through the woods. Dinna worry. He can stack the wood over there and sit on it 'til they both dry out."

"Ye are a stern taskmaster, sir." She returned to wiping the chipped plates that were already clean, chiding herself for speaking her thoughts in a manner that might be misunderstood as friendly teasing. Never would she consider such light-hearted banter. Not with the man who had helped her sister destroy all their lives. But trapped inside with this frustrating beast who had so far shown no despicable behavior was making it a chore to treat him with silent disdain.

He moved to the window and uncovered it to watch Evander's progress. "The lad is of an age where he feels the need to test the waters a mite too much for his good. Like a young buck challenging the old stag." With a satisfied nod at the soaked young man, he continued, "He'll learn, and I daresay my lessons are a great deal kinder than some."

"Can I go help him?" Keigan asked. "I dinna care if'n I get wet."

Entirely too many days of rain had worn on them all. It wouldn't hurt the lad, and it wasn't like everything wasn't damp as could be anyway. Brenna tilted her head toward the door. "Off wi' ye for a bit. Dinna get close to the steep banks alongside the stream. It will be swollen with the rains and swifter than the devil. And the ground could give way before ye know it."

As soon as he had charged out the door, she realized her error. Here she stood alone with the man she had wished dead more times than she could remember. From the look on his face, he found the situation as uncomfortable as she did. "My sister defended ye, saying ye traveled to earn yer way. A sword for hire. How do ye expect to raise my Keigan if he chooses to live with ye as yer son?" With the boys outside, now was as good a time as any to find out all she could.

"Should he accept me as his father, my mercenary days will be at an end." He idled his way around the fire, hands clasped behind him. "There's always room for another sword to guard the keep." A faint smile deepened the dimple in his cheek. "I'm nay too proud to join the MacCoinnich guards."

"Ye mentioned caves." She resettled her stance as though spoiling for a fight. "How do ye expect to keep a nosy wee bairn from making the same mistake as that pup?"

"Why…I would tell him he best not go there without me."

That error in his thinking caused her to snort. "Ye think just because ye say a thing, he will obey it without trying ye?"

"He does what ye tell him."

"*Most* the time, he does what I tell him," she corrected. "That's after years and years of scolding and smacking his bum for him. Dinna be fool enough to think he willna test ye to see what he can get away with." She stretched to peer out the window in search of either lad. "He might seem an angel, but let me tell ye, there are times aplenty when his wee horns knock his halo askew."

The wind chose that moment to switch directions and gust through the open window, dousing the table and tossing loose thatching from the roof across everything in its path.

"Saints alive! I had hoped to leave it open for a bit of fresh air." Brenna hefted the window's makeshift shutter back in place and wedged it shut with a stick of wood. Drying her face and arms with her apron, she turned, then froze in place. Astonishment struck her mute.

Magnus had already pulled the table aside, cleared away the soiled dishes, and wiped all but a few of them clean. "Have ye a bit of bark or something I can scrape this mess into?" he asked without looking up from slaking the debris to one corner of the table. When she didn't respond, he straightened a bit and frowned at her. "Brenna? Are ye unwell? Did something in the wind strike ye as ye covered the window?"

She shook her head. She hadn't been injured. Just rendered shocked at a man being helpful. Without a word, she retrieved a chunky length of bark she had fashioned into a trencher. "Here. This'll do." She held it to the table's edge while Magnus wiped the wet grittiness into it.

With one last swipe of the rag, he had the table cleaned and dried. As he straightened from the task, he held out a hand. "I'll toss that out the door, then move the table back." He motioned to the plates and bowls piled in a precarious stack on the stool. "I cleaned most."

"I'll finish them." She handed him the plank, snatched a dry rag from the rack beside the fire, and bent to the task. Eyes locked on the bowl in her hands, she wiped it dry within an inch of its life. Was this man truly this good? Or merely talented at acting the part? She watched him with covert glances as he dumped the dirt and returned the table to its place. When he turned back, she hurried to focus on the plates, holding up a bowl. "Ye did well. Thank ye."

He dipped his chin and gave her a faint smile that increased her edginess. Devil take him. How could he be so kind? So seemingly thoughtful?

So…friendly?

"Rain's coming down harder again," he said. "The lads will be soaked to the bone for sure." He easily scooped up the stack of cleaned dishes in his large hands and returned them to the table.

"I'll set them some broth to heating. Even though it be summer, they still could catch a chill." Head bent and gaze locked on the pot in her grasp, she turned and ran into his chest so hard, she bounced and stumbled toward the fire.

Grabbing her up in his arms, he swung her to safety, then steadied her on her feet. With a nervous clearing of his throat, he stepped an arm's length away. "Forgive me, lass. I didna wish ye to fall."

"It was my fault." She waved away his words and busied herself with stirring the coals and setting the dented pot among them. Her face burned, and it had nothing to do with the fire. "I should watch where I'm headed. This space is barely big enough for one, much less two." *Fool,* she thought. She and Keigan were two. "Two *grown* people, I mean." The devil take her and her senseless blethering. This rain needed to end before she lost her wits completely, and he carried Keigan away on the grounds that she didn't have mind enough to care for him. "Shout for them again, aye? They've been out there long enough, I think."

"I'll do one better," he said as he went to the

door. "I'll fetch them." Then he was out and had it closed behind him before she could respond.

"Thank God above," she whispered. "And give me the strength and patience to get through this," she added with a glance heavenward.

BRENNA COULDN'T BELIEVE her eyes. What in Heaven's name had she done to deserve such? Too late, she remembered a priest once telling her that she should never pray for patience. Because if she did, the good Lord would bless her with even more trials to pound the trait into her. She pointed at a spot on the floor. "Were ye not standing right there when I told him to stay away from the stream because the banks might give way?"

Positioned just outside the door, Magnus didn't answer, just blinked through the mud and rain streaking down his face. The man was so coated in muck, he could pass for a *bodach,* the mythical creature rumored to rise from bogs and steal away naughty bairns. Keigan stood to his left, coated in sludge to the point of having clumps of moss and grass sticking out of his hair and clothes. Evander, the only one not clothed in Scotland's soil, stood at his right, soaked to the bone and balancing a load of wood in each arm.

Two of the three needed their arses tanned for them, and it was all she could do to keep from sending Keigan to fetch her a switch to handle the task. She pointed at Evander. "Inside and by the fire with ye. Dinna stack that wet wood on the dry, ye ken?"

"Aye, mistress." Evander bobbed his head and hurried past her.

She jabbed her finger first at Keigan, then at Magnus. "The two of ye strip off yer muddy clothes and spread them out there on the bushes. If luck's with ye, the storm will wash them clean. If the rain stops, ye'll both be down at the stream washing them yerselves." Still blocking the door, she gave them each a stern up and down once over. "And rinse yerselves off the best ye can whilst yer about it. Ye'll nay be bringing all that mud in here."

"But the floor's dirt anyway," Keigan whined. "And—"

"Keigan! Hush, lad!" Magnus gave the boy's shoulder a gentle nudge. "If ye value yer arse, I think it best we do as she says."

Perhaps the man had a wee bit of sense after all. She arched a brow at Keigan. "Our floor may be dirt, but our blankets and pallets are not, now are they?"

The child stared down at his feet that were three times their normal size because of the wet earth clinging to them. "Nay, Auntie," he replied meekly. "They are not."

"Once ye rid yerselves of the muck, ye will have the fire, a dry blanket, and a cup of broth." She left the door open to make sure Keigan did as he had been told. She would not have a layer of mud covering everything in their shelter. After tossing several sticks of wood on the fire and handing Evander a blanket, she went back to the door to check on the lad's progress.

Her mouth fell open. Both Magnus and Keigan stood in the rain, bare as the day they were born, their pale skin glistening in the half-light of the gloomy day. They were at the large wooden barrel she used to catch rainwater. Magnus stood behind it. Thankfully, the height of the cask hit at his waist, shielding her eyes from the parts of him a proper lady wouldn't wish to see. Well, a proper lady wouldn't wish to see such things. But she hadn't been a proper lady in a long while.

She shook herself free of her wicked curiosity with a silent scolding. This was not the time to be ogling Magnus's man parts. The immediate problem was that her mud-covered child stood *inside* her barrel of precious rainwater that kept her or whoever else had to fetch water from having to walk all the way to the stream. The lad disappeared down into the keg, then reappeared free of his coating of filth.

"And just what in Heaven's name do the two

of ye think ye are doing?"

"Ye said ye didna wish mud inside," Magnus reminded with a sly wink. He lifted Keigan out of the barrel and stood him on a patch of grass. "There's nary a speck of filthiness on him now." With a wave toward the door, he sent the boy running. "Stay to the grass so ye dinna get yer feet muddy again."

Skittering the short distance to the door, Keigan hopped inside and ran to the fire. Teeth chattering, he inched as close to it as he could. "The fire feels good."

Brenna grabbed a blanket and wrapped it around him. "Ye know ye'll have to fetch water from the stream now that ye've muddied the water barrel?"

"It was my idea," Magnus said. "Dinna blame the lad."

Without thinking, she turned to berate him, then whirled back around and faced the fire, her face burning. "There is a blanket waiting for ye. There on the cot. Do me the courtesy of covering yerself, aye?"

The man had filled the doorway, his body sculpted and glistening, wondrous and muscular as a mythical god of old. He had stood there unashamed. Nay, not unashamed, but proud of his fine naked form.

She caught Evander grinning and threatened a step toward him. "I may not be yer mother, but

I'll still box yer ears for ye, ye ken?"

"Aye, mistress." His mouth clamped into a flat line, and he focused his attention on the fire.

"Have ye covered yerself?" she asked as she wrapped her hand in her apron and lifted the bubbling pot of broth from the coals.

"Aye, lass. I promise 'tis safe for ye to turn now."

The mirth in his tone made her consider flinging the soup at him. But, nay, she wasn't that foolish. He wasn't worth it, and it would be a waste of a good broth. Instead, she shoved around him, not sparing him a glance. "Move to the fire. I'll bring yer cup to ye."

"As ye wish, mistress." Before moving deeper into the room, he pulled the door closed. "Wind's picking up and changing again. Looks to be another stormy afternoon."

God help me. She poured a bit of broth into each of the cups, dividing the meager leavings from their midday meal between the three. It was a wonder there had been anything left at all. Two grown males impossible to fill, and Keigan doing his best to become a third. "Take this, and I'll fetch each of ye a crust or two for sopping, aye?" She served Keigan and Evander first. Magnus would be last as punishment for his brazen behavior.

"Thank ye, lass." He grinned, accepting the cup and bread as though she had handed him a feast. "As penance for my teasing, I'll wash our cups after we've finished and the dishes after supper, aye?"

"I would rather ye clean out the rain barrel, so the water willna be fouled."

"Aye, it needs dumping. I kinda peed in it," Keigan confessed, his words muffled by a mouthful of bread.

"Son!" Magnus stared at the boy as though he couldn't believe what he had just said.

"I couldna help it." The lad sipped his broth, smacked his lips, then dipped the last of his crust into the cup. "The water just made the pee come out afore I could stop it."

With a heavy sigh and shake of his head, Magnus rose, downed his broth, and went to the door. He arched a brow at Brenna. "Mistress? Yer back, please? I shall hang my blanket on the hook whilst I tend to the barrel."

She turned away from him, then stole a glance over her shoulder just in time to catch sight of his bare arse as he stepped out the doorway. He was indeed a finely made man. Once more facing the fire, she closed her eyes and rubbed her throbbing temples. But finely made or no', she prayed Keigan would soon send his father on his way. Opening her eyes to the two lads with their heads together, smiling and whispering, she feared her prayers would go unanswered. How could she compete with the life Magnus offered the boy?

"Yer rain barrel is clean and uprighted, m'lady," Magnus announced a few moments later.

"I have asked ye not to call me that," she snapped. Without looking at him, she retreated to her pallet and took up her mending. "Do me the courtesy of remembering, aye?" A glance up from her stitching told her every male in the room watched her as though they feared she had gone mad. "Forgive me," she said in a quieter tone. "This endless rain is wearing."

"Evander, once ye and Keigan finish yer broth, why dinna ye show him another game?" Magnus scooped up his stool and moved it to her side of the room.

"Which game?" Evander drained his cup and shoved the last of his bread in his mouth.

"I dinna care," Magnus said in a warning tone. "Something entertaining, aye? Later, we'll tell more stories. Like the ones from Sutherland's songs."

"Who is Sutherland?" Keigan asked as he took his empty cup to the bucket and washed it.

"Sutherland MacCoinnich," Magnus explained. "Youngest of the MacCoinnich brothers."

"Ye speak of them as though they're family," Brenna said before she could bite back the words. But in for a penny, in for a pound. "Ye are a de

Gray. How came ye to claim Clan MacCoinnich as yer own?"

"The four brothers and I survived many battles together." He took his cup and Evander's to the bucket, washed, then dried them. "Perhaps not brothers by blood, but brothers by battle and blade." Once back at the stool, he rested his forearms on his knees, watching the boys as he spoke. "I have no other kin. They are the only family I have ever known—other than my mother." The rickety stool creaked as his weight shifted. "When I call ye 'm'lady,' I mean no disrespect or teasing." With a kind sincerity she found very disturbing, he made a gallant tilt of his head. "I hold ye in the highest esteem, Mistress Brenna. I swear it. Ye have done more than well by Keigan, and I owe ye greatly."

She stabbed the needle into the cloth, wishing he would move his attention to the young ones. "I would still ask that ye bide by my wishes, aye?" Knotting the finished stitch, she cut the thread with her teeth. "I have my reasons."

"If ye've another needle, I can help with the mending." He motioned toward her basket, mounded with garments needing attention. "I'm sure my stitches are not as fine as yers, but they'll hold."

"Ye will not help with the mending." How dare he say such a thing? "Is this another of yer poor attempts at mocking me?" Men didn't mend. Men did nothing but create more work for women.

"Who do ye think mends my clothing when I'm off in the Highlands?" The storminess of his frown triggered a twinge of regret and irritation through her. "I'd be bare-arsed as the day I was born if I depended on someone else to tend to all my chores."

"Here." She plopped the basket between them, then pointed to a shelf above his head. "Needle and thread up there. In the chipped crock. Do as ye will." She didn't allow Keigan pouting, and she'd be damned if she tolerated it in another.

With a smug huff, he fetched the tools, pulled a tunic from the basket, and started sewing. Brenna watched him through her lowered lashes, keeping her head bent over her own mending. What a strange man, this Magnus de Gray. And try as she might, she couldn't find any deceit or meanness in him. The man wanted to know his son, be a father, and atone for his past sins. Plain and simple. Brenna shook herself free of the judgment. Nay. She had to be wrong. Kindness in this unfriendly world was rarer than the finest gold—especially in men. But she had yet to catch him in a lie or the slightest show of malice.

He cut the thread with his teeth, squinted, and pulled at his handiwork, then folded the garment and set it aside. "One done," he announced with a smugness that made her want to thump him. He pulled another item from the basket with a challenging look. "Ye're falling behind, mistress. Pick up the pace, or ye'll look the lazy layabout by letting a worthless man out do ye."

Before she could stop herself, she stabbed her needle into his thigh.

"Ow!" He jerked away, rubbing the spot she had impaled. "There's no call for that now. Can ye no' take a bit of teasing?"

"Auntie!" Keigan called out from across the room. "What did ye do?"

"She showed me a new stitch," Magnus lied. "Pay attention to the game Evander's teaching ye, aye?"

"Aye. I will." The lad watched them for a few moments, then returned his attention to the sticks and stones arranged on the floor.

"Forgive me," she whispered, swallowing her pride. "I dinna ken how ye manage to nettle me so, but ye are the most irritating man I believe I have ever met." Lord have mercy. She hated apologizing when she would much rather just stick him with the needle again. But nay, she was in the wrong. She should have held her temper and ignored the fool. That would have served him better.

Magnus's smile broadened so much his dimple became a crease. "Thank ye, lass. I do believe those are the kindest words ye've given me since we arrived."

She couldn't help herself. She stabbed him in the leg again.

CHAPTER FOUR

S TEADY RAINFALL STILL pattered outside. The mouth-watering aroma of fried bread filled the room. A pot on the fire gurgled with a heavy *glop* against its cracked lid—a hearty parritch, Brenna's standard morning fare. The subtle smokiness of a stirred fire added a homey feel to it all.

Magnus shifted in his seat, doing his best to watch Keigan without staring. The child intrigued him; the son he had feared he might never find, just as much as he had feared that he would— quite the double-edged sword.

He sipped at the steeped honey water Brenna had thrust into his hands without a word. The refreshing tartness of the lemon balm she added helped offset the cloying sweetness of the golden syrup. A smile came to him. He wondered if she realized lemon balm calmed and improved moods. In that case, the two of them needed the stuff by the buckets. He huffed out a silent laugh. Aye, she knew the herb's properties. That's why the lass kept a warmed pot of the stuff at the ready.

Even after several days spent in close quarters, a dangerous mix of pure dislike and leeriness still charged the air, threatening to blow the tiny dwelling to bits. An endless string of summer storms had trapped them inside until the idea of a good soaking appeared the lesser evil. Daily necessities of tending animals, fetching fresh water and firewood, or emptying the chamber pot from behind the blanket partitioning off part of the room provided too brief a respite from their forced close company.

The days had been tense, but the nights were worse. Long stretches of listening to each other breathe as minutes crept into hours. Rarely did the wary lass succumb to anything more than light dozing, startling awake at the slightest noise. Magnus hoped she didn't become unwell because of the unease he had caused her. He'd tried to make it better with teasing, but that had only made it worse. Only Evander and Keigan slept soundly each night, sprawled out like a couple of pups across their pallets.

"I love Granny Wick's raspberry jam," Keigan said around the huge bite bulging his cheeks. "It's the verra bestest in all the land."

"I imagine that's why she sent it to ye," Brenna observed as she ladled a serving of parritch into a bowl and pushed it toward him. "Oats, too, my fine young man. Ye willna grow strong on jam and bread alone. Remember?"

"Do ye never eat parritch?" Keigan asked Magnus, as though seeking an ally for another slab of jam-smothered bread rather than the bowl of boiled oats he fought against every morning.

"Yer auntie's right. Parritch will grow ye into a braw warrior." Magnus dodged the question. He hated the stuff. Only ate it if starving and had avoided it so far.

"Then ye shall have a share of it, too, this morning," Brenna said as she globbed a double spoonful into a dish and handed it to him. "Father and son eating the same breakfast, at last. A prosperous start to the day if there ever was one."

The woman's sly look gave her away. She had picked up on his aversion to the mash and took wicked pleasure in torturing him with it.

"Aye, a grand start," he said, accepting the stuff as though it were poison. Within the confines of the hut, there would be no dumping it without getting caught. Never one to cower from a challenge, he scooped up a bite with his bread and ate the foul mixture as though he relished it.

When he glanced up and spotted her gleeful look, it made the pasty clump of grains sticking halfway down his gullet almost worth it. It still amazed him how she bore no resemblance to her tiny, fae-like sister. Unlike her sibling, Brenna was a powerful beauty. Like a fierce warrior woman of the Norse. Tall for a lass and broad-shouldered, he had no doubt she would do well with a sword and shield if trained how to use them.

Covertly, he allowed his gaze to appreciate the fullness of her breasts and the generous curves of her hips. With hair golden as grain ripe for the harvest and eyes striking as vivid bluebells, he would've remembered meeting this fine lass and maybe even tried to charm her. His attention slid to his son. And if that had happened, this child would not exist. Stabbing at the oats, he wondered which meddling god had cast lots for this game. Everything might happen for a reason, whether good or ill, but the gods loved toying with defenseless mortals.

He forced the last bite of parritch down, chasing it with the last of his drink. Bowl and cup in one hand, he rose and patted his stomach. "Thank ye for another hearty breakfast."

"Ye are most welcome." Brenna accepted his wares with a smug tilt of her head. After a glance out the window, she turned to Keigan. "The rain appears to have let up at last. If ye wish to show Master de Gray yer skills with our stones, ye may do so, as long as ye stay in front of the window where I can see ye as I wash the dishes."

"Please, call me Magnus." He had lost count of the times he had asked her to use his given name. While he understood her dislike of him, he hoped that somehow, they could make peace for the child's sake. And perhaps not only for Keigan but for each other as well. He liked Brenna, and the more time he spent with her, the more he realized he needed her to like him, too.

"What do ye think I should call ye?" Keigan asked as he pushed away from the table. He glanced over at his aunt, frowning when she didn't comment. He turned back to Magnus. "Well?"

"Whatever ye feel most comfortable calling me." Although, after saying that, he wondered what Brenna had always called him in front of the lad. He noticed that although she remained silent, her cockiness from earlier had disappeared. She twisted a wet rag between her hands as though wishing it was his neck she wrung instead.

"I shall call ye Magnus for now," Keigan said with amazing wisdom and clarity for one so young. "After a while longer, once I decide for certain about being yer son, I'll know better then what to call ye, aye?"

"I think that verra wise. Sound judgment, indeed." Magnus opened the door, then turned back to Evander, who was still eating every crumb he could find. He pointed at the lad. "Ye've eaten enough, boy. Our mounts are just as hungry and needing their horse bread and water, aye? I dinna wish them to feel the urge to over-forage here. There're several trees and plants that'll bloat them fiercely if they get into them."

Evander shoved the last piece of bread into his mouth, bowed a thank you to Brenna, then rushed outside. Keigan scampered out after him. "I'll help with the horses first, then we'll throw stones," he shouted back over his shoulder.

"Is that why ye brought Evander?" Brenna asked as she soused a bowl in the wash bucket, then wiped it out with the rag. "As bait?"

"Bait?" Magnus knew what she meant but wished to get this poison between them out in the open and cast it aside once and for all.

"Aye," she said, adding the washed dish to the stack of clean ones on the back of the table. "Bait. Ye said there are many children at yer *Tor Ruadh*. I'm sure ye know how young lads love to take every step the older ones do. They look up to them as if they're gods." Her scrubbing grew fiercer as she continued. "Ye knew Keigan would go with ye easier if ye had *bait* with ye."

Hell's bells, the lass kept her rage well fed. "Actually," Magnus propped the door open with a stone, inhaling a deep lungful of the clean, rain-washed air. "Evander's mother forced him to come. Alexander, the chieftain, agreed, so the boy might learn that everything we do in this world has a consequence. Appears they caught him with the smithy's daughter, and Gretna doesna think him ready to be fathering a brood of his own."

"And they thought ye to be a good teacher of this important lesson?" The huffing noise she made echoed with bitterness.

"They thought me to be a good example. Not a teacher." He stepped closer and lowered his voice to ensure it wouldn't carry outside to the boys. "I understand yer anger. The resentment. Hatred even." He threw up his hands. "Whatever ye wish to call it. I canna imagine all that ye've had to endure these past few years—but I also canna undo a bit of it. All I can do is attempt to make what lies ahead easier. For Keigan and for yerself."

Turning to watch the lads untie the horses and head toward the stream, he thumped a knuckle on the window ledge, then held up a finger. "One time I laid with yer sister. One time because she hoped to use the loss of her virginity to trade the prison of a forced marriage for the prison of a lonely nunnery. I never once told her I loved her nor ever tried to seduce her. I considered her a friend—and she knew that." He rapped the windowsill again, harder this time. "But that doesna mean I willna honor my obligation to Keigan. I refuse to desert him as my father deserted me before I was born."

Brenna propped both hands on the table and stared down at it. "She loved ye as a dear friend," she said without lifting her gaze. "Said ye were the kindest man she had ever met." She looked up at him, her face filled with pain and sorrow. "Even when we were running, even when we were starving, she never once spoke ill of ye." The furrow between her fair brows deepened as she straightened and stared out the window. "And she also told me ye had never lied nor tried to deceive her."

"I am so sorry she died," he said, thankful that now the truth stood open between them.

"I am, too," Brenna replied, swiping away an escaped tear as she turned away. Head bowed and her back to him, she pulled in a deep, shuddering breath, then blew it out.

Magnus waited, giving her the time she needed to settle what had to be a terrible storm within her. He understood little about women, but he felt in his heart that this one had been through what amounted to a terrible battle. All because of him.

She turned and faced him, a vision of composure and determination. "I am finished in here. Shall we wait outside for the lads to return with the horses?"

Magnus managed a smile and stepped aside for her to exit in front of him. "A fine idea."

He meandered around the muddy clearing,

glancing at the overgrown path that had brought him to her. Every person he had spoken to in the nearby village had talked of her with enough awe and reverence to stir the memory of a terrible time in his life.

His mother had been a white lady. A fine healer everyone sought for cures from the mildest maladies to the worst. When she had erred by insulting the vain wife of the procurator fiscal by telling the woman there was nothing to change her enormous nose, they had accused her of witchery. The court had then ordered his beloved mother crushed between boards laden with stones. To squeeze the evil from her soul, the parish priest had said. Magnus had arrived too late to save her and never forgiven himself for leaving her so unprotected.

With a glance to ensure the lads had not yet returned, he motioned toward the path leading to town. "Superstitious folk can be dangerous when they perceive themselves wronged. Ye dinna fear witch hunters?"

Brenna frowned. "I have had no trouble so far. They have been nothing but grateful and share whatever they can spare for my herbs and remedies." Her chin lifted to a defiant angle. "Unlike many places where I sought help, including those on Nithdane land, the folk here seem generous enough. Our lives have been a great deal easier because of them."

But the way she fidgeted in place, folding her arms, then letting them swing free, told Magnus more than her words. "Something troubles ye. Pray speak it. Let there be no lies or deceit between us."

"No lies or deceit," she repeated with a snide cut of her eyes over at him. "That's the only way I have kept us safe and fed most of the time since the banishment." She began gathering up sticks and loose debris that had blown into the clearing during the storm. "Rest assured, I trust no one. I have learned the hard lesson of misplaced trust. Dinna doubt that I take the greatest of care with my healing and limit any dealings with the villagers. I let no one close, and neither does Keigan."

"What kind of life is that for a child?"

"A safe one," she snapped, hefting a stick as though ready to throw it at him.

"A lonely one," he corrected. He knew. His mother had done the same to him. That's why he had left to seek his fortune at such a young age. Ironic. Since now, he preferred the peace of solitude and shied away from closeness. Closeness meant pain. Loss of friends in battle. His mother's murder.

And yet now he had a son. A child to worry about and protect. While he didn't wish to live in the noisiness of a keep such as *Tor Ruadh*, he would do so for the sake of the lad. A child needed kith and kin. "He would have friends and safety at *Tor Ruadh*."

"I thought ye said it was his choice," she dared. "Deceit?"

He gave a slow shake of his head. "Nay, woman. If the lad doesna wish to come with me, I willna force my opinions on him. I have made many a mistake in my life. I hope to do right by my son and not scar him with the same choices that scarred me."

The tension appeared to ease out of her as she studied him for the span of several heartbeats. Without a word, she resumed her tidying of the area as though their conversation had never happened.

Magnus's hopes rose. At least, she seemed to believe what he had said. He hoped so. He also hoped if Keigan went to *Tor Ruadh* that she would come, too. It wouldn't be right to leave her here all alone—so vulnerable and unprotected. Nay, he could never do that and have any peace of mind. Not after all she had already endured.

Keigan's laughter warned them the lads would be upon them soon, so Magnus made a show of flicking branches and leaves back into the bushes. Funny how he hadn't noticed the noise of lashing wind and rain so much. He had been too distracted by the storm inside the dwelling.

"See the throwers Auntie made?" Keigan

asked, holding up several long shards of stone as he approached. "She chipped and ground their edges 'til they were sharp as blades and just the right weight."

Magnus examined one of the flint missiles, impressed with its design. "Fine work." He looked up and forced himself not to smile when he caught Brenna watching him, as though his opinion mattered. "How did ye know how to create such a thing? 'Tis quite impressive, and I'm sure, verra effective."

She gave a slight shrug. "Ye work with whatever the good Lord gives ye." With an affectionate nod at Keigan, she pulled several more from her skirt pocket. "We spent many an evening this past winter perfecting our workmanship. Did we not, Keigan?"

"Aye," Keigan said as he lobbed one missile at a nearby tree that had been used for target practice before. He closed one eye, aimed again, and threw another. "Auntie's better than me with making them, but I can throw them good as her." He motioned toward the target, then nodded at the stone Magnus held. "Ye try." With a wink, he added, "It's nay as easy as ye think."

Magnus hefted the shard, studied the target, then let the stone fly, missing the tree completely.

Evander guffawed. "Did ye miss it on purpose? It canna be that hard to hit a tree with a rock."

Irritated at both himself and Evander, Magnus jerked a thumb in the boy's direction. "He knows so much. Let him try." He stepped aside. The cocky little arse wipe would see it was easier said than done. The weight of the thing had a mind of its own, causing it to fly off-kilter.

Brenna stood quietly to one side, merriment sparkling in her eyes.

Keigan grinned and passed a stone to Evander. "Here. This is my lucky one. It never misses."

The cocky lad made a show of checking the weight of the rock and aiming at the target, only to miss it completely, just as Magnus had done.

"Why, Evander—did ye miss the tree on purpose to make me feel better? Ye didna have to do that, but I thank ye for yer concern." Magnus fixed the youngling with a smug stare, certain to rub his fur the wrong way.

"Gimme another one of those flints." Evander tried again, missing the tree by an even greater distance. "Son of a whore!" he growled.

"Evander!" Magnus strode over and thumped the boy on the back of the head. "Apologize for yer coarse language in front of a lady. I know yer mother taught ye better."

The lad ducked his head. "Forgive me, Mistress Brenna. I meant no disrespect."

"Ye are forgiven." The corners of Brenna's mouth twitched, betraying her struggle not to smile.

"Ye hold them like this," Keigan said as he took Magnus's hand and placed the rock in a specific position in his palm. "Ye keep yer thumb there." The boy folded his digit over the thick end of the shard, pressing it in a slight indentation of the flint. "And ye keep yer forefinger stretched out along it just so." He fiddled with Magnus's hold until it was set to suit him. With a nod, he stepped back. "Try it now. Dinna throw it hard. Just aim and let loose of it. Kinda sling it. The weight of the rock does the work."

Doing his best to follow the child's instructions, Magnus threw the missile, overjoyed when it thunked into the tree and stuck. "I did it!"

"Well done," Brenna praised. She nodded at Evander, who stood pouting a few steps away. "Now, help Evander. He needs to learn, too."

Magnus stepped out of the way, moving to stand beside Brenna. "With those stone knives, the two of ye would be dangerous foes."

She gave him a side-eyed glare. "Dinna make fun of us. We do what we must for protection."

"I didna speak in jest, lass. Yer crafted knives are verra impressive, and the way ye wield them, even more so." When he detected a hint of a smile and pride in her stance, he breathed easier. Winning this fair lass's trust would be no small feat.

Evander crowed, "I hit it! Look! I hit it!"

"Well done!" Keigan bragged.

"I believe he's prouder of him than he was of me," Magnus said so only Brenna could hear.

"Remember what I said?" With a superior air, she smiled at Evander. "The young ones think the older ones are gods. Ye and I are merely the parents who more often than not tell them what they dinna wish to hear and make them do their chores."

His heart warmed at the fellowship in her tone. Her forgiveness meant a great deal to him. At the end of his life, when they weighed and measured all he had done, he wanted Brenna and Keigan to be on the good side of the scales.

"Lady of the Wood! We have come for ye!"

Magnus stepped between Brenna and the threatening shout. The owner of the harsh words hadn't stepped into view, but from the rustling of the bushes and the pounding steps, whoever it was didn't travel alone. "Keigan and Brenna into the hut. Evander, hurry! Fetch our swords. I canna tell how many, but it's more than one."

Relief flooded through him when Brenna grabbed up the child and ran as he had bid. Then his heart fell when she reappeared at his side with her bow and quiver of arrows.

"I meant for ye to *stay* inside the hut," he said in a low tone as a trio of men shoved through the bushes.

"Keigan is armed, as well. He's a damn fine

shot from the notch in the shutter." She nocked an arrow, then stepped forward with a fiery glare fixed on the angry visitors. "I am the Lady of the Wood. Speak yer piece."

"We are the sons of Alfric and Morag," announced the largest of the three. "They are dead."

"Both lived a great many years," Brenna countered without lowering her weapon. "Be thankful they reached the end of their life's path together."

"They are dead by yer hand," the brother to the left growled.

"We know our mother came here to fetch more of the herbs that always eased our father's breathing," the man to the right explained. "This morning, we found them dead, in the bed with the pipe ye gave them and barely a sprinkling of the herbs left between them."

"I warned Morag that too much of the smoke would make her a widow," Brenna said. "She and Alfric chose their end, not I."

"They had years left with us!" the brother in the middle snarled. "Years! Instead, they are gone. Dead by yer poison."

"Yer grief blinds ye to yer parents' wishes," Magnus interrupted, taking another step forward, so he was closest to the men and not Brenna. "They feared loneliness. One left behind without the other. Surely, ye can see they wished to walk through the veil together."

"They had us!" the brother to the left retorted. "Neither wouldha been alone as long as one of us lived. Now, we have no one to cook for us or tend the goats. Who will mend our clothes? They knew we needed them and wouldha never left them without a roof over their heads or a warm hearth in the winter."

"It isna the same," Magnus tried to explain, deciding the three selfish brothers despised the idea of fending for themselves more than they grieved the loss of their parents. "No son, no matter how beloved, can take the place of a wife or a husband. Leave here and mourn for yer dead. Know that ye have our condolences."

"And just who are ye who dares to speak for the Lady of the Wood?" asked the largest man. His glare shifted to Brenna, and he spit. "Heartless murderess that she is."

"I am the protector of the Lady of the Wood," Magnus said, barely holding himself back at such disrespect.

"Protector," the brother repeated. "Husband? We always thought her alone. Just her and the fae child some have seen charming the animals of the wood."

If acting as her husband would guarantee Brenna's safety, then so be it. "War called me away, but now I have returned to my wife and son." He sliced the air with his sword, daring them to come closer. "Leave now. Go and bury yer kin. Honor them as ye should."

"I'll have ye know we've gone to the council about the poisons yer wife hands out," the brother on the right said, his tone calm but menacing. "This isna over."

"Ye will pay!" threatened the large one with a raised fist as they turned to leave. "We mean to see to it!" The woods closed in around them as they headed back toward the village.

"We must leave here as quick as ye can pack yer things," Magnus ordered, striding down the path several steps to ensure the men had departed for certain. "Keigan can ride with Evander, and ye can ride with me." When Brenna didn't respond, he turned to see why.

Arrow still nocked, she had lowered the bow and rested it against her skirts. She stared at the path, but Magnus could tell she didn't see a thing other than what had just happened. He recognized the fear and uncertainty storming in her eyes. Panic held her prisoner.

"Brenna," he said gently. "We will get ye from here safe. I swear it. Ye and Keigan both. But we must hurry before they return."

"But I...this is our home. We worked so verra hard to build it."

"I know, lass." The despair in her voice broke his heart, but there was nothing that could be done for it. "The two of ye made a fine life here, but it appears it is time to change—like the seasons. Ye know nothing ever stays the same."

"I had hoped we were done with running," she said as she turned and moved slowly across the clearing. "I am so weary of running."

Silently, he motioned for Evander to ready the horses, then moved to walk beside her. "Ye are nay running alone this time. I'll keep ye safe. I swear it."

"Auntie?" Keigan stood in the doorway, his eyes wide and troubled. "We have to leave our house?"

"I fear so, my dear one." She stopped and lifted her face to the sky, closing her eyes as though praying.

Magnus crouched at Keigan's level. "We are all leaving together. The villagers are angry and confused, and when folk get that way, they say and do things they shouldna do. But we mean to ride away before they return. I swear, Keigan, I will keep ye and yer auntie safe."

Keigan dove forward and hit his chest, clutching him tight. "I am afeared," he whispered. "Those mean men sounded like Mr. Wicklow when he called Auntie ugly names and hit her."

At first, Magnus didn't know how to react or what to say, but then instinct and a stirring warmth in his chest overtook him. He hugged the boy and picked him up as he stood. "I will keep Auntie just as safe and happy as I intend to keep ye safe and happy, ye ken? Ye can ride with Evander. Ye would like that, would ye not?"

The child sniffed and nodded but kept his face tucked in the crook of Magnus's neck.

He patted the little lad's back and held him. "But for now, we must gather our supplies. Ye dinna wish to leave behind what's left of Granny Wick's jam, now do ye?"

"We can take the jam with us?" Keigan lifted his head and wiped his nose on his sleeve.

Magnus nodded as he lowered the lad to his feet. "Aye, son. The jam and all the other supplies she sent, but we need to hurry so we can get on our way as soon as possible."

Keigan gave him a quivering smile. "I'll gather my things quick as a blink." Then he scampered off, grabbing up bits and bobs and stuffing them into a cloth sack.

"Where will we go?" Brenna asked quietly from behind him.

Magnus turned and risked taking her hand. She looked pale and suddenly very weary, but at least she didn't pull away. "I intend to keep my word to Keigan," he said. "For now, we will just go away from here to keep ye both safe. He still has the right to decide whether he wishes to be my son and return with me to *Tor Ruadh*."

Brenna stared at him as though trees had just sprouted from both his ears. "Ye would still give him his choice? Even when this madness could work to yer advantage?"

"I gave the boy my word." He gave her hand a gentle squeeze. "I gave that same word to ye." Pausing, he wrestled with what he knew needed saying, but the words would only bring him sorrow. Against his will, he forced the pledge out. "And if the two of ye decide ye dinna wish me in yer lives, I shall see that yer settled safe somewhere, any place of yer choosing, and then I will leave ye be." A sadness overcame him. "But I would ask if I might return and visit once in a while—just to see yerself and the boy. Make certain ye're faring well?" The thought of them living without his protection pained him, troubled him more than he wished. But he would keep his word, even though it would rend his heart in two.

"My sister was right," she whispered, easing her hand free of his and hugging it to her middle. "Ye must surely be the kindest man in all the world. And the most decent."

The stirring in his chest warmed even more. It swelled through him, threatening to cut off his air. It took a forced swallow to enable him to speak. "I dinna think I am any of those things, lass. I am just a man trying to do what's right."

CHAPTER FIVE

T HEIR MOUNTS SLOWED to a halt as they reached the summit of a steep rise. In silence, they looked back. The billowing column of smoke in the distance twisted like a knife in Brenna's heart. Her and Keigan's cozy home was no more. It had been little, but it had been theirs, and they had enjoyed many a happy time there.

"Why did they burn it?" Keigan asked from his seat in front of Evander.

"Because they're stupid bastards," Evander supplied before anyone else offered a more mature reply.

Magnus turned to scold the boy, but Brenna stopped him with a quick pat on his back. "Leave him be," she said, thankful for the unlikely saviors

Divine Providence had sent just in time. If Magnus and Evander hadn't shown up when they had, she wasn't sure what she would have done. The man she had hated since her sister's death wasn't the man sitting in front of her. Nay, that foul imagining had been a heartless monster who cared for no one other than himself. Magnus was not that monster.

She tightened her hold on his belt and patted his back again. "Let us be gone now, aye? What's done is done, and canna be changed. No sense staring at where we have been."

"We'll ride west for a while to gain some distance from them. Then cross back to the coastline for easier traveling south." He urged his horse onward at a good clip. "Three days to Inverness. We'll head that way 'til Master Keigan decides his future. Would that suit ye well enough, in case he decides the two of ye should go on without me?"

Her heart twitched at the way he said that. She felt and heard the melancholy in his tone. But it wasn't just that. The thought of Keigan casting Magnus aside almost made her sad. She shook away the dangerous tenderness, refusing to give it a minute more of her time.

"What say ye, lass?" Magnus urged, turning his head for her answer.

"Aye. That'll do just fine." Whatever the man thought best. She couldn't think straight. The past few days had been nothing but a wearying upheaval she hadn't foreseen.

Evander thundered past, pushing his horse into the lead. As they cantered down the rolling hillside, Keigan's laughter filled the air.

"No faster, Evander!" Magnus shouted after them. A disgruntled growl rumbled from him. "I swear that youngling keeps his head up his arse half the time."

His frustration made Brenna smile. "'Tis part of the trials and joys of parenting."

"How in the name of all that's holy do ye bear it?"

"Bear what?"

"The worrying about him." Magnus nudged his horse into a smooth gallop to catch up with the boys. Exasperation and wonder filled his voice as he shouted back at her, "Will he get hurt? Is he hungry? Is he ailing? Does he understand why I tell him what I do? God's beard! Does it never end?"

The ranting of his insecurities over the thundering gait made Brenna laugh. "I dinna think it will ever end," she called out. "Remember—this is my first time raising a bairn, too."

Magnus slowed the horse. Thankfully, they no longer needed to shout. "I thought women were born knowing."

"Born knowing how to raise a bairn?"

"Aye."

"Not *born* knowing but taught." An old bitterness flared, prodding her to add, "At least some clans teach women about bairns. If there's an elder who cares enough to offer advice." As soon as she shared her resentment, she regretted it because the conversation came to a halt. Perhaps it was just as well. In her current state, she risked saying more than she should. No one cared to listen to a snarling harpy, and she didn't wish to sound like one.

They rode on in silence for a long while. Warm sun on her back and the repetitive *thump* of the horse's hooves. The hypnotic combination lulled her past the point of caring about decorum. Perhaps it wouldn't be so wrong to just lean against him for a moment or two while she rested her eyes. Nothing improper about that. The linen of his tunic, soft from many washings, almost gave her a sense of comfort and safety. Or was it the raw power in the muscular body shifting beneath the cloth? And he didn't reek like most of the men they had forced her to tolerate. Nay, some sort of aromatic spice blended with his pleasant, manly musk. She breathed in deep, then tightened her grip on his belt and relaxed even more. Her cheek settled in the inviting dip between his shoulder blades. Surely, he would understand and not take offense if she rested against him for just a moment.

"Hold up!"

Brenna jolted awake, disoriented and shaken. "What…what's wrong?"

"Ye were about to slide off, lass," Magnus said with a gentle squeeze of her hand. "Come. Sit in front of me so I can keep ye from falling whilst ye rest."

"Nay, I'm…I am fine," she mumbled, blinking against the lingering sleepiness.

"Nay." Magnus twisted in the saddle, wrapped an arm around her, and pulled, sliding her off the back of the horse and settling her neatly in the front of him before she could argue. He tucked her snugly against his chest, then kneed the mount back into motion. "Rest yerself. There's no shame in it. The past several days have been a trial, and ye've slept verra little. What with my showing up. Angry villagers. Losing yer home. 'Tis no wonder ye're bone-weary. Grant yerself this time of rest whilst we ride. I'd say ye've more than earned it after everything ye've done to protect Keigan with no one to help ye."

"Well…" A humbling guilt filled her at such lavish praise. "I canna take credit for everything. Granny Wick was a great help. If not for her kindness, Keigan wouldha been born in a stable much like our Lord and Savior."

"Quite a few years have passed betwixt then and now." Magnus's arm tightened around her as they maneuvered across a ridge dotted with large stones. "I'd say the lion's share of the credit for the lad's health and well-being should still go to yerself."

"Ye're verra kind," she said quietly, hoping he wouldn't hear. At the very least, she needed to dislike this man. She had given up on hating him. But becoming his ally and helping him grow close to Keigan would only result in the loss of her sweet child.

If her wee one left for *Tor Ruadh,* what purpose would she have in this life? She tucked her chin and allowed herself to lean against Magnus, closing her eyes to prevent further discourse. The more he talked, the more he heaped praise and thankfulness upon her, the more unsettled she felt. Considering Magnus de Gray the enemy had become almost impossible.

Even though the idea of sleeping again seemed farfetched, the next time Brenna opened her eyes, the countryside had transformed. Gone were the rolling hills dotted with clusters of trees here and there. Dense woods had taken their place. Steeper inclines and gnarled crags. The long shadows where the sun pierced through the canopy of thick pines told her it was later in the day. She straightened, reluctantly pushing away from the warm muscular chest that had made quite a comforting pillow. "Where are we?"

"The heart of the northern tip of Scotland. Probably farther inland than ye've been in a while. Still about two days' ride from Inverness." He brought the animal to a stop. "This looks to be a good place to tarry for a bit. The horses need rest and water."

"And I need to make a pee," Keigan said, grabbing hold of Evander's sleeve and swinging down to the ground before anyone could offer a hand with his dismounting. He scurried to the nearest tree and let out a relieved groan as his stream hit a mound of pine needles.

"Best steer clear of that tree's shed for pallets," Evander teased. "He's done soaked them through."

"Ye dinna need to pee?" the child asked while still watering the base of the tree.

Evander joined him and, with his back to Brenna, set to releasing a stream of his own. "Aye, and this be a good enough place, I reckon."

Magnus chuckled, then offered his forearm to her. "Take my arm, and I'll swing ye down so ye might escape these two unmannerly heathens and tend to yer own needs."

"I thank ye." As soon as both feet hit the ground, she shook out her skirts and hurried off behind a thicket. She needed some relief after so long in the saddle. As she took care of pressing matters, she listened to Magnus get the boys started on several chores. Their conversations made her smile. The man claimed to know nothing about parenting, yet the way he handled the lads said otherwise.

A great deal more comfortable, she emerged from behind the bushes. Her feet sank into the soft thickness of pine needles as she looked around. A deep breath treated her to the sharp, clean scent of the trees. She'd be harvesting some of those long green needles for steeping. Chopped and steeped in boiling water, they made a pleasant hot drink to stave off a morning's chill.

She paused and glanced upward again, unable to get an unobstructed view of the sun's position through the treetops. "Will we spend the night here?" No sense gathering what she needed for the brew if they would soon be on their way.

Magnus studied the place as he walked around the naturally formed clearing the land had been kind enough to provide. "Aye. I believe so. We covered a lot of ground today, and whilst our beasts are fine and hardy, they're nay used to carrying two riders and all the additional supplies we loaded. They could use a good night's rest." He grinned. "And I'm not too proud to admit I would enjoy a brief stay here, too."

"There's fish!" Keigan's excited shout came from somewhere deeper among the trees.

"He's already caught one!" Evander crowed before the echo of Keigan's excitement had fully faded.

"They're supposed to be watering the horses," Magnus said with a failed attempt at sounding stern.

"Keigan loves guddling for trout," Brenna explained. "Almost as much as he loves eating them." She shrugged. "And the boy has a talent for it. I assure ye we shall eat well tonight, considering all we just heard."

Magnus stared at her as though he didn't believe what she had just said. "Five years old and already an expert at tickling fish from a burn?"

"Aye." His surprise pleased her. Most men didn't think a woman could survive alone in the wild, much less train a child to survive, too. "He's also adept with a bow and almost better at throwing daggers than I am. Ye saw him throw the stones." She squared her shoulders. "And I am none too shabby at daggers and stones either, mind ye."

Magnus shook his head, then trudged off toward the boys' shouts. "I reckon I best see to the horses and the filling of the water bags, myself," he called back to her.

Brenna knew better. If Magnus was like most men, he'd be down at that stream cheering Keigan on before she could blink twice. A sadness overcame her as she busied herself with pushing dried pine needles into piles for their pallets. A father and son would naturally share the joys of hunting and fishing. Keigan had enjoyed learning the skills from her, but now he and Magnus would be on equal footing and able to share in the hunt's thrill. They would quickly forget her.

Cutting a branch from a nearby tree, she used it as a broom to clear the area of broken sticks, pinecones, and whatever else cluttered the encampment. The longer she swept, the more she thought about losing Keigan. She wasn't a fool. As kind as Magnus had been, why wouldn't the lad choose to accept him as a father? After all, how many times had the boy asked about his parents over the years?

Brenna suddenly regretted that she hadn't instilled a deep, dark hatred for the man within Keigan. A bitter laugh escaped her. She hadn't painted Magnus in a good light, but neither had she raised the boy with the undying need to hunt the man down and kill him. Nay, she could never have done that. Her conscience wouldn't allow it. The fault of Keigan's begetting didn't fall fully on his father's shoulders. Her sister had known full well what could spring from her ridiculous plan. Brenna swept harder, attacking the ground with a vengeance. Aye, but there was no way her sibling could have known all the chaos that would spring from that one fateful decision.

A horse's snort made her turn. Magnus led both steeds while carrying the bulging water bags slung over one shoulder. "He's already caught enough for supper. Fine, fat trout. Now, he's helping Evander set traps for game and find ramps and mushrooms to go with them." He draped the straps of the leather water bags over a branch, then stretched a rope between two trees and secured the beasts. "I promised him I'd help clean the fish. He left them by the stream. I'll bring them to ye once I've finished."

"Verra good," was all she could reply through the misgivings churning within her. Her sweet nephew was lost to her for certain. Even though Magnus had offered her a home at *Tor Ruadh* as well, how could she accept such charity? For that matter, had he truly meant it? Nay, she wouldn't even consider such. Hanging on to Keigan like a poor relation begging for food and shelter would be nothing but an embarrassment to the child. Besides, Magnus probably had a woman at the keep ready to care for his son. *As well as himself,* she silently added.

With a stern rolling of her shoulders, she cast aside the self-pity. She would do what she must and do it with pride. What was done couldn't be undone. Tossing aside the crude broom, she hurried to start a fire and search out rocks that would help with propping the skewered fish and be flat enough to hold her poor battered pans.

A stick snapped behind her, and she whirled about. Keigan stood there, a worried look on his face.

"What's wrong with my lad?" Brenna rushed to him, chucking a finger under his chin as she searched him for injury. "Are ye hurt? Did ye eat something ye couldna tell what it was? I told ye never to test things without checking with me first." God help them both if he had eaten a dangerous plant. One that she might not be able to identify or counteract with the herbs she had packed. "Keigan, what is it?"

"My head's a weighing heavy on my heart, Auntie."

Rarely was Keigan without a smile unless he had done something he shouldn't. Brenna stepped back, folded her arms, and waited. Silence paired with a stern look usually worked best at convincing the lad to confess all.

"I havena done a thing wrong," he said as though reading her mind.

"Then what vexes ye?" Softening her motherly glare, she gave him an encouraging smile. "Ye ken well enough ye can tell me anything, my wee one. Now, what is it that's troubling ye so?"

He chewed on his lip for a long while, peering up at her with those pale blue eyes that so resembled his mother's. After puffing up with a deep breath, then blowing it out, he spoke. "I like Magnus."

Her heart shattered, knowing what he was trying to tell her but couldn't find the courage to say. Be that as it may, the child needed to learn to speak his mind, even when it might not be easy to do so. She forced herself to act as though his announcement was perfectly understandable.

"Magnus has been verra kind. In fact, I'm certain he saved us by carrying us away from those villagers so quickly."

The boy nervously shifted in place, avoiding her gaze and narrowing his eyes as though sighting in a target just past her shoulder. "Aye, but that's no' exactly what I meant."

"Then perhaps ye should say what ye mean," she prodded. "A man knows how to speak his mind clearly." She cleared her throat to cover the trembling in her tone. "Mercy! Stirred up a storm of dust making camp." With the threat of tears back under control, she gave him another nod. "Well, what is it, lad? Tell me now."

"I think I want him to be my da," he said so softly she almost failed to hear him. "I think he needs me for a son."

Brenna forced a smile. "Of that, I have no doubt. Any man would be blessed to have ye as a son."

"But what about ye?" He frowned and dug the toe of his boot into the soft ground. "If I take Magnus as my da, will I lose ye? I know ye have never liked him."

She crouched down and pulled him into a fierce hug. "Ye will never lose my love, no matter yer choice. Remember that always, my fine warrior—always, ye ken?"

He hugged her tight, digging his chin into the crook of her neck like he used to do as a wee bairn. "Aye, but since ye dinna like him, I know ye willna wish to come and live with us at his clan's keep. He said ye could though, ye remember?"

"I remember. But ye could always visit me wherever I decide to make my home," she countered with a reassuring pat on his back. "Besides, I doubt he really meant the offer of a home to me. Folk often say things they dinna mean when they're trying to win ye over."

"I damn well did mean it," Magnus declared as he stepped into the clearing. "If I hadna meant it, I would never have said it."

His interruption startled her, nearly knocking her back on her heels. She unwound Keigan's arms from around her neck and slowly stood, assuming a self-righteous air. "Eavesdropping is a verra rude habit."

"It also appears to be a verra necessary one." Magnus strode forward, his look thunderous. "I realize I have erred in many a way when it comes to Keigan, yerself, and yer sister, but I have never lied to any of ye, and I never will. I swore ye would always have a home at *Tor Ruadh* and the protection of Clan MacCoinnich, and I meant it."

Keigan took her hand, his proud grin betraying that perhaps he'd had this confrontation planned all along. "Ye see? We would all be together, and then my heart wouldna be so heavy with having to choose between the two of ye."

If the wee beastie had set this snare on purpose, she would tan his backside for him. "Keigan Ruari Maxwell—"

"—de Gray," Magnus added.

"What?"

"Keigan Ruari Maxwell de Gray," he said louder, saying the words slowly so she wouldn't fail to understand them. "That is my son's name."

"So, it's come to that, has it?" She shot him an angry glare, then turned her disapproval on Keigan. "Ye sided with *him*? Against me? Thought to trick me into doing what ye wished? Is that how ye treat someone ye love?"

"Keigan—" Magnus strode forward and pushed his way between them. His glare clashed steel with hers as he spoke with the lad. "Evander snared a pair of ptarmigans to go with the fish. Ye might help him clean them whilst yer auntie and I speak privately."

Keigan turned and ran as though the devil himself nipped at his heels. The boy was not a fool.

"Dinna ever speak to my son that way again." Magnus's voice was low, but his intent raged loud and fierce. "The lad's fear of losing ye is real. Have all yer trials hardened ye to his needs?"

"Keigan *needs* to know the meaning of loyalty to those ye love." The man's scolding grated like the cut of a rusty knife. Perhaps, she shouldn't have spoken so harshly to Keigan, but the wee one should have just been honest with her, not set up some foolish ruse to get what he wanted. "I wouldna have said what I did if he'd had the grace and courage to talk with me honestly—as he shouldha."

"He's a bairn," Magnus defended. "Ye're the only mother he's ever known. Not only does he love ye, but he fears losing ye and yer approval."

"Grand words from a man who just hours ago claimed to know nothing of parenting!"

"He wishes to be my son. Wants to come to *Tor Ruadh* and see how life with a family can be." With the force of a charging beast, he backed her up a step. "But he canna bear the thought of a day without ye, and as far as I am concerned, he doesna have to." He shoved his face close to hers. "Why, in the name of all that's holy, would ye refuse to come with us to the keep?"

"Because I'd be a burden," she shot back. "All would pity him for being tethered to an impoverished woman of no name, and I am sure they would assume *no moral standards*. They would gossip about how I cared for the both of us for as long as I did without a man at my side." She fisted both hands, tempted to strike him. "I willna put Keigan through that."

"Ye are a healer," Magnus retorted. "And it's also none of their damned affair how ye kept him fed."

"So, ye want yer son associated with a woman yer clan might brand as a whore, or maybe even a witch?"

Before she realized what he meant to do, he grabbed hold of her shoulders. Holding her tight, he spoke through clenched teeth. "My mother was executed for being a witch." He paused, the muscles in his square jaw rippling. "Gretna Cameron, Evander's mother, came close to being burnt at the stake for the same reason. Alexander has ordained that if any in Clan MacCoinnich accuses another of such, they damned sure better be able to prove it. True, factual evidence. Not the charades of a well-paid witch pricker." Nostrils flaring, his jaw flexed again. "And I willna grace yer other insult with a response. Folk always gossip. Their foolishness isna worth yer time or worry."

She could tell he wanted to shake her hard enough to snap her neck but held himself in check. Devil take him. The fool man couldn't even be accused of being abusive. Where in heaven's name had her sister found this oddity when it came to men? Managing to yank free of his hold, she shoved away and put an arm's length of space between them.

His nearness bothered her. Not because she couldn't stand him, but because no matter how hard she tried, she couldn't despise him either. No wonder Keigan already loved the irritating beast. Kindred souls attracted each other like bees to heather. She waved him away as though he were a midge. "Ye should be proud of yerself. Won him outright, ye have, and all will be just as ye wished. Dinna fash yerself, he will be fine with visiting me now and then. Ye'll see. He'll adjust. Bairns always do."

"I will *see* nothing." He closed the distance between them again and took hold of her. Locking his fingers in her hair, he tipped her face up to his and tightened his other arm around her waist. "I willna take him from ye, nor will I leave ye alone and unprotected. It wouldna be right, and I willna burden my conscience with such a deplorable act."

By heavens, if he was determined to churn her emotions into a storm, she would do the same to him. A futile shove to push herself free again only made his embrace tighten. "What am I to ye other than an annoyance?" she goaded, doing her best to vex him even more so he might release her.

"Ye speak the truth about that," he agreed in a low, dangerous tone that sent a breathtaking tingle through her, a tingle no man had ever triggered before. "Ye're a damned annoyance for certain." Teeth bared, he held fast for a moment longer, then his grip flexed in her hair. "But ye are the woman my son needs and..." His words trailed off as the space between them disappeared.

"And what?" she dared, digging her fingernails into the iron of his muscular arms as she squirmed to be freed.

"And ye are the woman I need, too, damn ye." Another growl escaped him, then he kissed her with such an intensity it shook her.

The action frightened her to the core. Not because she feared him. Nay, far from it. The only thing she feared was that he would let her go—and that feeling frightened her even more. Tossing both caution and fear to the wind, she clutched him tighter. Their delicious war raged, fire against inescapable fire. She reeled with its heat.

After an entirely improper amount of time, her good sense finally surfaced and freed her of his spell. For that's surely what it had to have been. Some sort of powerful witchery. Had to be. She had gotten her fill of men while working at Wickhaven. The stench of them. Their greedy pawing while she served them food and drink. All the men she had ever known, including her father, had treated their dogs better than they treated their women. She shoved at Magnus again, and this time he released her. Edging backward, one slow step at a time, she battled herself just as fiercely as she was prepared to battle him. Her ridiculous wants and needs would only lead to folly. "How dare ye! I will thank ye to never take such liberties again. Ye have no right."

"Ye will be coming to *Tor Ruadh*," he said softly, but somehow the quiet edict rumbled loud as thunder.

"Are ye asking or telling?"

He stared at her so long, she thought she would lose control and throw herself back into his arms, revealing all the loneliness and yearning to be cared for that he had uncovered within her.

"I asked ye before," he said. "Now, I'm telling ye."

"What if I dinna wish it?" she provoked. "What if I refuse?"

"Dinna challenge me on something ye have no hope of winning, lass." He took a step toward her. "Because I grant ye, I willna hesitate to accept yer challenge and win it for us both."

The suggestive innuendo in his tone made her shudder, but his self-satisfied smile stoked her anger. "I will go to *Tor Ruadh*—but for Keigan's sake. Not because ye ordered it. My sweet boy's happiness is all that matters."

Magnus had the grace to jerk a nodding approval. "Good. I am glad ye chose to come willingly."

"What is that supposed to mean?"

"Because I dare say…" The man's infuriating look turned into an even more irritating smirk. "Keigan wouldha been a damned sight embarrassed when we arrived at the keep with ye tied and thrown over the arse of my horse."

Then he turned and disappeared into the woods before she could wrestle her rage under control enough to speak.

"Damn ye to Hell!" she shouted after him.

His deep laughter echoed back to her through the trees, making her wish she had slapped him when she had the chance.

CHAPTER SIX

FOLDING THE LAST of his fried bread, Magnus sopped the drippings off the dented pewter plate Brenna had refused to leave behind. He glanced over at her as he shoved the food in his mouth. She knelt on the other side of the fire, scraping the last of their bountiful dinner into Evander's bowl. He couldn't fathom what the woman might be thinking. She kept her expression as blank as a fresh sheet of parchment. Not a word had passed between them since their explosive encounter.

What the devil had come over him? He ran his thumb along the dent in the plate, rubbing it as he stared at her. What the devil *hadn't* come over him? Already a beguiling temptation, she had become impossible to resist as she raged and threatened not to come with him and Keigan. Never had he reacted toward a lass in such a way before. A wry snort escaped him. Never had he been so inclined. But what stirred him even more, was the way this gloriously furious woman had responded to him. Fire and lightning straight from the heavens had filled that kiss.

He rose from his seat on a fallen tree and walked over to her. She acted as though he wasn't there, keeping her attention locked on her useless frittering of a stick through the softly glowing coals. Fine. He would leave her be for now. Without a word, he picked up the pile of soiled dishes and the iron skillet she seemed to cherish more than gold.

She started as though waking from a dream. "What are ye doing?"

"The lads hunted and fished. Ye cleared the camp and cooked. I intend to carry these to the stream and wash them. I do my part, aye?" Without waiting for a reply, he turned and walked away.

"Mind that skillet's handle," she called after him. "There's a crack on the underside that'll cut ye quick as a blade."

Keigan appeared at his side. "That's how she stole it out of the bin," he said in a loud whisper after a quick glance back toward the camp. "She's 'shamed about how she got most of our things before folk started paying for her healing. But I think she did good. Like treasure hunting for whatever we needed!"

"I think she did damned fine, m'lad." They walked alongside the gurgling stream until they reached where the embankment leveled out and opened into a shallow with small enough pebbles for scrubbing. Magnus submerged the dishes, leaving them to soak as he washed them one by one.

"Dinna be angry with her," Keigan blurted after a lengthy silence. "She loves me fierce, ye ken?"

"I am nay angry with her, son." He paused in his rubbing of sandy grit against the inside of the pan. "I admire yer auntie, but I also wish she would allow me to make her life easier. It is my hope she'll see that for herself once we reach *Tor Ruadh*."

"Auntie's the way she is because folks havena been all that kind to her." Crouched at his side, the youngster peered up at him with the wisdom of an old soul flickering in his eyes. "She cries a lot at night when she thinks I canna hear her 'cause I'm 'posed to be asleep."

"Why do ye think she cries?" Magnus set the skillet aside and reached for a dish. He had to keep the boy talking. The young one's insights about Brenna could be more than a little helpful.

Keigan picked up a plate and half-heartedly

swished it in the burn. "I reckon sometimes is 'cause she misses Mama." He filled the dish to the rim, then barely tipped it, and watched the water trickle out. "Before we left Granny Wick's place, she would always cry after mean old Mr. Wicklow hit her and made her go to the rooms I wasna allowed in. But I think that was 'cause she was angry at him, not 'cause he hurt her." After a thoughtful pause, he nodded. "Aye, most definitely 'cause of her ire. If ye ever see her crying when her temper's on the loose, ye best lie low. 'Cause her crying makes her rage even harder."

"I shall bear that in mind." Magnus hoped the boy kept talking. This information was golden.

Scooping up a handful of rocks, the lad clunked them into the dish and swirled them all around. "But now I think she cries mostly cause her heart's awful lonesome." The rattling pebbles inside the metal plate stilled as he looked up and met Magnus's gaze. "She doesna have a soul in this world that loves her 'cept me. Told me so herself." Dumping the rocks and wiping the dish on his shirt, he stood and added it to the stack of clean ones. He scooped up some larger stones, took aim, and threw them one by one across the water. "Do ye have a lot a folk who love ye?" he asked as he sent another pebble skittering along the stream's rippling surface.

With everything washed, Magnus stood and

started skipping stones, too. "Love is a strange thing, lad. The MacCoinnichs love me as if I'm their family." He smiled down at the boy. "I dinna ken if my falcon, Merlin, loves me, but he seems to like me well enough."

"Did ye love my mother?"

The question caught Magnus off guard so badly, the stone he threw landed in the water with a dismal kerplunk.

"Ye didna do that one verra well at all," Keigan observed.

"I did not," Magnus admitted, wondering how the hell the conversation had taken such a turn.

"Well?" the boy prodded. "Did ye love Mama? Is that why ye laid with her? Auntie says when I'm grown to be a man, I should never lay with a woman unless I love her enough to never, ever leave her. She said that's the way it's 'posed to be. Is she right?"

Hell fire and demon tails. "Aye, Keigan. Yer auntie's right."

"Then why did ye lay with Mama, then leave her?" He skimmed another rock across the water, then turned back and frowned up at him. "And did ye *ever* love her? Ye never said if ye did or no'."

"I cared about yer mother. Was verra fond of her. Considered her a treasured friend." Damned, if he wasn't babbling like a fool. Magnus looked all around, wondering where the hell Evander had gotten off to and why he wasn't here to distract Keigan.

"But ye didna love her," Keigan surmised with unnerving insight.

"Nay, lad. I did not love her," Magnus admitted. He had sworn to never lie to the boy, and he had meant it.

"Then ye should not have lain with her," the child gently scolded.

"Nay. I should not have." Magnus knelt to Keigan's level. "But if I hadna lain with her, then ye never wouldha been born, and this world wouldha been robbed of an amazing young man."

"And ye should never have left her either."

"Nay. I should not have. And for that, I have no excuse. All I can do is beg yer forgiveness and yer auntie's forgiveness." He would rather take fifty lashes across his back than continue this review of his poor choices. But he reckoned he deserved this, and all things considered, he had gotten the easiest share of the bargain. Keigan and Brenna had fought to survive because of the choices he made, and who knew what trials and suffering Keigan's mother had endured before she died.

The boy's head tilted, and his eyes narrowed. After what seemed like forever, he gifted Magnus with a precious smile. "I forgive ye—as long as ye promise to forgive Auntie whenever she yells at ye. She's kinda like a hurt animal sometimes, ye ken? Snarling 'cause she hurts inside, not 'cause ye've done anything wrong to her. She canna help it really. Just be kind and forgive her, aye? If we love her enough, maybe she can get better."

Magnus pressed a fist to his chest and lowered his chin in a solemn nod. "I shall forgive yer auntie each and every time she yells at me. I do so swear." And he meant every word of it.

Keigan beamed up at him. "Good. 'Cause she likes ye better than she does most folks."

More interested than he cared to admit, Magnus did his best to act indifferent. "Why do ye say that?"

The lad brushed off his hands and picked up the pile of stacked dishes. "Auntie never sleeps unless she feels safe. She never wouldha slept while riding with ye unless she liked ye and felt safe." His pale brows arched with an impressed seriousness. "Trust me. I know about these things."

"I am sure ye do," Magnus agreed.

"Keigan!"

Magnus shooed the boy along. "Best run now but mind those dishes. I'll bring along the skillet. Ye dinna want to keep her waiting."

The lad trotted ahead, hugging the plates and bowls to his chest.

Drumming his fingers against the bottom of

the frying pan, Magnus stared in the camp's direction, thinking back over all Keigan had told him. Brenna had not had an easy time of it. Never, from the sounds of it. Nithdane Keep had been no loving sanctuary—especially not for the women living there. And then he had made the situation even worse. He stepped up on the embankment, then came to a halt. Since Brenna had already agreed to come to *Tor Ruadh,* why the devil did this uneasiness still plague him?

He swallowed hard and stared down at the warped iron pan that belonged in the smithy's scrap bin. That warm stirring, the unnerving tightness the thought of her always triggered in his chest, squeezed him even harder than before. Brenna mattered. Her happiness mattered. What she thought and felt about him mattered more than he cared to admit.

"Dammit." How the hell had he allowed his heart to soften toward her? He knew better. "I am a damned fool," he muttered, knowing what had to be done. To undo the sins of his past and protect Brenna and Keigan both. She had to become his wife. But how he would ever get her to agree, he didn't have a clue. "She will never agree to it. Not after all I've put her through." Whacking the skillet against his thigh, he trudged back to camp, then came to a halt at the edge of the clearing. As silent as a breath, he eased behind a thicket, watching the comforting scene before him.

Brenna had Keigan sitting on a rock in front of her, washing his face with a wet rag. His chin trapped in her hand; the lad looked less than pleased about the scrubbing. But she had a serenity that only appeared whenever she dealt with the boy. She was the picture of a loving mother, taking care of her child.

Her child. Keigan was as much her son as his. More so, in fact, because she had raised the bairn. A heavy sigh escaped him. He had to make her realize he wanted to do better by her, and not just because of the lad. She mattered to *him.* He had to win her over. Without realizing it, his grip relaxed, and the pan slipped out of his hand. Its cracked handle sliced open his palm as it fell. A grunt escaped him at the biting sting of the cut.

"Who's there?" Brenna drew a throwing stone and pushed Keigan behind her. "Step out where I can see ye, or this stone'll find its way through the leaves, and I promise ye'll not like its greeting."

"Ease up now, lass. It's just me." He bent to pick up the pan, his heart nearly stopping when he noticed it lay in two pieces. "Shite!" he hissed under his breath. Her beloved pan. The handle and a good-sized chunk of its side had broken free from the rest. He was doomed for certain now. *Shite! Shite! Shite!* All he could do was confess and hope for her mercy.

"I didna mean to drop it. I swear I'll get ye a new one in Inverness," he said, stepping free of the bushes. "I'm sure we can find ye a fine one there." He held up the pieces, bracing himself for the arse chewing he deserved. "I am verra sorry."

Her open-mouthed shock made him feel even worse. How could he have been so careless with something she prized so dearly?

Trying to fit the two pieces back together, he slowly shook his head. "I dinna think we can mend it."

"Toss that useless bit of metal aside, ye fool man, and be quick about it. Ye're bleeding like a speared boar." She rushed over, grabbed hold of his hand, and spread it open wide.

"That hurts when ye do that!" He tried to pull away, but she held fast.

"Be still," she scolded, then turned to Keigan. "Fetch the whisky and one of my linen strips. This needs a good cleaning before I bandage it. I fear the cut's too ragged for stitches." With a brow arched higher than the other, she gave Magnus a look that made him feel like a lad caught stealing pies from the kitchen. "Did I not warn ye about the handle?"

"Aye. Ye did." He escaped her grasp and backed away until a safe arm's length of distance separated them. "It's not like I did it on purpose, ye ken? Leave off now. I can wrap it myself, and it'll be fine." He couldn't believe he had been so clumsy. "And I meant what I said. Soon as we reach Inverness, we'll find a shop where ye can have yer pick of pans. Any skillet that suits ye. Two even. I swear."

The bottle of spirits in one hand, Brenna held out the other as she walked toward him.

Damned if he didn't feel like trapped prey.

"Give me yer hand. It needs washing out before I bandage it." She marched another step closer. "And I'll be the one handling all the healing in this camp, mind ye. I'll no' risk any of ye falling ill because of neglect fueled by stubbornness. Now, show yer son how brave ye are, and let me tend to that, aye?"

When she put it like that, he had little choice. With his teeth clenched, he shoved his fist toward her.

"Ye'll grind yer teeth to dust if ye dinna relax and trust me," she said quietly as she pried open his fingers. "This'll sting a mite, but I'm sure it'll not be too bothersome for a grand warrior like yerself."

At first, he was insulted, then the searing pain of the tonic she poured across the cut made him forget. "Sons a bitches!" He tried to yank free of her hold and escape the liquid fire, but she had his wrist locked in an iron grip, and his arm hugged to her side. "What the hell is that? A red-hot iron wouldna hurt so bad!"

"It's just whisky." She blew on the cut and

held the bottle aloft. With a sympathetic smile, she hugged his arm tighter and squeezed his wrist. "Cheap whisky with herbs. A little honey. Oil of pine. Just a few things to make it better for healing. Hold yer breath now. One last rinse, and then it'll all be over."

Aye, it would all be over. As the pain from the wretched remedy faded, the soft warmth of her hugging his arm gave him an aching somewhere else.

"Here, Da." Keigan held out his hand. "I'll hold yer other hand so it doesna hurt ye so bad." The boy gave him an encouraging smile and squeezed his fingers. "It'll be done afore ye know it."

That accursed spot in the center of his chest swelled with a slow burn hotter than Brenna's foul whisky. It was the first time Keigan had called him *Da*. Magnus held tighter to the lad's hand. "Thank ye, son. Yer strength makes it a great deal more bearable."

The grateful look Brenna gave him made the tenderness in his chest rage even harder. Heaven help him, she already possessed a fearsome power over him. After his mother's gruesome murder, he had allowed nothing to give his heart the slightest twitching—until now. Now, he needed his son and this enigmatic woman protected and safe. For all time. By him.

"Ready to go now." Brenna released him and

picked up the bottle of liquid torture she had placed on the stump beside them.

"Ready to go?" Magnus stared down at his hand. He had been so occupied with the stirrings in his heart, he hadn't even realized she had wrapped his hand in a strip of bleached linen.

"We'll keep it wrapped until the cut seals over well." Still frowning at the bandaged wound, she shook her head. "Where ye're cut, isna good. The least bit of flexing, and ye'll break it right open again. We must watch it."

"Thank ye." He tucked it to his waist and made a formal bow. "And I beg yer pardon for my earlier behavior. Back in the woods. When we had words about Keigan and *Tor Ruadh*. I shouldna have done what I did to such a fine woman as yerself. Can ye find it in yer heart to forgive me?" If he were ever to win her, he had to make her know that he valued her and didna think of her as property or some wench for grabbing then tossing aside.

The way she looked at him made him shift in place as though he stood barefoot on hot coals. He wasn't good at this at all. But his son needed him, and Brenna did, too. It was just a matter of convincing her. Now was not the time to turn cowardly.

Brenna's attention moved to Keigan. She took hold of his shoulders and gave him a gentle nudge toward the horses. "Off wi' ye now. Find

Evander and enjoy what's left of the daylight, aye? He might need yer help with the beasts."

Keigan gave her a quick hug, then darted away.

When she turned back to Magnus, the look on her face made him swallow hard. A beauty when she raged, this calm kindliness made her even lovelier.

"And I must apologize for the way I responded. It was less than proper, and I am ashamed," she said. "Please forgive me."

He had never been one to dance with words. To him, the mumbling of social niceties and wordplay made as much sense as hunting with a baitless trap. They needed the truth between them—especially now that he had decided.

"I kissed ye because I could resist ye no longer," he confessed with a quietness that belied all he felt. "Yer fire draws me, lass. Tempts me. And I can protect ye and Keigan both." He braced himself for what he felt certain would be her adamant refusal. "I despise the art of gaming with words, so I'll just ask ye straight out. Could ye ever consider aligning yerself with a man like me? Especially after all the pain and loss I have caused ye?"

"Aligning myself?" she repeated in a tone that sounded as though he had just asked her to pluck gold coins out of her nose.

Perhaps he had worded his intentions poorly.

How else should he say it? He squeezed the bandages wrapped around his hand. "Aye. Align yerself, ye ken? Pair off. Consider yerself...uhm mine." There. That sounded clearer, and so far, she hadn't unsheathed her knife. A good sign for certain.

"As in yer wife?" She sounded as though she were about to laugh in his face. What the hell was so amusing?

"Nay, lass. I wouldna presume to ask ye to be my wife," he hurried to reassure. At least, he wouldn't ask her *yet*. He didn't wish to frighten her away. She needed time to know him better. Time to trust him and realize he meant only the best for her. "Ye've only just met me and discovered the truth about me."

"So ye mean to insult me by asking me to be yer mistress?" Eyes flashing and cheeks flaring a bright red. Now she looked as though she were about to draw her dagger and gut him. "Why, Magnus? Does yer woman not warm yer bed enough to suit ye?"

"What woman?"

"Yer woman! Back at the keep. Or should I say *women*?"

"I have no woman," he retorted, perhaps a little louder than he intended. "Or women. Back at the keep, nor anywhere else. Where the hell did ye come up with such an idea?" He had never said he had a woman anywhere. Why would she say such a thing? And how had she misunderstood him so badly?

"Ye expect me to believe that a man such as yerself doesna have a woman?" She gave him an insulting up and down look, then flicked her hand as though dismissing him. "Why, I'd wager ye've got a host of them longing for yer return. All sorts of lasses all across the Highlands."

"I dinna ken where ye would get such a notion. But let me assure ye, I dinna travel the Highlands in search of women to bed." Aye, he had found comfort now and then. That couldn't be denied. But compared to some, he might even be considered celibate as a monk. Apparently, he had fumbled his telling her what he meant far worse than he thought. "I wouldna dare ask ye to be my wife because ye dinna know me well enough yet, and I dinna wish to make ye bolt. Do ye not need time to know me better so ye can decide if ye would like me as a husband and protector?"

"What?"

He scrubbed his face with both hands, silently cursing himself for all those years of solitude. If he'd had any sense, he would've traveled with one or more of the MacCoinnich brothers to learn their art of wooing women properly. "I fear if I repeat all I just said that I'll mangle it worse than I did to begin with." He blew out a defeated breath and allowed his hands to drop.

She seemed calmer now. Almost pleased, even. "I heard what ye said. I'm just having trouble believing it."

"Which part?" Now it was his turn to be confused.

"The part about deciding. Because it doesna usually matter if a woman thinks a man fit to be a husband." She gave a half-hearted twitch of a shoulder. "At least not with most marriages." A sad smile trembled across her lips. "It rarely matters what a woman thinks about anything."

"My wife would be my equal," he said, wishing to take her hands but holding himself back. "She would be my partner. My helpmate. Mother to my children and likely as not, mother to myself when my conscience was found lacking, and I needed a good scolding." The look on her face spurred him on, giving him the courage to say more. "We value women for their strength and intelligence at Clan MacCoinnich." He risked sliding his fingers under hers and gently lifted her hand for a kiss. "After ye've had the chance to know me better, I pray ye'll consider taking my name. But I daren't ask ye now. It wouldn't be fair. Not while ye're so vulnerable." *Shite!* He should've left that part off. This brave lass hated for anyone to think her weak. He had seen proof of that repeatedly.

She stared at her hand, the hand he held. So very still. Not blinking. He swore she had even stopped breathing.

"Brenna?" he whispered.

She jerked as though startled, her lashes fluttering as she looked up, then eased her hand out of his. "Ye are a verra strange man, Magnus de Gray. Verra strange, indeed."

"Aye. Ye are not the first to tell me such." His hopes faltered at the way she had withdrawn, but he wouldn't give up now. He wondered if she meant his strangeness was a good thing or bad. She didn't seem *that* put off—yet. "So, will ye at least bear what I said in mind? A pairing until we've had more time together?"

"I willna bed ye until ye are my husband," she said as if throwing down a gauntlet. Her chin jutted upward, and her eyes narrowed. "And no more forced kisses either."

"If memory serves…" Magnus mimicked her defensive stance. Since she had drawn no weapons nor told him to take his offer straight to Hell, he felt surer of himself. Encouragement did wonders for a man's confidence. "I remember our first kiss as not entirely forced—leastways not once I got it good and started."

The genuine smile that sparkled in her eyes as well made her even more beguiling. "Aye, I might admit to such." But just as quickly, her look changed to puzzlement. "I just wasna certain what ye meant by *pairing*. That sounds more like the matching off of prized animals for mating."

"Betrothed," he sputtered. The word burst from him of its own volition. "I guess I didna say it that way before because I dinna wish to bind ye until ye see what a good man I will be for ye."

"Think that much of yerself, do ye?"

"Aye, I do," he said. He stood taller, puffing out his chest. "Ye are the only woman who ever set my heart astir, and I dinna intend to lose ye."

A coolness came over her, like storm clouds blanketing the sky. Jaw tight, she turned aside and stared downward. "Since we are speaking the truth and not dancing about with words, ye should know I am not a virgin before ye speak of betrothals or any sort of bindings." A bitter laugh forced its way free of her. "Ye might be a good enough man, Magnus, but are ye certain I am good enough for the likes of yerself?" She turned back to him, glare fierce, and standing as though she awaited a walk to the gallows and took great pride in the sentence sending her there. "I did what was necessary to keep my precious boy safe, warm, and fed. I am ashamed of nothing."

Magnus knew whatever he said next would either forge a path for them to walk together or build a wall between them that could never be torn down. He had to make her know that he understood and truly believed he had no right to condemn her for anything she had done to survive.

"A warrior does whatever is necessary to win

the war." He eased closer, taking care lest she decide to run. With the softest touch, he traced his fingertips along her tensed jaw, then gently cupped her face. "Yer battles made ye the woman ye are today. The lass I admire. The woman I want for my own. What is it ye said before? 'What's done is done and canna be undone'?"

The blue of her eyes shimmered to a darker shade beneath the sheen of unshed tears. When she blinked, a teardrop broke free and rolled down her cheek.

Magnus caught it on his finger and brought it to his lips. "Dinna cry, *mo ghràdh*, unless ye weep from happiness. I swear I will do my verra best to never give ye a reason for any other kind of tears."

"How could I have ever hated you?" she whispered.

"Easily, dear one." Regret for his poor choices would walk with him the rest of his days. "And I deserved it. Then." After a gentle kiss to her forehead, he smiled down at her. "But I swear to do my best to never deserve yer hatred ever again." Cupping her upturned face between his hands, he grazed another chaste kiss across her mouth before locking eyes with her. "So, we are betrothed now, aye—until I have proven to ye beyond a doubt how I'll keep ye safe and happy?"

"Aye." With a shy smile, mischief flashed in her eyes as she pressed a hand to his cheek.

"Aligned. Paired. Whatever ye wish to call it. We will see what the days ahead hold for such an unlikely match as ours."

"Unlikely?" He didn't much care for the sound of that.

"Aye. Unlikely." She tapped a finger on his chest. "A solitary man. A woman who hates people." With a glance past his left shoulder, her eyes narrowed. "And a wee lad eavesdropping in the bushes even though he knows 'tis rudeness itself!" One of her brows arched higher, and she blew out a heavy sigh. "Heaven only knows what lies ahead for the lot of us."

CHAPTER SEVEN

B RENNA STARED DOWN at her hand as they rode along. She kept her gaze locked on the ring encircling her finger, remembering the inscription Magnus had ordered engraved inside it. *Mo chridhe. M'anam. Mo chuid.* My heart. My soul. My all. A poesy ring—a symbol of the promise between them, he had said.

She could not speak when he slipped it on her finger. It fit perfectly—a prosperous sign for certain. The fine new skillet would have been more than enough, but he had insisted on the ring as well. He was determined to win her heart and wipe away all misgivings about the past. That made her smile. Silly fool. His kindness, honesty, and the way he was with Keigan had won her more quickly than she cared to admit. She might not fully love him yet, but she feared it wouldn't be long—especially when he treated her with more respect than she had ever known in her life.

"We should be there by midday." Magnus's arm tightened around her waist. "Dinna fret o'er much. I think ye will find Clan MacCoinnich most welcoming. Catriona, Mercy, Gretna—they're all kind and wonderful ladies." His pleased chuckling rumbled against her back. "All three are brutally honest, but they are each of them kind and good."

"Kind and good," she repeated, her misgivings churning harder with every thump of the horse's gait.

"Aye," Magnus continued. "In the past, they have all battled their own demons, so they're sure to understand how ye faced down yers." He paused as though searching for his next words.

His pause made Brenna smile. He worried so much about saying the wrong thing to her. Her amusement melted away as quickly as it came. In part, he agonized over everything he said because of his fumbling betrothal, but he also struggled to choose the right words because of her habit of thinking the worst about everything. She scolded herself as she glanced down at the ring again. Life appeared to be taking a turn for the better. It would only be good sense to enjoy this change of luck rather than ruin it by waiting for something ill to happen. She vowed to change her ways.

"Catriona is Alexander, the chieftain's wife. Kind but fierce as can be," he finally said. "Her brother tried to kill her when he failed at selling her to a Campbell chief before Alexander saved her." He fluttered his fingers in time with his musings, tapping them against her arm. "Mercy is Graham, the war chief's wife. She is sightless but brave as they come. She lost her sight when her lady's maid bludgeoned her. Mercy's father hired the wench to kill her. Gretna is the clan healer, married to Ian Cameron, cousin to the chief. She was a Neal, turned over to the witch hunters by her bastard of a husband, who faked his death." A growling snort clearly expressed how Magnus felt about that. "As I said, they've each of them fought their own battles and won. They all admire courage and tenacity. I think ye'll find them good friends once ye get to know them."

"That would nice." She wouldn't go into her misgivings. It had been her experience that women were often more vicious and territorial than men. But she would do her best to fit in and give everyone a fair chance—for Keigan and Magnus's sake. And she would do better about not thinking the worst unless it turned out to be so. She twisted the ring on her finger. "Will ye speak of us to them? About our...*pairing?*"

"Of course," Magnus said. "Since Evander knows, I promise ye, it'll be common knowledge in both the village and the keep before sunset. That lad couldna keep his mouth shut if his life depended on it."

"Aye, well, I suppose that's true. Keigan's been known to share everything he knows as well." She fell silent and attempted to calm herself by taking in their surroundings. The land was so different here. Lush green glens surrounded by dusky blue mountains. Thick woodlands with ancient trees bigger than what two men could wrap their arms around. Breathtaking crags and dangerous ravines echoing with the gurgling burns that had slowly carved them out of the land. It was all beautiful, but she missed the sea. Waves crashing against the shore. Terns crying overhead. The sharp tang of the salty air. A heavy sigh escaped her before she could stop it.

Magnus pulled their mount to a halt. "I think it's time we stopped and stretched our legs a bit."

Before she could comment, the boys came up alongside them.

"We stopping this close?" Evander asked as his horse danced sideways along the trail. It was as though the beast sensed its home stable within reach and was anxious to get there.

"Go on ahead with ye." Magnus waved them on. "But dinna be racing too fast across the glen and dinna enter the village until we catch up with ye, aye? I wish to be the one to introduce Keigan to one and all."

Evander grinned and tapped Keigan on the shoulder. "Ye dinna need to rest or make water, do ye? Wouldna ye rather keep going?"

His grip tight on the lip of the saddle, the lad bounced in place. "Aye! Let's be on our way."

"No racing!" Magnus ordered again.

"Aww," the boys groaned in unison.

Brenna turned and spoke low, so only Magnus could hear, "Let them run a bit—as long as they're careful. They've done well, and I trust Evander to keep Keigan safe."

Magnus still looked unsure but nodded. With a fierce glare, he pointed toward the glen. "Ye may run a bit, but take care, or I'll have both yer arses, understand?"

"Aye!" Evander grinned and took off before the adults changed their mind.

As the boys thundered away, Brenna twisted in the saddle and tapped Magnus on the chest. "Now, tell me why ye really stopped." His poor excuse of stretching their legs bordered on a bald-faced lie, and he had always sworn to keep the truth between them.

Without answering, he dismounted, then helped her down, keeping his hands around her waist long after her feet touched the ground. He looked down at her, eyes narrowing as though peering into her soul. "Ye're tenser than a newly strung bow. I feel yer worry. Hear the fear in yer voice. Tell me what I can do to make this easier for ye."

Grazing her fingertips across the stubble of his beard, she kept her gaze locked on the small silvery scar on his chin. It was a poorly mended slice from a dagger if she ever saw one. She daren't meet his gaze. So much compassion echoed in his tone. She feared she would lose control and confess all her troubles if she witnessed the same in his gaze. Her worries were hers to bear. Alone. She had nurtured them all these years, adding new ones with each passing day. She needed to keep them close until she could bury them away. They made her who she was.

"Brenna—talk to me," he whispered. "Let me help ye."

"I cannot." She patted his chest with both hands and forced a smile. "Dinna fret. I will be fine." Risking a glance upward, she swallowed hard, fighting to maintain control. "I am always fine." She patted his chest again. "Ye have already helped me more than ye know. All I ask for is yer patience, aye?"

He gathered her close and held her. "Ye have it and more," he whispered. He kissed the top of her head and tightened his embrace. "Ye are a wonder to me, ye ken?"

"How is that?"

He tilted her face upward. "As soon as I set eyes on ye, I knew in my heart ye had to be mine." His head lowered, he paused and whispered, "May I?"

"Aye," she breathed, hungry for the taste of him.

As soon as his warm mouth settled on hers, he stiffened, then jerked around, pushing her behind him.

"What is it?" She darted a glance around but saw nothing.

"Someone approaches." He drew his sword. "Listen."

Soft as a whisper, farther down the trail behind them, the unmistakable sound of hoofbeats.

"Are we not safe here? Is this not MacCoinnich land?" She drew out her throwing stones and dagger. "What about the boys?" A distant flash of red through the trees shot fear through her. "British," she whispered. "God help us." She'd had dealings with soldiers who had strayed as far north as Wickhaven, and the encounters had not been good.

"To the horse with ye," he ordered without turning around. "Ride like Hell's biting at yer heels, and dinna look back, aye? Get yerself and the boys to the keep. Warn Alexander."

"But—"

He whirled around and hoisted her up into the saddle. Without another word, he smacked the beast's rump hard and roared, "Hie wi' ye, now! Hie!"

Her weapons clutched in one hand and the horn of the saddle in the other, Brenna held on for dear life. The war horse might be enormous, but it moved with amazing speed. As the reins whipped through the air, she grabbed at them, finally catching them without losing her seat. She spotted Evander up ahead in the glen and leaned forward, praying Magnus's horse was the faster of the two. Thankfully, her prayers were answered. She cried out for the lad to stop as she came up beside him. "Evander!"

She slipped her throwing stones inside her belt but kept her dagger ready. "Get Keigan to the keep! Fast as ye can!" She turned her horse back in the direction she had just come. No time could be wasted by her going to the keep with them. "British coming. I dinna ken how many, but I'm going back to fight with Magnus. Have the chieftain send help quick as ye can."

Evander opened his mouth to argue, but she cut him off. "No arguing! Get moving! Now!"

When the boy had done as she ordered, she spurred her mount into a fierce gallop. She would ride back part of the way, then dismount and creep up on them on foot. Who knew what cowardly evil the redcoats might attempt on a lone Scot they came upon in the woods? It hadn't sounded like many approaching, and the flash of the uniform had been brief. She would do her best to maim however many there were, hopefully holding them off 'til Magnus could get to their horse and escape with her.

"Stay here and no snorting or stomping," she whispered to the mount as she led it into a thicket and secured the reins. Slipping a stone out of her belt and keeping her dagger ready, she crept forward with painstaking care through the treacherous leaf mold that risked giving her away with every crunching footstep.

Deep voices rumbled up ahead. Two men. Magnus and another. She tilted her head to better hear, then frowned. Their conversation was too low to make out the words, but it seemed unnaturally calm considering one was a Scot and the other a damned Sassenach. Was Magnus that artful in cloaking his feelings while speaking to the enemy?

She eased closer, then halted. Was that laughter? Sounds of genuine camaraderie? Silent as a beast of the woods, she shifted a branch and peeped between the leaves.

Magnus and the bloody redcoat stood side by side. All smiles. Heads nodding. Chatting like a couple of old women gossiping over their washing. Perplexed, Brenna watched them a bit longer to make certain her eyes didn't deceive her. The longer she stood there, the more irritated she became. That fool Sassenach had interrupted what had promised to be a very fine kiss. Damn him to Hell!

She couldn't stand it any longer.

"Are ye siding with the English now?" she accused as she shoved free of her hiding place.

Both men started and jerked around to face her, looking as guilty as if she had just caught them with another man's wife.

Magnus recovered quicker than the vile soldier. "I sent ye to the keep!"

"I came back to rescue yer sorry arse from the bloody redcoats!" With an angry jab, she sheathed her dagger and stones into her belt.

The 'bloody redcoat' found that uproariously funny, laughing out loud as he smacked Magnus on the shoulder. "Introduce me to your fine lady, my friend, so I might beg her forgiveness for causing such a stir."

Magnus reached for her and cocked a brow, his eyes daring her not to take his hand.

Ignoring him, she marched closer with both arms folded tightly across her chest. He had better learn she would never heel like a dog. Such would not be their relationship.

The redcoat turned aside and failed at hiding his amusement behind a fake fit of coughing.

Nostrils flaring, Magnus huffed out a frustrated snort. He stepped over to her until his arm rubbed against hers. With a nod toward the Sassenach, he said, "Allow me to introduce ye to an old friend and one of the few English I trust.

Commander Edward John Cunningham, 2nd Earl of Crestshire. He fostered with the MacCoinnich Clan. We're as good as brothers." With a tilt of his head in her direction, he continued, "Lord Crestshire, I present to ye Brenna Maxwell, a most irritating woman of fire and fury, who has seized my heart."

Lord Crestshire bowed. "It is my honor to meet a lady of such great power."

The smile he gave her seemed genuine enough, so she granted him a polite nod. "The honor is mine, Lord Crestshire. Pray forgive me, but I'm sure ye understand my reaction."

"I do indeed, madam." The commander hooked his hands onto his lapels. "Unfortunately, many of my countrymen do not appreciate the Scots for the fine, proud people they are and treat them most reprehensibly." He turned to Magnus. "Such is the reason for my visit to *Tor Ruadh*." His jovial air disappeared, and he turned grim. "My time at Fort William is at an end, I'm afraid. I am to be replaced as Garrison Commander by Lieutenant Colonel Thaddeus Barricourt. A most foul-tempered, brainless man if ever there was one. He angered his elder brother, the Earl of Estringham, and an extended assignment at Fort William is to be his punishment—and the Highlands' punishment, too, I fear. In fact, he has already arrived, stating he is ready to be apprised on the surroundings and management of the area's savages."

The man's *punishment* was his assignment to Fort William? She couldn't resist asking, "And why were ye sent to Fort William, m'lord?"

Lord Crestshire's grin returned, and this time, it was Magnus turning aside to hide a smile. "I volunteered to come here, madam. It was my honor to serve in the Highlands, close to those I loved and respected since I was just a *wee lad*."

Now, she felt a bit guilty about the question, especially since both men knew very well why she had asked it. "Again, I feel I must beg yer forgiveness. I fear my brazenness often borders on the rude."

Crestshire shook his head. "Trust me, madam, after dealing with Barricourt, I find such openness as refreshing as the air of this glen." He smiled at Magnus. "I am more than a little pleased for you, old friend." After a chuckle, he continued, "I must admit, I am surprised you finally agreed to give up a life of solitude, but I am glad that you did. You deserve such happiness."

Magnus clapped him on the shoulder. "Ye havena said what's becoming of ye. Where will the king's whims take ye next?"

"Barbados." The fair-haired man's self-assured look soured and appeared strained. "I am to be their new governor. My first duty is to quell the recent troubles surrounding the sugar plantations." His good-humored air disappeared completely. "Hopefully, my new bride's parents will convince her to join me before we are too many weeks into autumn, and treacherous weather makes travel at sea unthinkable."

"Ye've married? Congratulations, man!" Magnus thumped him on the back. "May the gods bless ye with many healthy bairns."

Crestshire shot a sideways glance at Brenna, one she didn't quite understand, but gave her suspicions. She had learned early on how to read a person's feelings by their actions rather than their words. Her ability to do such had been a means of survival. For whatever reason, Lord Crestshire did not enjoy wedded bliss.

"Does yer wife fear traveling by sea?" she asked, figuring that question innocent enough to give him an opening to share his burdens.

"Nay, madam. Nothing as simple as that." He blew out a heavy sigh and stared at the ground. "Ours was an arranged marriage and not a well-suited one at that, I'm afraid." Squaring his shoulders, he stood taller. "But we shall see. Time might change things." His good humor back in place, he smiled at Magnus. "That is why I am more than a little proud to see you have found a woman willing to defy your orders so she might protect you. That, my dear man, is a sure sign of true and heartfelt love."

"And maybe just a wee mite of stubbornness," Brenna couldn't resist adding. She could tell Magnus was still a little disgruntled she had disobeyed him.

"A wee mite?" he interjected, giving her a look that said all might be forgiven, but it would not be forgotten.

She slid her hand through his arm, then patted it. "I would attempt meekness in front of Lord Crestshire, but we would all know it for the lie it was."

"That we would," Magnus agreed.

Crestshire pulled a small silver watch from his waistcoat pocket and gave it a glance. "Duty calls," he said as he returned to his saddle. Reluctance and a sad wistfulness shadowed his tone and his movements. "As much as I'm tempted to leave Fort William in disarray for Barricourt, I dare not for my well-being." With a half-hearted shrug, he grinned. "I am already considered a sympathizer." His smile became more willful and broadened even more. "And I am damn proud of that reputation."

"May the gods protect ye and send ye happiness, my friend," Magnus replied. "Ye may not be a Scot by blood, but ye are one at heart." He lifted a hand in farewell. "A brother, forever."

"A brother, forever," Crestshire repeated, then gave a gallant nod to Brenna. "God bless you, madam. May you both be gifted with happiness and good health all your days."

"And ye as well, m'lord," she said, deciding that Lord Crestshire wasn't so terrible after all, even if he was English. As he rode away, she sent up hope and a prayer that the man would find happiness.

"I sent ye to the keep," Magnus repeated, his deep tone bristling with irritation.

"Aye. Ye mentioned that earlier." She turned to face the scolding head-on. It would be interesting to see what he had to say since he had become so leery about choosing the wrong words. "And I shall give ye the same answer I gave before, 'I came back to save yer sorry arse from the English.'"

Fair brows knotted over his narrowed eyes. He swelled with a deep inhale, then snorted it out.

"Ye know ye look like a Highland bull when yer nostrils flare like that." She pointed at his boots. "All ye need do now is paw at the ground."

"Disobeying me when I am trying to protect ye is not a jesting matter, lass."

She stepped closer, giving him a stern look of her own. "Ye best learn now that I dinna 'obey' well. I trust my instincts when it comes to protecting myself and those I care about. They have yet to fail me."

His demeanor immediately changed. It relaxed. Warmed. He closed the remaining distance between them. "So, ye do care about me then?"

"Aye, I do." She swallowed hard, nearly choking on the admission. How could she not? He had made it damn near impossible not to…to…dare she even think the word? Name that dangerous emotion? "I am not a fool. Ye think I would promise myself to someone I despised?"

He slid his hand along her cheek and laced his fingers in her hair. "It's fallen loose," he whispered.

"What?" Between the intensity of his touch and his intoxicating nearness, she struggled to concentrate on what he meant.

"Yer hair." With both hands, he fluffed her waist-length tresses through his hands. "Ye must ha' ridden hard to come back and save me."

"I did." She rested both hands on his chest, then slid them up the warm, muscular expanse to his shoulders. "Now, ye must give me time to tend to my hair, or yer kin will surely think ye have brought them a mess of a woman."

"I like it loose," he said as he leaned closer. "And I dinna give a damn what they think," he added in a husky whisper against her mouth. "May I?"

"Ye may stop asking permission before each kiss. I promise ye will know well enough when ye're not welcome to proceed."

His smile tickled across her lips until the heat of the kiss seared the tickling away. Never had she felt as safe and cared for as she did at that very moment. Surrounded by rock-hard muscles but held as gently as a babe, a breathtaking combination of fierce strength and warm tenderness swept her away on a wave of happiness. The longer the kiss lasted, the more she wished it never to end. Disappointment filled her when he lifted his head.

"We...should go," he forced out, his breathing ragged. "The lads."

"Aye." She blinked, struggling to pull free of the delicious daze. "The lads." With a reluctance born of few pleasures ever received, she stepped out of his embrace. A long ribbon snagged in the neckline of her shift reminded her of her hair. Hands flying to repair the damage, she turned and looked in the direction she had left his horse hidden. "Yer horse is that way. Straight through those bushes. Ye might fetch him whilst I sort out this mess."

He stilled her hands and fixed her with a look that also stilled her heart. "Not before ye swear ye will do as I ask from now on when I'm trying to keep ye safe." He paused, his gaze fierce and searing. "Ye forced me to acknowledge I still have a heart. Dinna rip it in two by getting yerself killed because of foolish stubbornness, ye ken? What if it hadna been Lord Crestshire? What if it had been a detachment of soldiers, and they laid claim to both of us? Where would that have left Keigan? Do it for him, if ye willna do it for me. In any other matter, I dinna give a rat's arse if ye do as ye damn well please, but when I fear for yer safety, I need ye to do as I say. Will ye do that for me, *mo chridhe?*"

As much as it hurt her to admit it, he was in the right, and she had been wrong—for all the reasons he had stated and more. "Aye, I admit I didna use good sense." Any other man would have beaten her for disobeying, and rightly so. But not Magnus. He had made his point painfully clear by speaking to her heart. "Will ye forgive me?"

"Aye, love." He framed her face in his hands but didn't kiss her. Instead, he arched a brow. "*This* time, ye ken?"

"I ken." She smiled, then nudged him away. "On wi' ye now, while I tame this rat's nest." She returned to smoothing back her blonde curls and twisting them into a neatly plaited bun.

A low pounding, loud as thunder and steadily growing stronger, startled them both.

"Come!" Snatching hold of her hand, Magnus plowed into the nearest thicket, then balanced them both as they slid down the hillside and took cover behind the broad base of a mighty tree uprooted and half fallen. He covered her body with his as he peered upward, watching the road.

Brenna recognized the sound now. Horses. Many horses. Galloping at a hard run. But then she heard an even more frightening sound:

silence. The drove of riders had stopped just above them. She held her breath, praying it was Lord Crestshire's men and not followers of the tyrant he had said would soon be in their midst.

"There!" came a shout. "See the branches?"

"Thank the gods," Magnus muttered as he pushed himself to his feet and offered her his hand. His reassuring grin calmed her pounding heart. "'Tis Alexander. The chieftain."

"Praise God Almighty." She held tight to him as they slogged up the steep hillside that had been much easier to slide down than climb.

"The MacCoinnich guards," Magnus announced with pride as they crested the shallow ravine and stepped out of the bushes. "Alexander!"

"How many men set upon ye?" asked Alexander, a large man with hair blacker than Satan's waistcoat.

"Are either of ye hurt?" asked a second man, who had to be a brother since he and the chief shared such a striking resemblance.

Pulling Brenna to his side, Magnus held up a hand and shook his head. "Ease yerselves, my fine brothers. All is well. It's naught but a wee misunderstanding."

"How *wee*?" Alexander asked.

"'Tis my fault," Brenna spoke up. "I thought Magnus set upon by redcoats and told Evander as much when I sent him to the keep. I didna discover until I returned to fight them that the man was a friend of yer clan."

"I thought the same, lass," Magnus said.

The chieftain winced, then scrubbed a hand across his mouth. "Lord Crestshire?"

"Aye," she said.

"It is both my pride and pleasure to introduce ye to my lady love, Brenna Maxwell," Magnus said as he gently pulled her closer. "It is all right, *mo chridhe*," he whispered. "Chin up, my brave one, so they can meet ye proper."

Inhaling deeply, she lifted her head and faced the men staring down at her from their fully armed warhorses.

The chief blessed her with a genuine smile and a noble nod. "I am Alexander MacCoinnich, chieftain to Clan MacCoinnich, and it is my true honor to meet ye, m'lady." A warm chuckle escaped him. "I am more than a little glad our brother Magnus, here, has finally found someone willing to watch over him."

"None of us thought that would ever happen, I grant ye that," said the man who looked so much like Alexander. "And I am Graham MacCoinnich." He tilted his head toward the chieftain. "Brother to this one, here, and clan war chief."

Her cheeks still burning, Brenna made a shallow curtsey. "Again, I am sorry. I didna mean to cause such alarm." She felt like a fool.

"Ye had no way of knowing," Alexander

reassured. His gaze traveled across the several men they had brought with them. "And it did us good." His expression hardened. "With Lord Crestshire leaving Fort William, we no longer have an ally among the English. 'Tis best we be prepared for the worst." Settling his scowl on Magnus, he asked, "Did ye speak with him and learn of what I speak?"

"Aye." Magnus resettled his stance and stood taller. "But it didna surprise me. We were lucky to have a sympathetic ear at Fort William for as long as we did."

Agreement rumbled through the gathering of men.

Alexander motioned back toward the direction from which they had come. "Back to the keep, men." As the group milled around to head out, he looked back and smiled at Brenna and Magnus. "We shall see the two of ye at *Tor Ruadh*. Catriona will be delighted to have such a fine reason for a grand feast. Dinna tarry, aye?"

"We will be right along," Magnus promised.

Watching the fearless guard ride away, Brenna shook her head. "Word will spread, and the entire clan will think me a careless fool."

"They willna think such." Magnus kissed her hand and tugged for her to follow. "If anything, they'll think ye the perfect addition to the clan since nearly every MacCoinnich wife wouldha done the same were she to find herself in yer place."

CHAPTER EIGHT

"A UNTIE! AUNTIE!"

"Thank the Almighty," Brenna whispered.

Keigan's shrill cry reached her over and over as they passed through the final stone arch of the protective barbican with its series of iron gates and entered the main bailey. The crowd's stares stung like biting midges, but with her dear lad charging toward her, she ignored them all and focused on him.

"Help me down, aye?" She patted Magnus's arm, eager to gather her precious child into a fierce hug.

"Down ye go, *mo chridhe*." He swung her to the ground as though she weighed less than a cloud, then dismounted and took his place beside her.

Keigan hit her at full speed, clutching her tighter than bark on a tree. "I was afeared, Auntie! Sore afeared the Sassenachs had gotten ye both."

She gathered him up and hugged him as tight as he clung to her. "It is all right, my dearest one," she shushed, pressing kisses to his cheek. "We are safe here. Safe as can be."

"I feared for the both of ye. Feared I would be all alone," he repeated in a hiccupping whisper. Keigan rarely cried. Whenever he did, his emotions came from so deep within, hiccups always followed. "I dinna want to be alone, Auntie. Not ever."

As much as she had dreaded meeting Magnus's clan, it struck her how right he had been to bring them here. With this new extended family, Keigan would never find himself alone if anything should ever happen to her. Aye, this decision had scared the living daylights out of her. Still did. But it was good. Holding Keigan close, she turned to Magnus. His pained expression showed how much he hurt for the lad. It also told her he watched with rapt attention to see what she would tell the child. Crouching down, she pried the boy loose and stood him in front of her. With a swipe of her thumb, she brushed aside his tears, then pulled a square of linen from her sleeve and held it to his nose. "Blow."

Keigan complied.

"Now, look me in the eyes, dear one. Look at me, so I know ye understand what I am about to say. Understand it without a doubt, aye?"

After a deep shuddering sniff, the boy nodded, then jerked with the force of another hiccup.

"Yer da brought ye here so ye would never be alone." She gently squeezed his hands and smiled. "Clan MacCoinnich is yer family now, too." With a nod toward the men, women, and children gathered around them, she forced herself to speak with a conviction she didn't yet feel. "Ye have cousins, aunties, and uncles by the droves now. None of these folks would ever leave ye out in the cold. And as soon as they get to know ye, they will love ye, true. I promise."

"As much as ye do?"

"No one could ever love ye as much as I do," she said. "But they *will* love ye, and should anything happen to yer da or I, they will take care of ye." She forced a calmness to hide all her doubts and fears. "I promise ye, Keigan. Ye know I would never lie to ye."

Magnus knelt beside her. He took hold of Keigan and turned him toward the crowd. He pointed out a beautiful, red-haired woman made even lovelier by the kindness of her smile. "Yer Auntie Catriona over there promised me before I left to find ye that she would take ye in as one of her own if need be." He chuckled. "With five bairns already, she said a sixth wouldna even be noticed." Then he motioned toward another lass with curly hair as bright as polished copper. "Yer Auntie Gretna there promised the same."

"And so did yer Auntie Mercy," said a woman whose empty gaze did nothing to diminish her loveliness. Tall and willowy with silky black hair and a serene smile, she held an ornate cane in one hand and stood with her face lifted as though sensing everything in the air. "Forgive me for interrupting," she hurried to add. With an arm around the shoulders of the wee lass beside her, she tilted her head in the child's direction. "My daughter, Effie, wanted to be sure and get in her bid for another brother since she has decided that her current sibling is no longer suitable."

"Ramsay is rude and tells me to go away when he wants to play swords wif William and Finn." The tiny girl, the image of her mother, puffed up her chest and folded her arms with a haughty jerk. "Thinks he's too good to play wif me. Ramsay's a mean old arse, he is!"

"Effie Marsalla!" Mercy exclaimed with a stamp of her cane. With a hand on her daughter's shoulder, she turned the child toward the keep, then firmly swatted her behind. She paused and partially turned back toward Brenna and Keigan. "Please forgive us. We shall welcome you properly once we have discussed *yet again* what words are appropriate for a young lady's usage and what words are not." One hand on the child's shoulder, the other swept the cane back and forth across her path as she marched the pouting tot inside the keep.

"Auntie Mercy's a bloody Sassenach," Keigan whispered loud enough for all to hear.

Brenna suppressed a groan as laughter rippled through the crowd. They would surely think her a terrible guardian for her nephew if he forgot to use his manners. As she rose from crouching beside him, she tapped his shoulder. "Keigan!"

"Leave the lad be," Graham said with a hearty chuckle. "She *is* a Sassenach, my boy, but a good one. Ye'll see."

Magnus took his place beside Brenna. The warm weight of his touch on the small of her back made her stiffen. It was time for the adult introductions. *Please help me say the proper things,* she prayed. *For Keigan's sake,* she added. Always one to speak her mind, she had never done well in social situations. Healing folks was her strength—not getting along with them.

"Catriona, Gretna." With a proud smile, Magnus nodded at each of the ladies. "'Tis my pleasure to present Lady Brenna Maxwell, my betrothed."

"Just Brenna Maxwell," she hurried to correct. Not only had the title never brought her anything but ill luck, the MacCoinnichs might think her arrogant or putting on airs.

Both women stepped forward and scooped up her hands, a genuine welcome beaming from them both.

"Welcome to yer new home, to *Tor Ruadh*," Catriona said. "I canna tell ye how pleased we are to have ye here."

"Aye, that we are," Gretna agreed with a friendly squeeze of Brenna's hand. "And we're even happier that Magnus willna be alone any longer." Her reddish-blonde brows rose to her hairline as the silver band on Brenna's finger caught the sunlight. "A poesy ring carved with hearts and thistles!" She aimed an approving nod at Magnus. "Well done, sir. I didna think ye had it in ye." With another squeeze of her hand, Gretna gave Brenna a smile that made her feel even more accepted. "I am so happy for ye, Brenna, but I'm even happier for us. Another woman added to the sisterhood. Yer strength will help us keep these stubborn MacCoinnich men in line."

Thank goodness both women chattered on with little or no urging because Brenna was at a complete loss for words. She had never seen such a kinship in her life. And what a welcome. Good gracious. Not the slightest dark glare or spitefulness from anyone.

With a snap of her fingers, Catriona whirled about and scanned the crowd. "Grant! Maxwell! Where ye be?"

"Here, Mama." Two young boys, both with hair as black as their father's and looking to be about Keigan's age, wiggled out from the sea of skirts and kilts.

"Ye can take Keigan to the kitchen now. He's had a long journey and a bit of a fright. I am certain he would love some bread and jam, along with a cup of fresh milk." Catriona coaxed the child forward. "Come, my lad, Grant and Maxwell will take good care of ye. Would ye like some of Cook's finest jam to hold ye over 'til supper?"

"Auntie?" Keigan edged closer and tugged on her sleeve. "Should I go?" he whispered.

"Aye, my brave one. Enjoy." Brenna patted his back, then nudged him toward them. "Mind yer manners, though, ye ken?"

"Aye!" Keigan scampered off, running alongside the twins without hesitation.

Brenna envied her wee one's ability to charge forward and make friends so quickly. Of course, the lad was young. He hadn't experienced all the ugliness human nature could offer—at least, he had only seen a little of it.

"They'll soon be close as pups from the same litter," Catriona promised. She urged Brenna forward while shooing Magnus away. "Come. I'm sure ye could use some refreshment, too, whilst the men tend to the horses and unload yer things." With a knowing tilt of her head, she lowered her voice. "They love their gossip as much as we do. I dinna care how much they deny it."

"That they do." Gretna gave a conspiratorial wink as she fell in step on Brenna's other side. "By the by, our refreshments will bolster ye more than a cup of milk." She grinned. "I'm sure ye're ready for a wee dram. I know I would be."

With barely time for a nervous glance back at Magnus, Brenna found herself flanked by the two women and herded into the cavernous main hall of the keep. *Tor Ruadh* was a grand sight, much larger than Nithdane had ever hoped to be. Built into the mountain of Ben Nevis, the enormous stronghold was a proper fortification.

Servants buzzed around the large main room, scouring the long dining tables, changing out candle stubs for freshly trimmed tapers, and sweeping the stone floors. A formidable woman of mature years marched through their midst with the look of a war chief planning a battle. Dressed all in black, her silver hair pulled into a stern bun, all it took was an arch of her brow to send a servant jumping to correct whatever she found lacking.

"Mrs. Fitzgerald," Catriona said as the matron altered her course to greet them. "This is Mistress Brenna Maxwell, Magnus's betrothed."

"Welcome to *Tor Ruadh*, mistress." Mrs. Fitzgerald's serious air melted into an expression of polite, but reserved, kindness. "Anything ye should have need of, please dinna hesitate to ask," she said with the slightest dip of her chin. Her attention shifting back to Catriona, she nodded again. "Their suite will be ready in no time, m'lady. I decided it needed a fair bit more scrubbing than we first thought. But I shall see it aired out, good and proper. Fresh water in every pitcher. Decanters filled and washed linens still warm from the sun for the beds."

"This keep would collapse into chaos without Mrs. Fitzgerald," Catriona said to Brenna, then turned back to the housekeeper. "As always, I know ye have everything under control. Would ye be so good as to have Cook send refreshments to the solar? We'll rest there until the suite is ready for Mistress Brenna's inspection."

"As ye wish it, m'lady." The matron bustled off. A snap of her fingers flagged down servants, and her orders sent them flying.

"Mrs. Fitzgerald is a true gem," Catriona said again as she looped an arm through Brenna's. "Ye can trust her with anything."

"She is that," Gretna agreed. "Loyal 'til death, that lady is."

Trust. Even though she managed a smile, Brenna struggled against a leeriness born of days past. Learning to trust this clan seemed a monumental task. Best not overthink it. *Handle a moment at a time,* she urged herself. *One moment at a time.* "Yer keep is verra fine, m'lady."

"Ye must call me Catriona, aye?" Catriona patted her arm. "As our newest sister-to-be, this is yer home now, too."

"We are so glad ye came here," Gretna said as they passed between the two rows of tables running down the center of the room. "Both Keigan and Evander mentioned there had been some discussion about the matter between yerself and Magnus."

Brenna failed at suppressing an embarrassed groan. "I can only imagine what those two shared with ye." She looked away, unable to face either woman. "Please forgive them. I meant no insult to any of Clan MacCoinnich."

"I dinna blame ye for having doubts. All ye've known is hardship, thanks to poor judgment from one of our own." Gretna shook a finger up and down with every word. "That is why I wanted Evander to see what can come from one moment of thoughtlessness. It isna fair for a man to go on his merry way, whilst a woman pays a price that either cost her life or lasts her a lifetime." With a shake of her head, she continued, "Why...we didna even know what might have happened to the wee tot or who could have him until Keigan told us about ye. We are so thankful ye were there to care for him." Her tirade paused, and she had the disturbing air of knowing more than she said. "We know it couldna have been easy for ye.

A woman alone. Trying to keep a child fed and safe. We are grateful for Magnus's sake that ye're willing to share Keigan with him *and* with us, after all ye endured."

Her speech gave Brenna pause. Could it hold a double meaning? Should she be insulted? She smoothed back her hair and tugged at her bodice. "I must look a fright. Forgive me."

Both Catriona and Gretna halted. "Nay, lass," Gretna said, color flaring to her cheeks. "Please forgive me for making ye uncomfortable. That was nay my intent. I said what I did because I know how hard it is to raise weans all by yerself. I did it for many years. I promise ye, we think ye brave as any warrior."

"That we do," Catriona agreed. "Never doubt how much we admire yer strength and ability to forgive. Not everyone wouldha given Magnus the chance to know his son."

Their seemingly genuine kindness touched her. "All I knew of Magnus was that he had fathered Keigan and left." After a deep breath and a silent prayer for composure, she continued, "But my sister's dying wish was for the lad to know his father, and after a time, I discovered why she had trusted him and loved him as a friend."

"Magnus is a good man," Catriona said as they ascended a winding tower staircase. "He has lived a lonely life," she continued as they climbed.

"It has broken my heart to see the loneliness in his eyes when he thought no one saw."

"Except for that annoying bird, he has had no one," Gretna added from beside her, then brightened with a wicked grin. "But now that ye'll be living here at *Tor Ruadh,* Merlin can roost with Keigan instead of my wee Finn."

"Merlin?" Brenna vaguely recalled her nephew mentioning a pet of some kind but had paid little attention since the boy befriended all creatures, be they furry, feathered, or covered in scales.

"Aye, Merlin," Gretna continued as they reached the chieftain's solar on the third floor.

Brenna stared down at the woven carpet of rich burgundies and blues that had surely come from some distant land. "I canna go farther as filthy as I am from travel. Is there somewhere else we might go?"

"Ye are no filthier than my five little heathens, who run through here daily." Catriona pulled her toward a cushioned couch, the likes of which Brenna had never seen. "Come and sit." She squeezed her hand and smiled. "Ye're family, lass. I promise ye're welcome here."

"Ye must tell us how Magnus asked ye to be his wife. He is always so reserved. I dinna think I have ever seen him even attempt to charm a lass." Gretna patted the cushion beside her, inviting Brenna to sit. "Did he stutter and stammer or just have Evander tell ye what he wished? Lord knows that child of mine has never been at a loss for words with anyone."

Perched on the edge of the seat for fear of soiling it, Brenna clasped her hands in her lap. She wasn't comfortable here. Everything looked too fine to touch. Evander had told her of Clan MacCoinnich's wealth, because of its specially bred horses, but she hadn't imagined the likes of this.

"He didna stutter or stammer," she said after realizing they both sat, looking at her, waiting for a response. "But he wasna quite clear at first—just asked me if I wished to align myself with him or be *paired*." The memory brought a smile. "I accused him of rudeness, but then he made himself clearer." Perhaps she shouldn't share so much. As soon as the words left her mouth, she worried that Catriona and Gretna might twist them to their own advantage.

Instead, both women laughed, acting as though they expected no less. Catriona rose and moved to a long buffet laden with decanters. She filled three glasses with a potent-looking ruby liquid. "Bless Magnus's poor, solitary soul. He doesna ken how to speak to women. He's better with warring and such."

"Ian told me the dear man barely spoke to anyone at all, right after his mother's murder," Gretna said as she rose to help with the drinks.

"Blamed himself for leaving her unprotected."

"Thank the saints he had the MacCoinnichs to help him through it," Catriona said as she strode across the room to answer a quiet tapping on the door. With a step back, she opened it wide and motioned for the young woman with a cart of covered trays to enter.

Once the lass positioned the repast beside the couch, she turned to Catriona with a modest bob of her head.

"Thank ye, Annie. Ye may go," Catriona said with a nod.

After stealing a shy glance at Brenna, the maidservant hopped a quick curtsey, then hurried out, closing the door behind her.

"Ye're in luck, Brenna," Catriona announced as she removed all the covers. "'Tis baking day." Eyes closed, she inhaled deeply. "I love the smell of freshly baked bread." She placed a steaming hot bannock slathered in butter and golden honey on a small plate and set it on the low table in front of Brenna. "Cook's finest will fill yer empty wame 'til supper! Enjoy this, my newfound sister."

"Cook is another of *Tor Ruadh*'s treasures," Gretna shared as she handed a folded square of linen and a silver fork to Brenna. "Yer Keigan will also soon discover that Cook loves giving the bairns treats."

Catriona laughed. "'Tis a wonder all of them

aren't plump as fine fat partridges ready for the spit!"

Palms sweating, Brenna clutched the linen and silverware in one hand and the treacherous goblet of wine in the other. She sipped at the heady drink, fearing her head would soon spin off her neck. This refreshment was much stronger than the cheap ale or whisky she had sometimes allowed herself. And she had watered those down even more to make them last longer.

"Keigan loves treats," she finally said, cringing at the lameness of her ability to maintain a simple conversation. They would think her a dullard for certain.

"Where did Magnus find ye?" Catriona asked, leaning forward with interest as she returned to her chair. "The lads didna say, and Alexander didna ken either."

"A fair bit north of Inverness." Brenna slid the fragile goblet to the table alongside the plate. No way in thunder would she be able to force down a single bite and didn't dare try. She unfolded, then refolded the square of linen, then folded her hands on top of it, battling the urge to twist it. "Keigan and I had built a shelter just inside the coast, about half a day's journey south of *Inbhir Ùige*." A hard swallow did little for wetting her dry mouth, but she daren't take another drink for fear of losing the ability to remain upright. *God help me through this*, she prayed, hoping her pair of hostesses hadn't already decided their precious Magnus had chosen a fool for a wife. She didn't mean to be such a poor excuse for a visitor. So much had happened, was still happening. Everything had set her head to whirling, making it pound.

Gretna and Catriona shared a glance. Catriona gave the slightest nod.

With her hand resting on Brenna's arm, Gretna scooted a bit closer. "When a body has fought for survival so long," she paused, compassion and understanding filling her eyes, "It can be a hard chore to open up and trust anyone." She leaned in even more. "Dinna fash yerself about trying so hard to fit in. Ye are among family now. Ye have all the time in the world to get to know us."

Catriona set her glass on the table and clasped her hands atop her knees. "It is our hope, Brenna, that with time, ye'll feel safe here at *Tor Ruadh*. Trust us. But until then, we understand. Anything ye dinna wish to speak about—don't." Her smile appeared genuine. "We respect ye, lass, and hope to be yer friends, but we also know it must come about in its own good time."

A sharp knock tapped the door, then Magnus stepped inside. "Ladies, might I interrupt?" He perked like a dog spotting scraps when he saw the cart filled with all manner of breads, cheeses, and sweets. "I see Cook's been busy."

Brenna had never been so relieved to see anyone in her entire life. "Do come sit with us," she said, cringing at the pleading sound of her voice. As soon as the words left her mouth, she glanced at Catriona. It wasn't her place to invite Magnus into the solar. 'Twas Catriona's. "Forgive my rudeness," she said with an apologetic shrug. She hated the fearful, bumbling fool she had become. But with stakes higher than she had ever faced before, all courage and boldness had left her.

"What rudeness?" Catriona waved Magnus forward. "Always speak yer mind here, lass. Eh, Gretna?"

"Absolutely," Gretna agreed, lifting her glass in a toast. "To speaking our minds." She cast a wicked grin in Magnus's direction. "God help every man at *Tor Ruadh*."

"Indeed," Magnus observed dryly as he went to the buffet and poured himself a drink before joining the ladies.

"Sit here beside yer betrothed," Gretna said as she moved to a chair. "Ye have done well, Magnus. We are verra proud of ye."

Brenna didn't miss the side-eyed glance Magnus shot in Gretna's direction as he settled down beside her. His gaze lit on her untouched plate of food, then he turned to her. "'Tis a lot to take in, is it not, dear one?"

His ability to read her had become keener

with each passing day. "Aye," she said softly but then sat straighter and managed a smile. "But everyone has been kinder than kind." She gave both Gretna and Catriona a thankful nod. "Just as ye promised."

"It takes time to adjust to such a grand change," Catriona volunteered. "But I am certain all will be well."

"Aye," Brenna agreed with more conviction than she felt. She would do better and make it so. "Once I am settled, I promise I willna act such a fool."

"Ye've nay acted the fool," Gretna said as she rose and headed toward the decanters of wine. "Catriona and I often forget ourselves and overwhelm the bravest of souls." She laughed. "And it's even worse when Mercy joins us."

"That it is," Catriona chimed in. "And soon, ye'll be right there with us. We shall be the fearsome four rather than the terrifying trio."

"Ye know of yer titles?" Magnus noted, failing at hiding his smirk behind his glass.

"Aye," Catriona said. "We know a lot more about the private conversations in Alexander's library than ye think." She pulled a face that made Brenna smile. "They say they're talking clan business, but often they're doing naught but drinking and telling tall tales."

Magnus cleared his throat and shifted so he faced Brenna. "Mrs. Fitzgerald said they have finished with the floor Catriona allotted us. I'm sure they've scoured the rooms from top to bottom. I had them leave yer things untouched in yer chambers. I thought ye would rather unpack them yerself."

"Aye, I would." Fidgeting, she wondered how much longer this initial visit would last. It had come to her early on that introductions were a great deal like healing remedies—best tolerated when taken in small doses. "Some herbs I brought require careful handling. I must see that they're stored properly."

"Herbs?" Gretna perked like a cat spotting a mouse. "Be ye a healer?"

"I am." At first, she wondered at Gretna's interest, then remembered Magnus had said the woman was the healer to Clan MacCoinnich. "Magnus told me ye are the healer here. Perhaps, we can share remedies?" Some healers didn't take kindly to sharing their lore, but Brenna had always felt the more who knew, the more who could be helped. She hoped Gretna felt the same.

"Aye, that would be grand." Gretna beamed at her with a broad smile. "Soon as yer good and settled, I'll take ye to my healing room and show ye around. Since my helper Flora just had her bairn a few days ago, there's no one but me tending to all in need. Now, there'll be two of us until Flora can return, and then we'll be three taking care of the clan."

"Three healers," Catriona repeated with a thoughtful look. "As far as I'm concerned, the more, the better. Especially, with us losing Lord Crestshire from Fort William."

Another polite tapping at the door interrupted them, then it opened enough to reveal Mrs. Fitzgerald. Her gaze searched the room until she spotted Catriona. "The floor is ready, m'lady, for whenever Mistress Brenna and yerself wish to inspect it."

Catriona and Gretna hopped to their feet, both motioning for Brenna and Magnus to follow. "I thought the second floor of this wing would suit ye best," Catriona said. "Since yer Keigan is so close in age to Maxwell and Grant, I feel certain they'll keep the stairs betwixt the floors busy."

Magnus offered his arm with a reassuring smile. "Come, lass, and if ye find anything amiss, dinna hesitate to say what ye need, aye?"

Taking his arm, she held tight and paused, her head swimming both from the day's events and the strong drink.

"Are ye unwell?" Magnus steadied her, his concern stirring that twitchy feeling that made her heart beat faster. "Do ye need to lie down?"

"What's ails ye, lass?" Gretna hurried back to her.

Her cheeks flaring hot at causing such a stir, Brenna waved them away. "I am quite well—just unused to such potent drink."

Magnus shot a glance back at her plate. "Ye didna eat a bite when ye fed the rest of us this morning. Nor did ye touch yer refreshments, I see. As soon as ye've settled in our rooms, we'll send for a tray. At least some broth and bread, aye? Ye'll fall ill if ye dinna eat."

With a knowing smile, Gretna returned to stand beside Catriona. "He has this well in hand," she observed.

"Aye. I do." Magnus held Brenna closer, his chin jutting to a defiant tilt. "Did ye expect anything less?"

"Please dinna make a fuss," Brenna said, wishing the floor would swallow her up. She knew she should have at least managed a bit of bread, but her nervous worries wouldn't allow it. And something else Magnus had just said set loose even more fretting. "Ye said *our* rooms?"

"Aye."

"But we're nay wed yet." She waited for the import of her words to sink in. He had to remember she had sworn they wouldn't share a bed until they married. What would people think?

Understanding lit in his eyes. "The suite will be *ours* once we have wed. My quarters, the rooms I always use whenever I'm here at *Tor Ruadh,* are in the south tower next to it." He smiled. "We are separated by a proper hallway and staircase that I am sure the servants will watch and update all in the clan regarding any sneaking about. When we unloaded the horses, I had them place my things there."

"Am I so easily read?"

"It's nay that I read ye easily, *mo chridhe*." He turned her so he might cup her cheek in his hand. "It's that I know how ye deserve to be treated." He paused, his gaze locked with hers and charged with so much emotion, she felt pulled into his inner storm. "Ye awakened my heart, dear one, and I mean to awaken yers."

He brushed a chaste kiss across her mouth, then lifted his head and smiled after a glance at the doorway. "It appears Catriona and Gretna have left us alone. A true welcoming kiss is in order."

Before Brenna could argue, she found herself swept away and rendered dizzier and more weak-kneed than any drink had ever made her. The heat of him, his urgency and longing vibrated with a heartbeat all its own. Saints have mercy on her soul. If his kisses had such an effect, what would happen when she allowed him so much more?

CHAPTER NINE

"TELL ME, MO *chridhe*…what do ye think of life here at *Tor Ruadh*?" She seemed happy enough, but Magnus needed to hear her say it. Learn her thoughts. Her hopes. Any remaining fears. Then he could hone his plan and coax her into completing their commitment and becoming his wife. Last night, while staring out into the darkness, he had worked out all he would say, but he needed more information to be sure.

All plotting left him as sunlight lit her face, making her even lovelier. The bright summer's day lent a golden glow to the heavy braid she had pinned into a tight bun. Her full lips shone juicy as ripe berries.

Heaven help him, he wanted her. For all time. He needed this precious woman more than he had ever needed anyone or anything before. His determination, armed with all his planning, made a valiant surge through the beguilement of her beauty. If he expected to win her completely, he best keep his head about him.

"Well, lass?" he gently prodded.

Brenna rested her hands on the top rail of the paddock fence, her gaze following the meanderings of a tiny bird hopping across the packed dirt, scratching and pecking for bugs. "*Tor Ruadh* is verra nice," she finally said. She stole a glance at him and paired it with a faint smile. "Catriona, Gretna, and Mercy are by far the kindest, most generous women I have ever been blessed to meet."

"Then why do I sense an unspoken *except* at the end of yer sentence?" He loved the way the corners of her eyes crinkled when she struggled to find the right words.

After a dismissive shrug, she added, "'Tis early yet. Folks could still change and show their true selves." Her eyes tightened into a squint as though the sun blinded her. "I have experienced such before."

"If anyone *changes*, I'll have their head on a platter, ye ken?" And then a stinging worry reared its ugly head. One he didn't wish to acknowledge. But he had learned early in life that fear could only be overcome if faced head-on. "Is it me, then, that gives ye pause?" He braced himself, hoping it wasn't true. "I willna change toward ye, lass." Well, that was a lie. His feelings for her changed with every rising of the sun. "Nay, I spoke in error. I do change. I care more for ye with each passing day and will do so until I'm lowered into the grave. Tell me the truth. Ye dinna wish yerself free of our promise?"

She faced him and took hold of both his hands. Her loving smile cast the weight of his worries away. "Nay, *mo ghràdh*. I dinna wish my freedom. Far from it, I assure ye." The slightest frown puckered her fair brow. "It's just that so much has happened so verra quickly. I need a little more time to know I am truly fit and ready to be yer wife. A wee bit more of yer patience is all I ask. Can ye manage that for me?"

"Aye, m'love." He pulled her in for a kiss. "For ye—I can manage anything." She smelled as sweet as warmed honey and tasted even better.

"Master Magnus! Master Magnus!"

With an irritated groan, Magnus ended the delicious kiss and lifted his head to seek the breathless cry.

A young maidservant holding a cloth-covered platter above her head kicked at the cluster of hens blocking her every step. "Shoo, I tell ye! This isna for ye." She plowed through them, but the persistent birds stayed with her, their indignant clucks and flapping wings interrupting the peacefulness of the courtyard. "Get on wi' ye now!" she cried. "I fed ye hours ago!"

Pitying the poor girl, Magnus stomped and clapped. Brenna joined in, flapping her apron. They charged at the flock, scattering the birds in every direction.

"Thank ye ever so much." The flustered maid curtsied, then held out the plate to Magnus. "'Tis yer favorites, sir. Just pulled from the oven."

Surprised by such special treatment, Magnus stared at the girl, not sure what to do.

"Dinna just stand there." Brenna nudged him. "Take it from her. Cook must ha' sent them." She leaned in and hid her words behind her hand. "Ye know how the fussy thing favors ye."

Brenna was right. The dear old woman spoiled him as though she were his doting grandmam. There was naught to be done but accept it. "I thank ye, lass." He lifted the cloth. The tantalizing aroma of meat pies greeted him, their golden crusts split and bubbling with rich brown gravy. Four of them nestled in the center of the platter, surrounded by odd-shaped pieces of broken crust glistening with butter. "Did Cook send these?"

"Nay," the girl said with a shy smile. "I brought them 'cause they're best straight off the fire." She pushed a lackluster brown curl behind her ear. "Baked them for ye myself whilst Cook was at the smoke pit. I remembered from before how much ye relished them."

From before? He struggled to recall the young woman's name but couldn't. Hellfire, had his memory left him in his prime?

"Eat them whilst they're hot," the maid urged, watching him with gleeful expectation. Her excited smile brightened her round, freckled face, her nose still smudged with flour.

Still puzzling over who she was, he bit into one of the scalding hot pies, then huffed and blew to get it cooled before it scarred his tongue permanently.

Brenna reached for the platter. "Here. Let me hold it for ye whilst ye enjoy yer treats. Fan yer mouth, aye?"

The young girl, slight of body and a full head shorter than Brenna, shoved in between them. She brushed Brenna's hands aside. "Nay. These are for Master Magnus alone. I shall hold the plate whilst he eats them."

Mouth opened in shock, Brenna backed away without a word. She stared at the maidservant as though the lass had just snarled at her like a beast on a short chain.

"Ye would do well to remember yer place, young woman." Magnus handed the platter to Brenna, then turned to the girl. "If ye ever behave in such an impertinent way again, ye will no longer work here at the keep, ye ken?"

Brenna sidled closer, interrupting him with a touch to his arm. She gave the maid a tight smile, then nodded toward the path leading back to the kitchens. "Perhaps, ye best return to yer chores, aye? Mrs. Fitzgerald will be looking for ye."

The sullen girl's eyes narrowed the slightest bit. A hostile air settled across her before she gave a half-hearted curtsey. "As ye wish, mistress." Then she stomped away, immediately swarmed by the flock of chickens.

Magnus returned the half-eaten pie to the platter. The thing had been a flavorless, underdone mess, and he was none too sure what sort of meat the girl had used. For all he knew, it could have been rat. He whistled for the dogs and tossed the pies to the ravenous hounds.

"I am sorry, m'love," he said as he placed the empty dish on top of a barrel beside the fence. "I swear I will speak to Catriona and Mrs. Fitzgerald both about her behavior. I'm sure they can find work for her down in the village, so ye willna have to deal with her rudeness again."

"Nay, my champion. Let it pass, aye?" Brenna looked thoughtful as she returned to watching the persistent little bird scour the paddock for bugs. "Catriona told me about that girl. We should bear her some extra patience, I think."

"I refuse to tolerate anyone treating ye with such disrespect." He rested a fist on the fencepost.

"Who is she? She spoke as if I should know her."

"Ye do know her. Her name is Cadha. Remember?"

"Cadha?" Magnus still didn't remember the girl with the tangled brown hair and eyes dark as obsidian.

"The lass ye found wandering along the shores of Loch Shiel just this side of Glenfinnan? Winter before last, remember? Catriona told me all about the poor child. How ye found her nearly frozen and so starved she couldna keep down anything more than broth for days."

He remembered now. While traveling alongside the loch, he had come upon a half-dead waif searching the icy shoreline for anything to eat. The poor mite's head had been shaved, and her meager clothes were so rotted and torn, he could see bruises and rat bites all over her. She had been so thin, he thought her a lad escaped from a poorly run orphanage. But on the way back to *Tor Ruadh*, the child had whispered her name and said she had escaped her parents, who ran a public house in Glenfinnan.

Scrubbing a hand down his face, he shook his head. "I remember her now, but that still does not excuse her behavior. She has been here long enough to know what we expect of her."

"Let it pass this time, aye?" Brenna traced a finger along the rough wood grain of the fence. "It was the smallest slight and meant nothing. I promise." A disturbing sadness softened her eyes. "She and I have a great deal in common, I think." The sadness left her as she gave the top rail of the fence a pat. "Now, where is this surprise ye promised me?"

Magnus didn't have to answer. He pointed as Evander emerged from the stable. The lad led a massive dapple-gray warhorse, with Keigan in the saddle. Evander's rope would control the beast if necessary, but Keigan sat tall and proud, holding the reins and guiding the animal with ease. The child had improved so quickly, he could ride without assistance. But to relieve Brenna's fears and convince her the child was safe, Magnus had kept Evander in place for a bit longer.

Pride swelled in Magnus's chest as he watched his son and the great horse move as though of the same mind. It was time. "Evander, release him. He's ready."

"Aye, that he is for certain." Evander grinned as he unhooked the safety lead and stepped away. "He's been ready for days, ye ken?"

"Ye are in full control now, Keigan. Dinna make me regret it," Magnus warned.

"Dinna fash yerself, Da." Keigan rode his mount around the paddock, as though he had been born in the saddle.

Brenna clutched her hands to her chest as if trying to keep her heart from escaping. "Are ye sure, Magnus? My precious one looks like a flea on that beast's back."

"He may be small, but look at him." With an arm around her waist, he pulled her closer. "Look how proud he is. Fierce and braw as can be. A natural rider."

She watched the lad with her bottom lip caught between her teeth. A mix of emotions played across her face, straining her brow tighter than a drawn bow. She looked as though watching the child ride around the paddock pained her. "He looks so grown," she whispered. "No longer the sweet little bairn I once cradled and sang to in the wee hours of the night."

Magnus envisioned the scene as easily as if it were his own memory and understood her bittersweet aching. "They canna stay babes forever, dear one," he gently offered. "Take joy in how well ye've mothered him. Take heart in knowing what a fine man he will be because of yer loving care. He'll charge into the world, fearless as a warrior, because of ye."

"Aye, but it's such a dangerous world that awaits him." Her hands, still clutched to her chest, tightened into fists. "I fret for him and all he has yet to face."

"I would think that is the woe of every parent." Magnus brushed a kiss to her temple. "We can only prepare him the best we can, m'love."

"And pray," Brenna added.

Magnus was none too sure about that. As far

as he was concerned, if a single powerful god did exist, he had abandoned this world long ago. But for Brenna's sake, and to ease the heaviness in her heart, he would agree with her. "Aye, dear one, and pray."

"Can we ride into the glen?" Keigan called out as he guided his mount closer to them. "Luchie is bored with the paddock."

"What say ye, love?" Magnus understood the lad's yearning, and it was a fine day for a ride, but he would leave that to Brenna to decide.

"Please, Auntie?" Keigan beamed at her, using the lethal charm possessed by all small children and beloved pets. "Ye can ride with us, too. I wasna meaning just Da."

"Why, thank ye, sir," Brenna replied in a tone that said she knew full well what the child was up to. After hesitating so long, Magnus feared she was about to refuse him, she smiled. "It would honor me to accompany such handsome men."

It only took a short while to ready his horse and a sweet-tempered mare for Brenna. Magnus wasn't sure who was more excited, Keigan or himself. The lad led the way out the front gate. Once they passed through the village, he tossed them both a wily grin. "Luchie would fancy a good run, ye ken?"

"Would he now?" Brenna's knuckles whitened as her grip tightened on the reins.

It wouldn't hurt the boy to give the horse its

head, but Magnus feared she was about to refuse. "What do ye think, love? A steady run. No racing, but fast enough to get his blood moving. We'll ride on either side of him."

She gave him a sharp cut of her eyes. "Betrothed or no', if my precious one comes to harm because of a deed ye've allowed, I will kill ye." Her glare turned so serious it sent a chill down his spine. "Ye ken?"

After a roll of his shoulders to dispel the uncomfortable feeling, Magnus nodded. "Aye, mistress. I assure ye there is nay a doubt in my mind." He urged his mount abreast of the lad's. "Ye've only today gotten off the safety lead, so there willna be any racing. We'll keep to a good pace. A safe, steady run." Remembering the rebelliousness of his own youth, he added, "Mind my words, son, or ye willna ride again for a fortnight, understand?"

With a dark glare and a frustrated huff, Keigan nodded. "Aye, Da."

They took off across the rolling glen. Magnus kept an eye on Keigan's seating, proud at the way the boy and horse moved. Brenna rode on his other side, stealing glances so often it was a wonder she didn't unseat herself.

Keigan slowed and pointed at the horizon. "Look! Smoke rising. Black as can be."

Magnus studied the dark, billowing omen. At this end of the glen, in such close proximity to

Fort William, the only thing that could render such a sight was a trio of shelters sometimes used by the herders when moving the stock. Thankfully, none of the clan lived at this end of the glen since no one wished to abide this close to the English.

"Stay here," he ordered, urging his mount forward. Recalling how poorly Brenna had followed orders in the past, he came to a halt and turned back to her. "I beg ye—stay here whilst I ride ahead and see what's what." After mulling the possibilities of what he might find, he added, "Swear ye will head back to the keep as fast as ye can ride if ye sense the slightest thing out of place, aye? Swear it?"

"I swear." Brenna rode up beside him, latched hold of his shirt, and pulled him toward her. "A kiss for protection?"

The churning in his gut paired with the warm sweetness of her mouth made him debate taking them both back to the safety of the keep before seeking the source of the smoke. He suddenly realized from now on, there would be no more rushing into anything. Brenna and Keigan came first. Life wasn't just about him anymore. "We should return to the keep, so I'll know ye both safe. Then I'll come back here with Alexander. He'll wish to see this."

Her gaze shifted to the ominous column of gray growing ever wider the higher it billowed.

"Aye, we should. I would feel easier knowing ye're not riding alone into whatever lies past that ridge."

That settled it. He locked eyes with Keigan. "Keep at my side and ride hard, ye ken?"

The child gave a quick nod, then turned his horse back toward the keep.

It took them half the time to cross the glen as it had before. "Sound the alarm," Magnus shouted to the guards manning the barbican. It might be rash, but he didn't care. The horns would bring Alexander running, so they could be on their way.

"Ye will be safe and return to me," Brenna ordered as she grabbed hold of his arm and pulled him over for another kiss. "Swear it!"

"I swear I shall do my damnedest, my fierce love." He kissed her hard, just as Alexander charged out of the inner bailey, already armed and astride his horse.

"Who attacks?" he shouted as he spared a glance at Brenna and Keigan hurrying their mounts inside the protection of the skirting walls.

"We have yet to discover that." Magnus motioned him forward. "With any luck, no one."

"What the hell does that mean?"

"Ye will see." Magnus turned his mount toward the glen and spurred him into a hard gallop.

They thundered toward the smoke, now

visible as soon as they reached the other side of the village of *Ruadh*.

Halting just before they topped the last rise, they studied the landscape, noting every sound and swaying blade of grass.

"None of our people live this close to Fort William," Alexander mused, resettling himself in the saddle.

"All I know in this area are the shelters for the herders." Magnus unsheathed his sword. His steel at the ready always made him feel better. He urged his horse onward. Enough wondering. Time to find out.

It was as they thought. The trio of shelters, as well as a wagon left from the last time the herders had passed through, crackled and roared with raging flames.

Magnus sheathed his sword and drew his pistol instead. Alexander did the same. Too much of the three structures still stood upright. Whoever had started the fire couldn't be that far away. With a nod toward a pine-tarred torch hissing and popping in the sedge, Magnus circled the carnage, more to study the surroundings than to look at the blaze. He had already seen enough to know the thing had been set. This was no act of stray lightning.

"Who would do this and why?" Alexander cast a murderous glare toward Fort William.

They both suspected the same culprit. The

new garrison commander. A hater of Scots and, from what they had heard about the man, stupid enough to believe that such an act would trigger Clan MacCoinnich into reacting rashly. Idiot Sassenach. When a Scot sought revenge, he took his sweet time, savored it, and planned well, so it became a fine story to tell his bairns on a long winter's night.

"The better question is, what shall we do about it?" Magnus said.

"Precautions," was Alexander's only reply as he turned his horse back in the direction of the keep while still holding his pistol at the ready. His one word spoke volumes.

Magnus understood completely. He had fought at Alexander's side long enough to know they would not ignore this attack. "And what shall we tell the people?"

"The truth as we know it." Alexander urged his mount forward. "This side of the glen is no longer safe and should be avoided until I decide otherwise."

"Ye know they dinna call me *the ghost* just because of my pale skin and hair?" Magnus shoved his pistol back in his belt. Instinct told him they were now safe since they had ridden to the center of the glen, and the village was in full view. The coward who had set the fire wouldn't dare risk an attack this close. "Perhaps, a few night wanderings are in order. Maybe even a visit inside Fort William itself," he said, rubbing his chin as he plotted. "I've been there before. 'Twould be easy enough to slip in, listen for a while, and then slip back out."

With a squinting glance back at the smoke, Alexander shook his head as his mount slowed. "I'm none too sure about that plan." He sidled a glance toward Magnus. "If I get ye killed afore Catriona's had the chance to see ye wed and expecting another bairn, there'll be hell to pay for certain. Besides—I want them to think we Scots are a bit slow. Nothing cripples an enemy more than when he underestimates his prey."

While Magnus agreed, he still felt it wouldn't hurt to gather as much information as he could. Chances were since there was nothing else on that stretch of the border to burn, there would be no further trouble. At least not from that direction. But it never hurt to watch things for a day or so. "No one will know I'm about. I've done such a thing a thousand times and never been caught. Ye ken that well enough." As they rode through the barbican, he thumped a fist to his chest. "And I swear to do nothing that endangers yer arse when it comes to yer wife, aye?"

"Ye best not," Alexander warned. "Because mine willna be the only arse at risk."

While Magnus looked forward to revisiting his old days of sneaking about to gather information, what Alexander hinted at was sobering. If Brenna got wind of what he was about to do, she would not like it, and that could be—unpleasant.

CHAPTER TEN

EVERY CHILD IN the keep crowded the corner of the large open rooftop of the tower. Well, almost every child, as near as Brenna could tell. She counted eleven tousled heads, a colorful assortment of inky black, coppery red, and golden blonde. The only wean not present was Gretna's three-year-old daughter, Malina Kirsteen. She was napping in the nursery. Her lively playmate, Catriona's three-year-old Maisie Leanna, bounced on her mother's hip, begging to get closer to Magnus and Keigan.

"Nay, I said," Catriona scolded. "I fear ye'll fall since Willa said she already caught ye crawling into the crenels to see the glen. Now, be still, or ye will go to yer cot, and there ye will stay and miss yer supper."

Maisie quieted, but her pouting informed everyone that she wasn't happy that her twelve-year-old sister had betrayed her.

Brenna wasn't all that pleased with Keigan's position on the roof's edge. Thankfully, the tall merlons rising from the stone battlement reached well above his head. As long as Magnus kept the lad from doing as Maisie had done, climbing into the spaces between them, she'd hold her tongue. Especially since they appeared to be enjoying themselves.

"Hold out yer arm," Magnus instructed, adjusting the straps on the heavy leather glove he'd had made for Keigan. The long thick cuff extended up over the boy's shoulder, protecting it and the rest of his small arm from the falcon's sharp talons. "Now whistle sharply like I taught ye. Merlin's waiting."

Pressing two fingers of his gloveless hand to his lips, the lad attempted a loud whistle but only succeeded in a soft shushing shower of spittle.

Brenna bit her lip to keep from laughing. Poor Keigan. One of his front teeth had come out last night and impaired his ability to summon the bird. Magnus ducked his head, struggling to contain his amusement as well.

"Can I just call him by name?" the boy asked after drying his chin on his sleeve.

Magnus peered up into the sky, his narrowed

eyes locked on the dark speck soaring above them. His head tilted as he watched the bird. "Try it. He knows ye well enough by now and seems to favor ye."

The falcon did favor Keigan. It had taken to roosting in the rafters of the lad's room. Brenna had caught Keigan hurrying to scrub droppings off the floors on more than one occasion. She'd not scolded him or forbidden the winged beastie from his quarters. As long as the lad cleaned up after the thing, she would allow it.

This day was a special one. It was the first time Magnus had given Keigan full control over his feathered companion. The lad stood taller and lifted his gloved hand. "Merlin!" he shouted. "Come ta me!"

An answering cry split the air. The tiny speck grew in size as the falcon's rapid dive brought him downward. With another piercing screech, it lit on Keigan's arm, then sidestepped its way up to the lad's shoulder.

"Well done!" Magnus praised, looking over at Brenna to ensure she had witnessed Keigan's victory.

It made her smile. She couldn't tell who was prouder, Magnus or Keigan.

The other children clapped and cheered. Gretna's sons had often worked with Merlin, even looked after him whenever Magnus feared his travels might be too hazardous for the bird.

But the rest of the wee ones at the keep gave the falcon a wide berth. Too many had seen the ease with which the feathery hunter tore into its prey and ate it. Talons sharp as steel and beak as deadly as a dagger, most at the keep admired Merlin from a distance.

"Red comin' this way!" shouted Rory, Gretna's second son, as he pointed at the horizon.

"Aye, just there. Across the glen," confirmed Ramsay, Mercy's eldest. "Headed toward *Ruadh*. Reckon we should tell the guards to sound the horns and warn the villagers?"

No sooner had the lad spoken, then the alarm horns blared long and loud, echoing down the mountainside and into the town below.

"Inside!" Magnus ordered. "Everyone goes with Brenna and Catriona. Now!"

Heart in her throat, Brenna helped Catriona herd the young ones into the keep and deliver them to their respective quarters. All but Evander. Unfortunately, at fifteen, the lad was old enough to take up a sword if need be. Brenna prayed it wouldn't come to that because if worst came to worst, Rory, Finn, and William, even at the tender ages of fourteen, thirteen, and twelve, might be called to bear arms, too.

Times such as these made her despise the cold cruelty life sometimes served. With the kindness and support of all she had met here at *Tor Ruadh*, she had settled into a peaceful routine.

Found her place. Discovered that contentment did, in fact, exist and waited for her to claim it. She resented anything that threatened to steal it away.

"Auntie, Merlin and I can help," Keigan argued as she ushered him into their chambers.

"I know ye're a fine fighter, my brave one. Ye protected me with both bow and stones many a time." She smoothed back his hair and pecked a kiss to his forehead. "But here at the keep, the guards protect us first. We have to help them by doing as they ask." Accompanying him to his room, she pointed at the wooden chest at the foot of his bed. "What say we check yer stones and see if any need their edges honed, 'case we should need them?"

"I guess we can," he grudgingly agreed. He stepped closer to the bed and held out his arm. "Ye can either sit here and watch or go high, Merlin. Whichever ye wish."

With a twitch of his feathery head, the bird blinked its dark brown eyes, then flapped its way up to the rafters.

Noise in the sitting room made Brenna snatch up a stone and rise from where she crouched beside the chest. "Stay here," she ordered in a tone she knew the lad would never challenge. They had been through enough during Keigan's brief life for the child to know when circumstances demanded complete obedience.

As soon as she stepped out of the room and spotted Magnus and a maidservant bearing a tray of food, she sagged back against the door she had closed behind her. "Thank the Almighty. I didna ken who might have entered without my permission."

Magnus hurried to her, while the maid held back and waited beside the entrance to the suite. "Forgive me for startling ye," he said quietly. "One of our outliers just arrived. 'Tis Commander Barricourt, along with what must be his personal guard from Fort William, headed this way. Alexander means to offer them a meal with all of us present in the hopes of starting off right with the man. Show him a united front of calm, respectable horse breeders, ye ken?"

"But Lord Crestshire said it would do no good. Said the man was beyond despicable."

"Aye, but we are stuck with him, so we'll do what we can to keep the peace until forced to do otherwise. Our lands run next to Fort William. For the sake of our people, we shall attempt to forge an alliance." He waved the maidservant forward. "Greer brought Keigan's supper and will stay with him while we are downstairs."

While Greer was a kind enough lass, Brenna hated leaving Keigan while the vile British were in their midst. Her stomach knotted as she looked at the girl, then turned to Magnus. "I dinna wish to leave him. What if something happens? She's but a slip of a girl. How can she protect him?"

"I know all the passages, mistress," Greer assured in a voice much stouter than what she looked. "If aught goes amiss, the lad and I'll hie to the tunnels and hide until it's safe to come out. I swear it." She gave a firm nod. "I willna let yer bairn be taken, I grant ye that."

"She'll keep him safe, *mo chridhe*." Magnus rested his hand on her arm. "I would never entrust her with my son otherwise."

"Ye'll run like the wind with him?" Brenna asked the girl, pressing a hand on Keigan's bedchamber door as though to bless it.

"I swear it, mistress."

While Brenna understood the soundness of the plan, her heart pounded in denial with every beat. She was the one to protect Keigan. Always had been.

"Come. Let us tell the lad that we're needed in the hall. We must make haste." Magnus opened the door and gently nudged her forward.

Still kneeling beside the opened trunk, Keigan looked up from his collection of throwing stones. He jumped to his feet, both hands filled with the flint missiles. "Are we to fight, then?"

"Nay, son." Magnus rested a hand on his shoulder. "At least, not yet. But I do have a very important task for ye."

Suspicion narrowed the boy's eyes as he peered up at his father. "Aye?"

Brenna remained silent, clasping her hands to her middle. Keigan was a canny lad, wiser and more mature than his years. God bless the poor mite. He had already been through so much. It would be best if Magnus didn't try to shield the boy from what might happen if things went awry.

Magnus motioned for Greer to join them. "Mistress Greer has brought yer supper so ye dinna have to listen to the boring Sassenachs the chief has invited to dine with us."

"Aye, and the task?" Still clutching his weapons, Keigan folded his arms. Brenna could tell by his stance that the child was onto his father's tactics.

"Keep Greer safe until we return, aye?" Magnus rubbed his hands together as though proud of the way he had worded his weak deception.

"If the Sassenachs are boring and just coming to eat, why wouldna Mistress Greer be safe? We're here in our private chambers. Second floor of the chief's wing. Why would the soldiers come up here?" Keigan sheathed the stones in his belt, then bent and fetched more, stuffing them into his sporran. He paused and looked at Brenna. "Do ye need more, Auntie? Ye shouldna go below without plenty in yer pockets."

"I have enough, thank ye." Brenna nudged Magnus aside. If they were to make haste and join the others, she best handle this. "We dinna know for certain why the English have come, Keigan. 'Tis our hope all will be peaceful, but we canna know until we've met with them. If aught goes wrong, Mistress Greer knows all the secret passages running through the keep. Go with her and hide until it's safe, aye?"

"Secret tunnels?" His interest perked, Keigan turned to the maidservant for confirmation.

"Aye." The lass set the supper tray on the bed, then went to a wall covered with a colorful tapestry of a hunting scene. She reached behind it and did something none of them could see. But a low rumbling, the grinding of heavy stone against stone, rewarded her efforts, and the wall opened. With a glance back at Keigan, she smiled. "Come see."

The lad disappeared behind the tapestry. "Can we explore them?" he asked, his voice echoing as though he stood inside a cave.

"After yer supper, we can explore a bit," Greer promised.

"Come here, Keigan," Brenna called.

The lad emerged with wide eyes and a big grin. "Secret tunnels, Auntie. I bet I can find some rats for Merlin."

"That is indeed grand." She waved him forward. "Now, tell me what ye're to do whilst yer father and I are down below." With his excitement about the tunnels, she had to be sure the boy understood the gravity of the situation.

He grew quiet as he looked up at her. "If

aught goes wrong and the Sassenachs attack, Mistress Greer and I are to hide in the tunnels 'til it's safe to come out." He threw himself against her as if suddenly realizing things could become dire. His arms tightened around her. "Hide with me, Auntie. Da, too. Please?"

Heart aching but satisfied that her precious one finally understood, Brenna gently untangled herself from his hold, then crouched down in front of him. "We canna hide with ye, my fine wee warrior. This is one of those things we *must* do. Remember how we've talked of sometimes having to do things whether or not we wish to?"

Keigan scowled at her, then wrapped his arms around her neck and hugged her tight again. "I remember," he whispered. "But I dinna like it."

"Neither do I, my brave one." Brenna closed her eyes, memorizing the feel of this blessed child she loved more than life itself. If aught went wrong, at least he would be safe. At least, she prayed so. His safety was all that mattered.

"We must go now," Magnus said quietly.

"Ye've got plenty stones, aye?" Keigan said as he eased out of her embrace, his little hands knotted into fists.

"I do." Brenna stood, already missing the feel of this precious bairn safe in her arms. "But ye might give me a few more, if ye like."

The child brightened and pulled a pair of the longest flint daggers from his belt. "My best ones.

They'll keep ye safe for certain."

She tucked them both into the front of her bodice, then patted the spot where they nestled between her breasts. "I feel safer already. Thank ye, Keigan."

The child smiled, then turned a serious scowl on Magnus. "I fear ye dinna throw them verra well, but would ye like some, too? Just in case?"

"I would." Magnus shifted in place, looking both relieved and proud that his son had included him and hopefully forgiven him for acting like the boy was too young to understand.

After selecting another pair of stones from the trunk, Keigan held them out. "These should tuck nicely into yer waistcoat. I know they're small, but that doesna mean they're nay sharp or deadly."

Magnus accepted them, then knelt to look the lad in the eye. "It pains me that ye speak as a man when all ye should know are the joys of a child. Forgive me, Keigan, for everything."

Keigan rested a hand on Magnus's shoulder. "I forgive ye. Just dinna get yerself killed today." His lower lip trembled, but he didn't cry. "Please," he said, soft and low. "I need ye and Auntie both safe for me, ye ken?"

"I swear we shall do our best, son." Magnus scooped the boy into his arms and held him tight.

Brenna blinked hard and fast, willing herself not to cry. Damned English. Nothing but trouble.

"Yer supper's getting cold," Greer interrupted, then cleared her throat. "Forgive me." She tucked her chin and retreated a step while lowering her gaze to the floor.

"Mistress Greer is correct." Magnus released the lad and rose to his feet but kept a hand on Keigan's shoulder.

"Aye." Keigan backed away, averting his eyes. "I willna watch ye leave. Auntie says 'tis ill luck."

"That's my good lad," Brenna said with forced calm. She turned and hurried out the door, determined to get through this and return to her sweet boy as soon as she could. Magnus caught up with her, looking as grim as she felt.

"Hell's fire, he talks as if he's grown," he said as they rushed down the stairs and into the hallway.

"He's seen more than a child should." Brenna had learned long ago that the less she spoke about the past, the easier it was to move forward. With a hand fisted to her chest, she pressed Keigan's daggers against her breastbone. The feel of them strengthened her, a reassurance she sorely needed right now. "I pray this goes well."

Magnus took hold of her arm and turned her to face him. With a loving touch to her cheek, he stared at her with a combination of frustration and longing. She held her breath, wondering what he meant to say before they entered the hall. Instead of speaking, he gathered her close and kissed her hard. Barely lifting his mouth away, his urgent whisper thrilled her like a lover's touch. "Say ye will be my wife. Soon as the priest can say the words over us, aye?" The need in his eyes held her captive as he waited for her answer. "We are meant to be one, *mo ghràdh*. Do ye not feel it as well?"

"Aye, I feel it." Life could be so fragile and short. She suddenly regretted making him wait as long as she had. "I will be yer wife, *m'eudail*." She sealed the promise with a tender kiss, then smiled up at him. "As soon as the priest can join us."

With a resigned sigh, Magnus glanced toward the hall, then back at her. "But for now…to battle."

"To victory," she corrected with a squeeze of his arm.

They stepped through the archway, and both her steps and her heart stopped. "God help me," she prayed under her breath, then crossed herself while fighting the urge to run.

"What is it?" Magnus steadied her as he glanced around to see what had caused her reaction.

"Well, bless my soul," boomed an oddly high-pitched voice for a man. "My little virgin whore came to welcome me to the Highlands."

All sound, all movement in the great meeting room ceased as the tall, broad-shouldered British officer sauntered forward with a self-assured air. A menacing smile twisted his strangely distorted mouth as he gave an arrogant tilt of his head toward one and all. "Awfully kind of you to plan such a surprise for me. Really, it is. However, I have already had this one, you see. I've really no interest in using her again." He tapped a finger on the wide scar splitting his bottom lip. The puckered red line continued down his chin and across his throat until it disappeared behind his neckcloth. "I'm sure you understand. After all, maidenheads don't grow back to be ripped through again at one's leisure." Flipping a hand toward the handful of soldiers behind him, he continued, "Of course, these men might feel differently if you'd like to offer her to them." With a gloating chuckle, he fixed a lusty smirk on Brenna. "I know my men at Wickhaven enjoyed her wares once I tore open her package."

With a guttural roar, Magnus whipped out his sword and charged forward. "Enough!"

Barricourt drew his blade, as did every soldier with him. "You dare draw upon an English officer?" he screeched. The man sounded more like a shrieking hag than a warrior.

Gunfire sounded, halting the clash of steel.

"Ye will leave this keep at once," Alexander roared, his smoking pistol still pointed upward as he held the other trained on Barricourt. "The English are always welcome here, but not when they come bearing insults."

Graham stepped to Alexander's side, both his pistols aimed at the man, as well. "The MacCoinnich guards will be happy to see ye out, Commander." A band of brawny, armed warriors stepped out of every archway, stairwell, and shadow in the room.

"Do you have any idea what you risk with such behavior?" Barricourt sneered. He pointed the tip of his sword toward Brenna. "Over a whoring, little bitch?"

"He is defending our own," Lady Mercy said, rising from her seat and moving out from behind the head table with more grace than any sighted person. "While I have not been to court in quite some time, I still have connections there, Lord Barricourt. Do not make the mistake of thinking I will hesitate to use them."

The commander stilled, glowering at Lady Mercy, as if trying to decide if she spoke the truth. "Lady Mercy. Daughter of the late Duke of Edsbury and favorite of King William—who is also dead, I might add."

"And well-acquainted with Her Highness, Queen Anne." Mercy held herself with a calmness Brenna found amazing.

"Ye are dismissed, m'lord," Alexander said. "Leave of yer own accord, or ye can be escorted. The choice is yers."

"This is not over." Barricourt shoved his

sword back into its sheath, then spit at Brenna. "All over a whore—and a sorry one at that. She was barely an amusement." Whirling about, he stormed out the double doors, his men following close behind.

"Have them followed," Alexander told Graham. "Make sure they leave our land."

"Done." Graham sent forth the guard, pausing halfway across the room. He turned and gave Alexander an arch of a brow that spoke volumes. "Ye know there are a great many ravines betwixt here and Fort William. A body could be lost. Forever."

"Not yet," Alexander said with a coldness that promised he wouldn't hesitate to make that decision if needed.

With a tip of his head, Graham departed.

More ashamed and humiliated than she had been on the day that Barricourt and his men had so brutally used her, Brenna bowed her head and covered her face with both hands. "I am so verra sorry to have brought such misfortune to Clan MacCoinnich. Ye have all been so welcoming. So verra kind." She closed her eyes tighter, cursing the day she was born. "I promise to leave immediately, but please allow Keigan to stay. None of this is his fault."

Magnus took hold of her shoulders. "Brenna..."

"Nay." She twisted away, covering her eyes

so she wouldn't have to see how much he despised her. "I have brought shame and danger to Clan MacCoinnich. I am sorry, and I shall leave at once."

"Everyone out!" Alexander bellowed. "Leave them their privacy or deal with me."

Chairs and benches scraped the floor. Hurried footsteps shuffled loudly, then faded away. Brenna kept her head bowed and her face in her hands, waiting for whatever punishment Magnus chose. She would not weep or beg for mercy. This betrayal was hers. She should have told him all. His anger was well warranted.

"Brenna." Magnus gently squeezed her arms. "Look at me, lass. Please."

Lass. Not his usual Gaelic endearment of *my love* or *my heart*, but *lass*. After a deep breath, Brenna dropped her hands and lifted her head. The compassion and sorrow in his eyes touched her like warmth from the sun. It nearly shattered what little control she had left. She didn't know which was worse, his pity or his hatred.

"Please protect Keigan as much as ye can," she said. "I know how folk can be." She looked back down, unable to face him any longer. "Dinna do it for me, but for him. I fear he'll meet with cruelty because of what was revealed here today."

"I will not." Magnus swept her up into his arms, cradling her like a babe. After three long strides to the nearest table, he sat her down on top of it and planted his hands on either side of her. Leaning close, he forced her to meet his gaze. "I willna do so because ye'll nay be leaving *Tor Ruadh* unless Keigan and I go with ye." His jaw flexed then tightened, making her lean away. "Or did ye lie to me when just moments ago, ye said we would wed immediately?"

"Ye would wed a woman revealed as a common harlot in front of yer clan?" Trembling, she tried to scoot away and escape him, but to no avail.

He took hold of her and forced her back in front of him. "A bloody Sassenach insulted ye. Ye think I give a damn about what that man said?" He thumped his chest and bared his teeth. "Or that I care what anyone but my heart thinks?"

"But it is all true," she choked out, turning her face aside. Shameful tears escaped and, once started, refused to stop. "The weaver nor the stables would pay me any longer for my work. They feared Wicklow, vile tyrant that he was. All in the village feared him." She closed her eyes, still able to hear her precious wee one crying clear as day. "Dear Keigan was so verra hungry," she whispered. With an angry swipe at the tears, she stiffened her spine, determined to finish her confession. "Wicklow said I would work for him or no one. Then he threatened his wife and all in the village if they gave me any food for my precious tot. Even made sure I couldna steal any scraps." Rage burned through her, as hot and fierce as it had that day. "The cruel bastard hated that I had held him off as long as I had. Him and every customer he wanted to sell me to." Fingernails digging into her palms, she stared down at her trembling fists as every sensation from that terrible day rushed back to her.

The shame. Bile burning at the back of her throat. Coppery taste of her own blood. Barricourt and his men had used her for what seemed like forever. "I didn't know their names. Not any of them. When they finished, each of them threw a crown on the floor beside me. Barricourt gave me a guinea." A bitter laugh escaped her. "Said my maidenhead was worth a guinea."

"Wicklow thought to take the money." She lifted her chin but still didn't meet his gaze. Instead, she kept her focus locked on a banner fluttering from the railing of the gallery across the room. "I kept the money by stabbing the bastard with his own blade. Then Keigan and I ran away." It took all her courage to look Magnus in the eyes. "I dinna think I killed him, but I wished him dead—so, I'll burn in hell for it just the same."

Magnus stared at her, hands still planted on either side of her hips, muscular arms hemming her in. He didn't blink, just looked deep into her soul with those cold, steel eyes her sister had so oft described with wonderfully romantic words. If only her sibling could see the doubt in those eyes now.

"Say something, damn ye," she uttered, unable to stand it any longer. "Give me leave to go, beat me, or kill me. I no longer care, as long as my precious Keigan is safe."

Magnus straightened and threw back his head, staring upward. A startling growl started somewhere in the back of his throat, then roared free, echoing to the rafters.

Brenna cringed, bracing herself for whatever his anger brought next.

He lunged and pulled her into a crushing embrace. "Forgive me, my dearest one, I beg ye. Please, forgive me," he said in a ragged whisper. It took a long moment for her to realize the trembling came from him and not her.

His heartbeat hammered hard against her as he rained kisses into her hair and across her forehead. "Dinna leave me, *mo ghràdh*. Search yer heart, I beg ye. Can ye find it in yer heart to forgive me and still be my wife, even after all the suffering I caused ye?"

"Ye have gone daft." The words escaped her before she could stop them. But surely, he must be tetched in the head to still wish to wed her. Had he not heard a word she had said?

"If wishing to make such a rare, courageous

woman my wife means I am addled, then aye, that I am."

"But what about…"

He stopped her with a finger to her lips and gave a sharp shake of his head. "All that matters is that the two of us and Keigan are together as a family. Nothing else, ye ken? Well…that and yer forgiving me. Yer forgiveness matters to me more than ye will ever know."

More damned tears fell, unbidden and uncontrollable. She hated the weakness they betrayed. "The only thing I canna forgive ye for is making me cry. I hate to cry, damn ye."

"Keigan mentioned that," he said with a faint smile.

"I am sorry," she whispered, still unable to believe his reaction. "I have placed everyone here in grave danger. Yer clan will never forgive me, and I dinna blame them."

"They will forgive ye, and I swear, all will understand if ye choose to tell them all that happened." Magnus helped her down from the table but kept an arm tight around her waist. "This isna the first time this keep's been at risk, and I daresay, it willna be the last." He half led, half carried her to the long cabinet behind the head table, and poured her a drink. "Besides," he said as he handed her a whisky. "None of this wouldha happened if I hadna fathered Keigan and left Nithdane. The fault isna yers, m'love. It is mine."

"If ye make me cry again, I'll smack ye." She didn't mean it, but it was so much easier to say that than admit how much she loved him. God help her. She did love him. Loved him fierce.

"I love ye, too, my dearest one." He leaned in for a gentle, whisky-flavored kiss. "Through this life and the next," he added. "Nothing, not even death, shall part us."

CHAPTER ELEVEN

"I FEAR THERE'S a problem." Alexander offered him a glass filled with a generous portion of MacCoinnich's best.

If that much whisky was needed to start this conversation, it couldn't be good. "What problem?" Magnus accepted the liquid bribe, downed it, then held it out for another.

Alexander hesitated, then refilled both glasses to the brim.

"*That* dire?"

After sidling a glance toward the library door, Alexander picked up his drink, then stepped back and pointed at Magnus's. "Get yer own. I dinna wish to waste a drop of this. Damn near spilled this one." As he sipped, he looked toward the entrance again.

Magnus left his whisky untouched on the sideboard, placing his hand on the hilt of his sword instead. A hot tingling, one that had nothing to do with the drink, stirred his hackles. "Who waits beyond that door, Alexander?"

The fidgeting chieftain worked his jaw as though tasting something bad. Without a word, he thunked down his glass, strode to the door, and yanked it open. "Get in here. The lot of ye. I refuse to do this alone."

Magnus braced himself as Father William, Graham, and Ian filed in, each of them giving him a look that clearly marked him as doomed. With the priest present, this had to have something to do with Brenna. Brothers in battle or not, if they thought to have their holy man dissuade him from marrying her, he would enlighten all of them on just how wrong they were. Then he, Brenna, and Keigan would leave *Tor Ruadh*. Forever. "What is this?"

Father William, short and gnarled as an ancient walking stick, marched forward with the boldness of a beast about to attack. "I informed the MacCoinnich that I willna perform the marriage ceremony betwixt yerself and Mistress Brenna."

Magnus managed a forced calm, but his grip tightened on the hilt of his sword. He had never killed a holy man, even though he had been sorely tempted a time or two. Christianity. He snorted at the word—what a hypocritical religion. Preached kindness and forgiveness, then tormented poor innocent souls. "Dinna make me kill ye, priest. I'll not allow a wonderful woman like my Brenna upset by yer deceitful beliefs that cause more harm than good."

The father's determined look puckered into a scowl. "I am nay refusing because anything's lacking with Mistress Brenna." The bushiness of his wild brows knotted tighter. "I am protecting the woman. She is a fine Christian lass. Confessed her sins and, from what she has told me, has more than paid her penance." With one hand clutching the large wooden cross dangling from a cord around his neck, he chopped the air with the other as though preaching to a crowd. "I refuse to bind her to a heathen such as yerself." His large, knobby nostrils flared. "Repent now or face eternal damnation, I say!" He dipped his chin again. "And face it alone because I'll be telling that poor lass to run as far from ye as she can get."

"What?"

"Ye heard me," Father William declared, lifting the cross higher as he stalked closer. "Repent!"

Alexander, Graham, and Ian all stared at the floor, clasping their hands in front of them. The three of them looked as guilty as lads caught stealing pies.

"Are all of ye such cowards that ye let a priest run this clan?" Magnus tossed back his drink. He had never expected such a ridiculous attack. "Ye know damned good and well why I dinna follow yer God," he continued when no one had the courage to answer him.

"Ahh," Father William cracked a smile. With a smug nod, he shuffled another step forward. "So, ye do believe in the Almighty. That's a fine start, my son." He pulled a vial from the pocket of his simple brown robe and sent the cork flying with a flip of his thumb. "Now, might I assume ye also believe in our Lord Jesus Christ and the Holy Spirit?"

"All I believe is that yer followers murdered my mother!" Magnus stormed toward the wiry little man, burning to knock the holy relics aside and throttle the arrogant fool. But something held him back. Something inexplicable. A tolerance instilled in him long ago by his beloved mother stayed his hand. "Lying hypocrites, inciting hatred. That's all the lot of ye do."

Father William looked up at him with so much compassion it made him even angrier. "I am truly sorry about yer mother, my son." He gave a sad shake of his balding head. "No Christian is perfect. And I freely admit, there are those who use God's word for their own cruel benefit. But ye mustn't blame the Almighty for the wicked ones who walk this earth. They shall receive their judgment, I promise ye."

Magnus turned away. He couldn't bear the sight of the man or his meaningless babbling any longer. He poured himself another drink and went to the wide window overlooking the chieftain's private garden below. Walled in and a guard at the gate since Barricourt's visit, the youngest of the keep's children played among the trees and flower beds, Keigan among them. His son. His precious son.

The sight of the lad romping with Alexander's youngest twin boys eased Magnus's soul better than any Christian version of a promised hereafter. His son's maturity bothered him. No bairn his age should possess such wisdom because of all he had witnessed. Where had Father William's God been then? Why had the Almighty allowed so much death and suffering? Magnus shifted his gaze to the last dredges of whisky in his glass, swirling them in the sunlight. Of course, to be fair, he should also ask why *his* mighty gods hadn't protected those he cared about, either. Every entity had failed him.

"We live in a broken world, my son," Father William said as if reading Magnus's thoughts. Somehow, the wily priest had moved to stand beside him without his even noticing. The man smiled down at the children playing. "Only when our Lord and Savior returns will all pain and suffering end. Come now. Ye believe in Almighty God. Allow me to baptize ye." He shrugged. "Who knows? Maybe one day ye'll be on speaking terms with our wondrous Creator again."

Magnus snorted. "Ye're too late, priest. Mother had me baptized when I was but a few days old and stricken with a fever she couldna cure." A sad fondness overcame him at the memory of her telling him of her panic. "She feared I would die. So, she thought to protect my soul in any way possible." He drained the last of his drink and upended the glass with a thud on the windowsill. "Magnus Jedidiah de Gray. I dinna ken what happened to the record of it. I can only assume it's recorded in a kirk somewhere."

"Jedidiah." The Father laughed. "Ye ken yer name means 'friend of God'? Aye, well, even friends fall out now and again and stop speaking to each other for a while." He patted Magnus's shoulder. "If I had known this about ye, I would nay have come at ye with the holy water. Forgive me, my son. It would honor me to say the words to bind ye with Mistress Brenna."

"She doesna wish a big affair." Magnus focused on the children at play. "But I dinna think we should hide away as though we're ashamed." He spared a backward scowl at the three where they now stood beside the cabinet with all the decanters and glasses. "I am not a coward like some in this room."

"I am not a coward," Alexander argued. "I merely know my limitations. Converting heathens isna one of my many strengths."

"Nor mine," Graham said.

Ian grinned. "I volunteered to help hold ye down 'til they had yer soul properly saved and watered, but Father said it wouldna work that way. So, I thought it best I keep quiet."

"Hold me down?" Magnus repeated. "Dare I remind ye who tossed yer arse during the games at the last gathering?"

Ian's grin widened into a toothy smile. "I let ye win. Respect for me elders, ye ken? I didna wish to shame ye."

Catriona threw open the door, silencing their banter. "Is it done yet? Mercy and I dinna wish her to see the dress."

"Is *what* done yet?" Magnus growled, even though he had a fair idea. If not for Catriona, he would tell the lot of them to kiss his arse. "If ye're asking if I'm still bound for Hell, I would say that's debatable."

"From that comment, I would say it is done," Mercy said. She stepped into the room but turned and faced back toward the hallway. "Perhaps, if we show him the gown, that will improve his temperament."

"Hurry! Bring it inside. We dinna ken how long Gretna can keep Brenna busy in the healing room." Looping her arm through Mercy's, Catriona moved them both to one side as a pair of maidservants brought in a long bundle wrapped in yellowed linen. As soon as they had cleared the door, she hurried to close it behind them. "Quick, unwrap it."

While he approved of the rich shade of blue, other than that, Magnus didn't know what to say. It was a dress. All that mattered was if Brenna liked it. "It seems nice enough."

"Seems nice enough?" Catriona repeated with a look that shot a chill through him.

Noting the varying levels of indignation flaring across all the females invading the library, Magnus backed up a step. "I am not an expert on dresses." As Catriona and Mercy opened their mouths, he hurried to continue, "However, I am amazed that ye managed to fashion it in one night's time. I canna fathom how ye did it." There. That should save his arse, especially since the rest of the men, including Father William, had retreated and left him to fight alone. "I feel sure my dear one's heart will be touched by yer kindness." He relaxed and felt a great deal safer when all the women smiled.

"I am just proud I had not yet used the silk damask, or we never couldha managed it," Catriona said. "'Tis simple, I'm afraid. There wasna time to fashion a proper mantua, but it turned out lovely, I think. We sewed nonstop to make it so."

"We hope it pleases her," Mercy said. "And lets her know how much she belongs here."

"We've a proper feast planned for this evening. If she still wishes a private affair, ye can marry in the chapel with only us as witnesses and then come to the hall to celebrate." Catriona gave a flip of a hand. "After all, we must all have supper anyway, aye?"

"Aye." The wily women's plans seemed plausible enough. He circled the gown, finally noticing the intricate detailing, layers of lace, delicate pleats, and gathers. Never again would he underestimate the power of women united by determination. "Ye say she's in Gretna's room?"

"Yes." Mercy pointed at the door. "Go convince her to agree so we can help her get ready."

"We've already had the bath taken to her chambers, and Mrs. Fitzgerald's set the laundress to boiling more water." Catriona gave him a stern look. "A tub and ample soaps have been taken to yer room as well. Hot water will be there soon enough. Make use of it, aye?"

"Welcome to our ranks," Alexander said with a knowing smirk.

Graham laughed. "Aye, man. Yer life will never be the same."

"A scrubbing before the feast wouldna be amiss for yerself, dear husband." Catriona slid her unrelenting glare to Alexander.

"And you as well," Mercy said with her sightless eyes trained on Graham. "I can tell where you are by your *scent*."

"Makes a man thankful to be a priest," Father William observed as he poured himself a healthy share of whisky and headed out the door. "I shall be in the chapel. Come to me when ye're ready, aye?"

Magnus escaped the room, wondering if he should've done as the priest and brought a drink with him. Alexander's library had always been a haven for the men. After today, Magnus had his doubts it would ever be so again. But he had to admit, with a feast planned and a dress readied, they had lifted considerable weight and worry from him. Maybe now Brenna would see that the past didn't matter to any of them. Truth be told, not a one of them had the right to judge her. He snorted out a wry laugh. As the priest would say, none of them were without their sins. Now, if only he could convince her that was how they all felt.

Descending the narrow stone steps to the bottom level of the north tower, Magnus paused outside the door to the healing room. He couldn't make out the conversation through the heavy oak door, but he could tell by Brenna's giddy laugh that the visit was going well. Head bowed as he listened, what he heard made him smile. Gretna sounded just as happy. In fact, both women chattered back and forth like a pair of contented hens clucking over their morning feed.

He pushed open the door and entered. "Ladies."

"Merciful heavens!" Gretna took hold of Brenna's wrist and stopped her work with the mortar and pestle. "Flora asked me to come 'round today. I told her I'd be there early, and here it is well into the day. Would ye mind ever so much if I left ye for a wee bit?" Without waiting for a response, she whirled about and snatched up a covered basket. "I know ye can handle anyone who might come needing help. Why—ye know more about healing than I do!" With a sly glance at Magnus, the woman was out the door and gone before either of them could speak.

With a puzzled frown, Brenna stared at the door. "Well, for goodness' sake, I guess it slipped her mind until now."

"She is a busy woman. Keeps up with a great deal." He moved to stand beside her at the long worktable in front of the window. A glance around explained all the odd smells. Shelves with tightly wrapped bundles, dark glass bottles, cloth-covered crocks, and small wooden boxes filled every available space. Dried herbs hung from the corners of the low ceiling. The cot in the corner beside a table set with fierce-looking saws, knives, and awls made him cringe. "I canna say that I have ever been in here before—thankfully."

"'Tis a fine healer's room." Brenna smiled, beaming as though she had just stepped through Heaven's gates. She resumed grinding the mixture in the mortar, pulverizing what looked like dried sticks and leaves. Her smile faded, and her mixing slowed. "And Gretna didna act any different toward me because of yesterday."

He set aside the pestle and took her hands in his. "There is only today. That is why I am here."

The puzzled crease returned to her brow. "Ye're not making sense."

He kissed her knuckles again, deciding he liked the pungent aroma the herbs gave her skin. "Aye. I am making sense." Still holding both her hands, he rubbed his thumb back and forth across the gold band on her finger. "We decided to marry at once. Did we not?"

Her gaze dropped. "Aye," she said quietly. "But with a new day, if ye've had a change of heart, I understand."

"My only change of heart is that I love ye more today than I did the day before."

"And ye've made me love ye more," she whispered. She blinked fast and hard against her unshed tears. "Dinna make me cry."

"Catriona, Mercy, and Gretna are waiting to help ye get ready." Magnus gently pulled her away from the table and steered her toward the door. "Alexander, Graham, Ian, and the priest are already in the chapel." He had decided the best way to move this fine day forward was to sweep her into it before she could refuse. "We shall wed in the privacy of the chapel, just as ye wished. With the six of them as our witnesses. Then we shall celebrate with all, in the keep." Gaining momentum, he walked her up the hall to where Catriona, Mercy, and Gretna clustered together, their faces wreathed in smiles. "Tonight will be our first feast as husband and wife."

"But—"

"Nay," he hushed her as if she was a child. "I am more than a little proud to have won such a woman." With the gentlest of kisses, he tickled the words across her lips. "*Mo chridhe, m'anam, mo chuid.*"

"My heart, my soul, my all," she repeated, then turned her face aside. "Ye are certain?" she softly asked, staring at the floor as though unable to believe in such happiness.

"More certain than I have ever been about anything."

She briefly closed her eyes while a tremulous smile played across her lips. With a squeeze of his hand, she opened her eyes to his, then turned toward the trio of females barely containing their excitement. "I am ready."

The ladies swarmed her and swept her away on a sea of lilting chatter.

Magnus headed for the peace and quiet of his

modest room, thanking the gods he had been born a male where scrubbing and dressing was a private affair.

"YER EYE IS sharp as ever, Catriona," Gretna said as she and Mercy encased Brenna in the silk damask bodice and overskirt. Holding the garment together at the waist, she eyed it with a critical frown. "I dinna believe it'll take any tacking in or letting out at all. With the lacing good and tight, 'twill be a perfect fit!"

"Mind the sleeves," Mercy cautioned. "We wanted yer lovely shoulders left bare, so we used the same lace we overlaid across the silk of yer underskirt and stomacher. There wasn't time for proper smocking on the sleeves, but the lace adds a perfect drape." She moved the delicate material back and forth through her fingers. "So soft and lovely, but also very fragile."

"It's the most beautiful dress I have ever seen," Brenna whispered as the women tugged, fluffed, and adjusted to ensure the perfect display. She smoothed her hands down the snug bodice that came to a point right above the creamy lace layered over the matching petticoat underskirt revealed by the open cut of the gown. The dark blue of the silk damask draped perfectly, the overskirt made even fuller by tight pleating at the waist. Deep flounces of the material gathered back at the hips, then bunched into a bustle at the small of her back. The ladies had even managed a modest train to flow behind her. Never had she possessed such finery.

"I wish we'd had time to add a wee bit of boning to the bodice," Catriona said as she examined their handiwork. "But I think yer stays will do. I believe I like this better than a full-on mantua." She stepped back a few paces, tilting her head, first one way, then the other. "Aye, this'll do just fine. Ye're a vision of loveliness itself." A happy sigh escaped her. "And that dark blue is yer color, lass. Matches yer eyes and makes yer hair shine even more golden."

Words didn't exist for her to make them understand how much their acceptance, generosity, and kindness meant to her. "How can I ever thank ye?" She pressed the corners of her eyes, willing the threat of tears to abate.

"Dinna ye dare cry!" Gretna said, jumping to hold both hands under Brenna's face. "Ye'll spot yer lovely silk." She looked over her shoulder. "Quick! The lass needs a cloth. Ye know as well as I there'll be tears. I've never seen a wedding without one."

Catriona placed a lacy-edged handkerchief in her hand. "Here. Tuck this into yer bosom. As Gretna said, this'll be a day for happy tears, and ye'll need it." She stepped back with another satisfied nod. "And ye can thank us with yer friendship and trust, aye? We're truly happy Magnus found ye."

"Time for Fenna?" Mercy asked.

"Aye," Catriona and Gretna agreed in unison.

Mercy moved to the door. "Fenna, Mistress Brenna is ready for you."

"Fenna?" In all the excitement, there had been so many maidservants helping her bathe and wash her hair, Brenna's mind whirled. She couldn't remember who was who.

The tiny lass with the shortest hair and the largest smile bounced into the room, toting a basket of brushes and combs. "Mistress Brenna, ye look most becoming. Master Magnus is a verra lucky man." With a sharp nod, she continued, "Dinna sit. Ye might crease yer dress and flatten the pasteboard we sewed into the bustle to make yer rump all grand and flare that train good and proper when ye walk."

A maidservant so forward she gave orders and made personal comments? Brenna didn't mind, but it had been her experience that such a thing was rarely tolerated. "Thank ye. I hope he thinks so."

"Fenna is my lady's maid," Mercy explained. "She is very outspoken." One of her smooth dark brows arched higher. "I wouldn't have her any other way—most of the time."

Lady Mercy might be blind, but she noticed more than those who had two good eyes. Brenna wondered if the woman possessed the second sight. "Such an unusual clan. Treating all with respect and kindness? No matter their status? Especially women? Verra rare indeed."

"Kindness and respect make for strong kinship," Catriona explained. "'Tis our belief it strengthens us, helps us overcome any obstacle we face."

"A strong kinship," Brenna repeated as the maid brushed out her curls and arranged them. A contentedness filled her. She knew in her heart her sister was smiling down from heaven, happy that her son had accepted such a family as his own.

"There now," Fenna climbed down from the footstool she had used to reach Brenna's hair. "I know 'tis simple, but yer hair is so lovely, I thought it fitting for this special day."

"Ye've made me feel grand as a queen." Ever so gingerly, Brenna reached up and ran her fingertips along the fine ivory combs sweeping her tresses up high, then freeing the curls to cascade down her back.

"And dinna ye fret about Keigan," Catriona said as she offered her a small goblet of wine. "Maxwell and Grant have already built a fortress for the three of them in the nursery." She laughed. "Little do they know that wee Maisie plans to attack them later on this evening." With a reassuring flip of a hand, she continued, "I've warned Willa and Nanny to ensure there are no injuries." She made a face, and her voice took on an amused but warning tone. "My sweet Maisie can be a vicious wee mite. They best not underestimate her."

Catriona's assurance that Keigan wasn't her responsibility tonight increased Brenna's nervousness. A wedding night. With Magnus. The sharing of the marriage bed. She swallowed hard, forcing down a choking knot of worry with a sip of the wine. Everything she knew about such matters came from a darker time. Survival had bid her lock that vileness away and never think of it again. She prayed Magnus wouldn't find her lacking.

"I'd say it's time we all got to the chapel, aye?" With a proud smile, Catriona took the wine away and set it aside. "Yer groom's a waitin'."

"My groom," Brenna repeated under her breath, willing herself to walk as gracefully as she could. The black leather shoes, tied with a bow that matched the silk of her dress and adorned with cream-colored heels, threatened to send her tumbling. Either that or pinch her toes clean off. May God have mercy on her soul. The cursed things squeezed her feet tighter than a starving dog's bite on a bone. And Gretna had secured her stockings with ribbons tied so tight above her knees, her legs had gone all numb. "Help me not fall on my face, aye?"

"Ye willna fall," Catriona reassured, strolling along beside her.

"We've surrounded ye," Gretna added as she and Mercy took their places alongside her. "And Fenna's at yer train to ensure it's set off good and proper."

"I canna believe I'm doing this." Giddiness filled her, threatening to send her head spinning. Swallowing hard, she fanned herself. "'Tis verra warm, aye? I'll soak my chemise through."

All the women laughed. "We felt the same, dear sister," Mercy reassured her. "And if need be, we have two more chemises ready, should you need to refresh before retiring with your husband."

"Aye," Gretna said. "Just give us a nod, and we'll have ye sorted and dry, quick as a blink." She grinned like a proud parent. "The women of Clan MacCoinnich prepare for everything."

Attempting any level of gracefulness with pinched toes and the weight of the gown proved quite the challenge. But the longer Brenna walked, the better she adapted to the shoes they had shod her with. She looked forward to their removal at her earliest opportunity.

The servants formed a line along her route to the chapel, all of them smiling and nodding, as though she were royalty itself. How kind they all seemed, and try as she might, she didn't detect a single disparaging glance. Except for one. Cadha stood at the very end of the line closest to the archway leading to the kirk. That lass gave her a sour-faced scowl that left no doubt she thought Brenna lower than the earth upon which she trod.

Brenna held her head higher. She assumed a disinterested air that informed the girl her opinion mattered less than a sputtering candle. That festering hen had no idea what she had survived. Nor was it any of her affair. She stored away the girl's insulting attitude for future reference. It would be a frosty day in Hell before she ever defended that surly maid again.

"Well done, lass," Catriona lauded under her breath. "And dinna fret, I'll be having a word with that wee chit on the morrow." She spared a glance back at the bothersome girl. "She should know the MacCoinnich way by now. Mrs. Fitzgerald and I shall offer her the choice of embracing it or leaving the keep." With a squeeze of Brenna's hand, Catriona gifted her an excited smile. "Today is a day of celebration, and I'll let nothing spoil it. God bless ye, sister. May only good things come to ye from this union."

"Thank ye," Brenna said. "For everything." After a deep breath, she faced the elaborately carved doors of the chapel, struck mute by their grandeur. Beyond waited Magnus. Her groom.

The man with whom she would spend the rest of her days. God help her. She prayed this was the right thing to do. Just because she had an overwhelming tenderness for him didn't mean they could survive whatever lay ahead. But she would do her best. Not for her sister. Not for Keigan. But for her own aching heart. Life would be so much easier to bear with Magnus at her side. God help her—how she loved him. She only hoped he felt the same tender aching for her.

"On wi' ye now," Catriona whispered as she pulled open the door to the right.

"God be with ye," Gretna said as she swung the left door wide.

"Welcome home," Mercy called out softly from behind her. "God bless ye and Magnus with good health, happiness, and strength to face whatever the future may hold."

"Wait!" Fenna called out. "Marcie made a lovely nosegay for ye."

A wee lass that could pass for a mirror image of Fenna except for her wild curly hair rushed forward with a bundle of ivy brightened with blossoms of blue, lavender, and pink. "'Tis heather, miss. I nurtured it where we seed the plants for the garden. I hope ye find the early blooms lovely."

"Thank ye, Marcie. It is perfect." Brenna accepted the bouquet, smiling down at the symbols of fidelity, prosperous luck, and protection. "Thank ye so much." Now, all she had to do was keep from shaking off all the blooms as she trembled her way down the aisle.

The young girl smiled, then scampered away, disappearing down the hall toward the kitchens.

"It's time," Catriona urged with a tilt of her head toward the doorway. "God bless ye, lass."

After sending up a quick prayer, Brenna entered the church's narthex. She halted as soon as she stepped into the nave. The sight of Magnus, strong and sure, waiting in front of the altar, swept away every worry. Striking as ever in his black jacket, brushed 'til not a speck of dirt could be found. Dark waistcoat. Tall, polished boots. His startling white tunic and neckcloth made her smile. The man preferred black, even when it came to his lèine. But now creamy ruffles peeped out of his coat sleeves. And even though his neckcloth was knotted and tucked, she knew it, too, had the ruffles reserved for the most special of occasions.

He wore a tartan of blue bands, some so dark they almost looked black, crossing others light as the sky. A length of it crossed his broad chest, the folds draped over his left shoulder and secured with a bronze brooch. His hair, pulled back and neatly tied, shone like polished silver. Her pounding heart shook the posies she clutched to her breast. Such a fiercely handsome man. Her true Highland warrior.

One hand propped on the buckle of his belt, he held out the other. "Come to me," he said. Or maybe he didn't. Maybe it was just the way he smiled as he waited to take her hand.

CHAPTER TWELVE

GOD'S TEETH, HOW could this fine woman have agreed to take him as husband? Magnus refused to blink. He didn't wish to miss a single moment of her walk toward him. Aye, the gown was fair enough, but it was the light in her eyes, her barely parted lips, the complete wonder of her that made it impossible to look away.

He stayed in place as long as he could bear it, then went to her, meeting her partway down the aisle. "I have never witnessed such beauty," he said with a reverence that came from the depths of his soul. Taking her hand, he led her back to the altar. "Thank ye, m'love."

"For what are ye thanking me?" Her fingers trembled in his, and the porcelain curves of her breasts lifted as she hitched in a nervous breath.

"I thank ye for accepting me, precious one." He kissed her hand, then held it to his cheek, reveling in loving contentment he had never felt before. No one existed but Brenna. "Ye made me whole again, m'love. I canna imagine life without ye at my side."

"Then I must thank ye as well," she said with a shy tilt of her head. Her words, soft and breathless, were sweeter than any music. "For ye have made me feel the same."

Father William cleared his throat. He thumped a finger on the open book he cradled in one hand. "Well, then…now that ye each spoke yer own vows, shall I speak the Lord's and make this official in the eyes of the church?"

"Aye, priest. Say yer words," Magnus said without breaking his gaze from Brenna's. In his mind, their souls were already joined for all time. Grudgingly, he faced Father William, and Brenna did the same.

The holy man uttered an imperious *har-rumph,* then lifted his tattered book higher. "As ye all ken well enough by now, we gather here to unite these two in the sacred bonds of marriage." He passed a glance around the sanctuary as though giving a sermon to a full church rather than just the chosen six standing in front of the first pew. With a bushy brow hiked to a stern angle, he looked at Magnus. "Do ye, Magnus

Jedidiah de Gray, take this woman as yer honored wife and helpmate? Swear to always provide and protect her? Keep her at yer side, whether ye be rich as a king or poor as a pauper, ill as a bloated beast or fit as a fine Highland day, until death so parts ye?"

"Yer book uses those words?"

"Never ye mind. Just answer the question." The priest drew himself up, looking as though he was about to rain down hellfire and damnation. "I shall have ye know I've married a good many souls in my day." His eyes narrowed at the witnesses trying not to laugh out loud. "My words stuck well enough, I reckon." With an imperious jerk of his head, his voice grew louder. "Count their bairns and their years together, aye? Now, do ye take this woman or not?"

"I most certainly do." Magnus pressed a kiss to Brenna's hand. "For all time."

Father William swatted at their hands with his Bible. "No more kisses 'til I say." He shifted his attention to Brenna, and his stern gruffness disappeared. "And now, my child, do ye bind yerself to this man? Hardheaded, infuriating soul that he is? Vow to stay at his side through prosperity or suffering? Cherish him all yer days 'til death shall part ye?"

"I do." She blessed Magnus with a loving smile. "Forever and a day."

The priest snapped his book shut and tucked

it into the crook of one arm. He resettled his stance with a pleased bounce. "Verra good, then. In the eyes of the church and the record books of Scotland, I now proclaim ye man and wife. Let no man tear asunder what God Almighty hath joined." He pointed at Alexander. "And all God's people said?"

"Amen!" Alexander bellowed, and the others echoed the same loud and clear.

Father William graced Magnus with a perfunctory nod. "And *now* ye may kiss her proper."

With the greatest of care not to crush her wee bundle of heather and ivy, Magnus cradled her face between his hands and eased forward to seal their vows. His heart stuttered when she brushed away his touch and turned aside.

"Catriona?" She held out the flowers.

With happy tears and a big smile, Catriona hurried to take them, then returned to her place beside Alexander.

"I shall let nothing come between us." Brenna slid her arms around his neck. "Not even flowers."

"I dinna believe I couldha married a wiser woman," he observed, then shared a kiss that forged their union with the heat of a smithy's forge.

"Well done!" Alexander cheered.

Graham and Ian roared Clan MacCoinnich's battle cry, nearly shaking the rafters with their chanting of *je ressuscite!*

"To the hall!" Alexander waved Magnus and Brenna forward. "The couple shall lead us to their banquet."

Magnus noticed Brenna's hesitation and how her hold tightened on his arm. He leaned in close as though kissing her cheek but whispered, "It will be all right, m'love. Show them yer courage. How ye fear nothing—most especially how ye dinna give a damn about any judgments they have no right to make."

With a loving touch to his cheek, she smiled. "How can ye read me so well?"

"Because we two are a proper match."

"All are waiting," Catriona gently called out from behind them.

After leaning up for a quick kiss, Brenna pulled in a deep breath and blew it out. "I am ready."

She lied, but Magnus admired her for the effort. He held tight to her hand, walking proudly beside her. They made their way to the main hall that had already filled with people. Word of their private ceremony and the celebration feast had spread like fire touched to dry tinder. Folks continued to mill into the room in a seemingly endless line of arrival.

Two long rows of tables, running parallel down the center of the massive room, had several seated. Benches along the walls and beneath the gallery were almost full as well. Servants bustled among the guests, ensuring everyone's tankards didn't run dry. Food wouldn't be offered to those at the tables and benches until the chief and his guests at the head table had been served.

Torches and candelabras burned brightly, even though the sun still hovered above the horizon. Its brilliant beams poured in through the windows lining the upper gallery. A trickle of sweat started between Magnus's shoulder blades, trickled down his spine, and pooled in the crack of his arse. Even with no fire in the hearths, the room had warmed with the heat of the late August day, and so many assembled.

He fought the urge to keep walking once they reached the head table. It would be easy enough, just power through the archway and escape up the stairs to their chambers. Nay. He daren't do such. Brenna might think him ashamed of her. Instead, he helped her maneuver the abundant yardage of her gown so she might sit. He took his place beside her after scooting her close enough to reach the table.

"Thank ye." Brenna drew a lacy cloth from between the cleft of her breasts and daubed it against the back of her neck, then her throat. "'Tis verra warm in here," she said, shielding her words behind the kerchief. "How could so many arrive this quickly? The hall was almost empty when I passed through."

"Food, drink, and gossip are impossible for most to resist. Especially this time of year. The days are long, and the weather fair enough to make a walk from the village and even farther just a wee stretch of the legs." Magnus motioned for a servant to fill her glass. "At least the chief's candles are already lit. Pray they burn quickly. Alexander promised one round only."

"Chief's candles?" She looked at him as though he had gone addled with the heat.

After plucking a juicy slice of pear from the platter of fruits and cheeses, Magnus pointed it at the candelabra burning on their end of the table. "Those are the chief's candles. When they burn out, everyone knows the gathering is at an end, and it's time to leave." He offered her the bite of pear. "For longer celebrations, more candles are added and lit. As long as the chief's candles burn, all are welcome to stay and enjoy the festivities."

"But Alexander promised only one round, ye said?" She nibbled at the tidbit of fruit as though she feared it poisoned.

"Aye." Unable to resist, Magnus reached out and caressed her cheek. "But we can retire before then. 'Tis expected of us."

She dropped the fruit to her plate and cut a fearful glance at him. "They dinna do the—" She interrupted herself with a deep draught of wine, then held out her glass for more. A smiling maidservant appeared from behind them and filled it. After another hearty drink, she slid the goblet to the table, then stared down at it in silence.

"Dinna do what?" The high color on her cheeks had drained away. Poor lass looked as though she had just seen a headless ghost. "Shall I call Gretna over? Are ye unwell?" He feared the heat had overcome her.

"Nay." She waved away his words but kept her gaze on her plate. "I had forgotten about the bedding ceremony," she whispered. "I fear I am nay prepared for it." After a hard swallow, she bowed her head lower, tucking her chin to her chest. "Father lived for weddings at his keep. He took great pleasure in helping the men strip the poor bride naked and enjoyed the consummation of the marriage as much as the groom."

Hell's fire. No wonder the color had drained from her. Magnus had witnessed the brutal custom once and couldn't imagine putting Brenna through such a thing. Ever so gently, he slid a finger under her chin and lifted her face. "I would never allow such a thing. Not ever. What passes between us is no one's affair but ours."

"Truly?"

"I swear it."

"Ye are the kindest man I have ever met." Her relieved smile warmed his heart, as well as the rest of him.

A loud clanging silenced the room. Alexander

rose from his seat and held his tankard high. "A toast to the newly wedded couple." With a wry grin, he waved his glass toward Magnus. "All of us feared our brother would die alone. Somewhere in the Highlands. With no one to grieve or pray over his bones other than wild animals." His gaze slid to Brenna, and his grin became a broad smile. "But thankfully, our prayers were answered. He found this fine woman." He held his drink high as if it was a scepter. "May God bless ye and keep ye both in perfect peace. May He grant ye many years of happiness, as well as many sons and daughters. *Slàinte mhath!*"

"*Slàinte mhath!*" everyone roared, with so much pounding and stomping, the entire keep seemed to quake.

In answer to the toast, Magnus leaned close until his lips brushed the velvet of her cheek. "*Mo chridhe, m'anam, mo chuid,*" he murmured against her ear.

With a tender smile, she framed his face between her hands and kissed him long and slow.

The hall went wild with even louder cheering.

"Let us go, aye? Neither of us wishes to be here." He held out his hand as he slid back his chair and stood.

Brenna took his hand and rose to her feet.

After a meaningful look shared with Alexander, Magnus led her from the dais and through the archway beside the long cabinet bearing all the bottles and pitchers of spirits for the evening. A glance back made him smile. The MacCoinnich guards had formed a barrier in front of the head table, one that stretched across the room, so none could follow and cause any mischief.

Just as they reached the end of the narrow hallway leading to the turret staircase of the south wing, Brenna stopped him. "Wait! I canna bear this any longer."

Her words hit him like an icy blast of winter's worst chill. "What?"

With a pained expression, she glanced back down the hall, then lifted her foot, fighting back the layers of silk and lace. "These shoes. Lord have mercy on my poor feet. I am miserable. 'Tis a wonder they havena crippled me. I have to be rid of them. Now."

Magnus bit the inside of his cheek to keep from laughing, but she spied his amusement.

"Ye think my torture funny?"

"Nay!" he lied, struggling to assume a woeful look. Best help her before she found a weapon. "Steady yerself on my shoulders whilst I relieve ye of the offensive things, aye? I'll have them off ye in no time." He knelt at her feet, sweeping her skirts aside and cradling her lovely ankle in one hand. His man parts took particular interest in the feel of her leg encased in her stockings, making it necessary to adjust his crouch to allow more room for his rising cock.

"Hold still afore ye knock me to the floor!" She clutched at his shoulders. "Forgive me. I didna mean to speak so harsh. Just hurry. I beg ye. Undo those terrible ribbons, pry them off, and I'll leave the infernal things on the steps for Catriona." She patted his back. "I didna mean to scold, but ye might as well know, ye didna marry a woman used to such trappings. Saints alive, I canna understand how she bears these fool things."

Magnus squinted, trying to decipher the dark ribbon's knot hidden in the shadows of her skirts and the poorly lit hall. Brenna's foot had swelled around the ties until they cut into her flesh. "No wonder ye're hurting. These look to be about three sizes too small."

"Just get them off me. Please." She sagged forward, resting her brow on his shoulder as he struggled with the embedded knot. "Catriona thought they would be fine. I didna have the heart to tell her my feet are big as a pair of war shields."

"This is madness," he said through gritted teeth. Wrapping an arm around her legs, he draped her over his shoulder and stood.

"What are ye doing?" She thumped his back, squirming to get down.

"Be still with ye." He swatted her rump and strode to the stairwell, charging up the steps. "I canna see a damned thing in this shadowy hallway. If I cut them off ye here, ye're liable to lose a toe."

"Cut them off?" she squeaked. "Ye mustn't damage the leather. They're Catriona's, and I'm sure they're dear to her."

"Aye, well, I'm thinking she'll live past losing a pair of slippers." By the time he reached the second-floor landing, he had worked up an even heartier sweat than before. He took hold of the latch and shoved, ready to be rid of his full dress of clothes and those damnable shoes. Why the hell did women put themselves through such foolishness? It couldn't be to impress men. Who gave a damn about a woman's feet when their bodies had so much nicer things to offer? The door did not open. "The key, Brenna?"

"Key?"

Her tone told him everything he needed to know.

As gently as he could, he slid her off his shoulder and plopped her rump to the floor. "Cover yer face in case wood goes a flying."

"Ye dinna mean to break it?" She stared up at him, wide-eyed and horrified. "Ye canna break it! What will Alexander say?"

"I dinna give a damn what Alexander says. He'd do the same if it were him." Magnus had had enough of uncomfortable fancy clothes and barred doors. He was ready to strip down, stand in front of a good strong breeze, and drink a whisky before he settled down to the pleasurable task of consummating their vows. Shoulder lowered, he charged into the door, ramming it with a determined grunt.

Wood split and crackled, but the door didn't give. Magnus backed up as far as he could on the stairway landing and dropped his shoulder again.

"Ye're going to knock yer shoulder clear out of its joint!" she scolded. "Just run fetch the key, aye?"

"Nay," he growled from between clenched teeth. The locked door had become the enemy. "The locks are weak. 'Tis the bars across the door that keep out real intruders." He hit it full force. It sprang open and sent him sprawling across the sitting room floor. He rolled up to a sitting position, rubbing his shoulder all the while. It appeared he needed to spend more time in the practice yards. Damnation, he had gone soft. Either that or feckin' doors had gotten a great deal harder than they once were.

Bunching up her skirts, Brenna crawled over to him. "Are ye all right? Let me see." She moved to his side, pinching his fingers under her knee.

Yanking his hand out from under her, he bit back a yelp and forced a chivalrous smile. "Nay, m'lady. I wish yer comfort to come first." Ignoring the minor aching in both shoulder and hand, he pulled his *sgian dhu* from his boot. With a pat to the floor in front of him, he held up the knife and smiled. "Yer feet, m'love?"

With a wiggle that made his mouth go dry, Brenna plopped down on her rear with both feet sticking out in front of her. Skirts hiked to her knees, she leaned forward and took hold of both legs. With an earnest look, she scooted closer. "Do ye think ye can cut them free without damage to the stockings? Mercy said I could keep them."

Her fair breasts nearly spilled out over the top of the stomacher, robbing him of all reason. "Uhm…" was all he could think to say.

"Can ye at least try to save them?"

"Aye," he managed to utter. "I shall do my best." Tearing his eyes away from what he would rather be holding, Magnus forced his attention on the too small shoes and his lady love's tortured feet. With the tip of one finger, he found enough slack in the leather below her ankle and above her arch for the width of his blade. There was no helping it. Her feet had swollen too much, making it impossible to cut or untie the string itself without injuring her. His dagger made quick work of the thin leather, loosening the slipper enough so he could peel it aside and sever the ribbon at the eye of the shoe. He tossed the offensive thing away, then massaged her poor foot. With a reassuring wink, he dipped his head toward her legs. "Ye've at least got one good stocking, m'love. I didna damage this one."

Her eyes closed in sheer bliss. "That feels so good," she said with a relieved groan.

In response, his cock hardened to the point of demanding relief. Soon. He cleared his throat and held out his hand. "And now the other foot." Dispatching that shoe the same way. He wondered how many wedding nights had ever started like this.

With a relieved sigh, Brenna returned to her knees, shoved the yardage of her dress out of the way, and crawled back to his side. "And now yer shoulder. I saw ye rubbing it, so I know it's hurt." Grabbing hold of his jacket, she pulled it back with a yank that hit a tender spot that made him wince. "Ye see? I told ye to fetch the key rather than maiming yerself like ye did."

He took hold of her hands and gently sat her back on her heels. "Allow me, aye? I promise, it's naught but a little soreness that a dram will chase away."

She gave him a look that called him a liar but remained silent.

Determined to prove he had not done himself any harm, he took his time unpinning the brooch at his shoulder, piling the extra length of his plaid in his lap, and shucking off his jacket. Belt and sword cast aside. Waistcoat and neckcloth soon joined the jacket on the floor. As he peeled off the tunic and tossed it, a grunt escaped him. *Dammit.*

Much to his surprise, Brenna didn't say a word. Just stared at him. Her lips barely parted. Eyes wide. A rosiness tinting her fair cheeks.

"What's wrong, lass?" She had seen him bare-chested before but had never looked at him quite like she did now.

"Wrong?" she repeated, as though waking from a dream.

"Aye." Magnus grinned, enjoying this effect he had on his new wife. He rolled his shoulder and flexed his arm. "Ye see? Not a bit hurt."

With an upward tilt of her chin, she blinked faster, then cleared her throat. "Bruising can take a while. Especially if the damage is deep." She leaned closer, smoothing her hands along his back and shoulder. The coolness of her fingers across his overly warm flesh increased the aching beneath his kilt. "By morning, ye'll most surely be black and blue. Mark my words."

Whisky and standing naked in the cool night air could wait 'til after. He couldn't resist her any longer. With a gentle tug, he pulled her into his lap. "Surely, ye must be sweltering in all those clothes," he coaxed while brushing kisses along her bare shoulder.

"It is verra warm in here." She trailed a finger along his collarbone, torturing him with her touch. "It'll be a far sight easier if I'm standing, and I may need a tad bit of help."

"I am yer servant, m'love." Without rising, he helped her to her feet, pleased that his words had made her cheeks glow even brighter. As he stood, his plaid fell to the floor, leaving him in nothing but his boots. He quickly dispatched those, working them loose with toe to heel, then kicking them away.

Brenna spun around, giving him her back. With her head bowed, she spoke so softly he couldn't make out the words.

"Dear one?" Something had changed. He didn't know what had gone awry, but he felt it.

Lifting her head, she straightened her shoulders but kept her back to him. "Forgive me. I know I am nay a virgin, but I have never done what we are about to do with someone I care for. I fear ye will find me lacking because I dinna ken how it should be betwixt a husband and wife." Head bowed, she stared at the floor. "All I had to do before was lay still and keep quiet or suffer a beating." She spared a glance back over her shoulder but still didn't turn. "I dinna ken what ye require of me. Ye will have to tell me what ye wish." Pain, fear, and so much more echoed in her whisper. "I am sorry," she added.

What the hell was wrong with him? He had rushed her without a thought as to how her past had hurt her. Left her with scars he couldn't see but scarred just the same. Ashamed of his callousness, he scooped up his lèine and yanked it back on, thankful that the length of it hit him mid-thigh.

"All I require of ye, m'love, is that ye be happy." He went to the sideboard, poured himself a whisky, and filled a goblet with wine. He carried it to her along with a tender smile. "A marriage bed should be a sanctuary for both partners—not a place of fear or dread." Careful to keep an arm's length of space between them, he sipped his drink, then added, "I wish to love ye, pleasure ye, make ye want my touch as much as I want yers. But I will wait as long as it takes. I willna touch ye 'til ye're ready. The pain of yer past is because of me." Before she could reply, he turned and strolled to the window seat and pushed open one of the tall panes.

A cool night breeze blew into the room like a spirit bearing gifts of peace and calm. He settled on the bench, sipping his whisky and watching stars flicker into view as the sun slipped below the horizon. He had meant what he said. While he ached to bed his beloved wife, he would not touch her until she was sure and ready.

"Ye are a rare man, Magnus de Gray." Her skirts rustled with a quiet shushing as she joined him on the bench. "Here." She held out the whiskey decanter. "I thought ye might like more."

"What about yerself?" He topped off his glass and placed the decanter on the windowsill beside them.

After a sip, she held up her half-full glass of wine. "I still have plenty, thank ye."

Turning back to the view, he watched her out of the corner of his eye. He could tell she wanted to say more but hadn't yet worked up the courage. Another breeze brushed across his face, reminding him of his promise of patience. Aye. He would wait as long as it took. She was more than worth it.

With a nervous clearing of her throat, she rose to her feet. "Would ye wait here for me, whilst I go to the bedchamber and don my nightdress?"

"Of course, m'love." He remembered she had mentioned needing help but didn't wish to make her think he might go back on his word. "Shall I fetch a maid?"

"A maid?"

"Aye, a maid. Ye said ye might need help with…" He made an up and down motion toward her gown. "Laces and things." There was no telling what held that dress together or what might be layered underneath to hold its shape. He had never been with a woman dressed in such finery but remembered quite a few interesting stories from those who had.

She shook her head while sidling toward the bedchamber door. "I've thought more on that. Surely, it must be easier getting out of the thing than it was getting into it." Upon reaching the sideboard, she downed the rest of her wine and poured herself another. With a polite smile, she lifted her glass and continued on her way. "I'll sing out should I need help, aye?"

"Aye, lass. I'll be right here." He settled more comfortably into the pillows of the windowsill, hoping he had handled the situation properly. In his heart, he felt he had. But that didn't matter. All that mattered was that Brenna felt the same.

CHAPTER THIRTEEN

Damn her shaking hands.

Brenna plucked at the satin ribbons holding the lace-covered stomacher in place. Thank heavens, the MacCoinnich women had neither had the time or materials to add additional whalebone to either it or the gown's bodice. The pasteboard sewn inside the triangular-shaped cloth had some give to it, making it somewhat easier to escape her elaborate cocoon.

"Thank God Almighty," she said as the snug bodice relaxed and the gown sagged away. Bearing in mind Mercy's warnings about fragile parts and not wishing to dishonor their loving act of kindness and hard work, she eased off the sleeves and stepped free of the silky mound. With the greatest care, she draped the lovely creation across a large leather trunk in the corner. Still encased in the lace-layered underskirt, extra petticoat, stays, and chemise, she hurried to the window beside the bed and pushed both panes open wide. Fluttering her damp neckline, she bent forward, hoping to direct the breeze to where she needed it most. She closed her eyes as the cool night air kissed her overheated body. "Saints alive, that feels so much better."

Her conscience tweaked her. Shame on her. Making her husband wait for that which was rightfully his. All his words came back to her. How all that mattered was her happiness. And a marriage bed should never hold fear or humiliation. As far as she was concerned, the man had earned sainthood when he had sworn he would wait as long as she needed. He had meant it, too. She had seen the truth of it in his eyes.

Mind made up and determination stoked, she pushed away from the window and set to untying the waistbands of her underskirts and petticoat. She refused to allow those Sassenach bastards of her past to ruin this chance at happiness. They had taken all from her she would allow. "No more!" she swore from between bared teeth.

"It will be different with Magnus," she assured herself as she took off her stays and tossed them on top of the rest of the layers she had piled on another trunk. She peeled off the damp chemise and ever so carefully removed the finest stockings she had ever worn. A stronger breeze gusted into the room, washing across her nakedness as though blessing her intentions.

With the washbowl filled, she soaked a cloth, wrung it out, then patted it across her heated flesh. A wry thought came to her. Her attempt at cooling down would all be for naught if her hopes and plans worked as she had played them out in her head. As she emerged from the private area, partitioned to conceal the chamber pot and washbowl stands, she clenched her hands until her nails bit into her palms. The room had far too many candles lit for her liking. While she enjoyed peeking at Magnus's breathtaking bareness, she feared her determination and courage weren't quite ready for him to see her in the same state. At least not in the blinding brightness of several blazing candelabras. She paused, second-guessing herself after snuffing most of them out. Would he need some light? Two candles remained lit. She moved one to the mantel and placed the other on top of the high dresser on the other side of the bed.

The room was dim but still lit enough for safely moving around, especially with the soft light of dusk and the rising moon casting a silver-blue path across the floor.

"My wine." She glanced around, searching to

find her glass. There. On the table beside the bed. She drank down every drop, then wished she had brought the bottle as she stared at the empty goblet, then placed it on the table. A change to her plan was needed to mend the oversight. Her stomach gurgled and churned, threatening to send the drink back out. After pulling in and blowing out several deep, calming breaths, she tiptoed to the door and opened it a crack. "M-Magnus," she called out, cringing at her ridiculous nervous stutter. "Could ye come here?"

"Aye, lass."

The deep rumble of his voice sent a rush of heat through her that no cool cloth in existence could ever ease. "And bring the wine!" she added, then clicked the door shut, vaulted across the room, and dove into bed. Wiggling her way under the sheets, she clutched them up over her breasts and scooted back into the pillows piled against the headboard. Breath held, she waited, straining to pick up the slightest sound of movement in the other room.

The door swung open. Light from the sitting room flooded the bedchamber, its wide golden channel illuminating the bed. Brenna blinked at the sudden brightness. *Fool!* She had forgotten about light from the door. Scooting deeper into the pillows, she pulled the covers higher. With a nervous flick of a finger, she glanced toward her glass. "Would ye mind pouring more wine for me?" God help her, she sounded like a squeaking mouse.

Slow and seductive, Magnus moved across the room, his expression unreadable in the shadows. The light from the sitting room outlined his muscular form through the light weave of his lèine. After he filled the glass, he set the bottle beside it. Seating himself on the edge of the bed, he picked up the drink and held it to her lips. "M'love," he said softly as he tipped the goblet so she might sip. Then he took it away and set it back on the table. He made no move to rise, just sat beside her. Silent. Motionless except for the steady rise and fall of his chest.

Fortified by both the wine and his gentleness, Brenna risked touching his arm. "Might ye remove yer lèine again?" She swallowed hard, then held her breath.

Without speaking, he stood and stripped it off over his head, then returned to his seat. Still watching her. Still silent.

Pushing away from the pillows, she sat straighter with one arm clamping the bedsheet up over her breasts. Fingers outspread, she drifted her palm over the corded muscles of his arm and ridges of his chest. She didn't touch him but held her hand close enough to draw in his heat. His strength. His very essence. Such a good man. Nothing to fear. Both her heart and her loneliness urged her on. Curling her legs beneath her, she went to her knees and leaned closer. "Will ye help me learn?" she whispered. "Help me discover the joy two people can share?"

"Aye, dear one." He grazed a fingertip along her jawline, then cradled her cheek in his hand. Brow furrowed, he studied her, as though trying to decide what to do next. "As long as ye are certain?"

"I am certain." And she was. He had set loose a hot aching inside her, a yearning for him to burn away all the years of suffering. But it was more than that—something she could never put into words. "Make me yer wife," she said, pulling him toward her. "Make us one."

With a kiss that tasted of wine, whisky, and unquenchable need, he eased her back across the bed. She laced her fingers in his hair, holding him, allowing all her doubts and fears to fall away. This was right and good. This precious man would never harm her.

Her breath caught as he raised up and shoved the sheets out from between them. "Ye are loveliness itself, dear one." His gaze raked across her. Sliding a finger down her arm, he took hold of her hand, lifted it to his mouth, and pressed a lingering kiss into her palm. "Ye are still certain, aye?" His head tilted over her, and she felt his encouraging smile even though she couldn't see it in the shadows.

"Aye, my fine husband." She shifted and moved, aching to know the complete wonder of him. "Fear and dread are gone. Only love and yearning remains."

"*Mo ghràdh*," he breathed as he stretched across her. "My precious love."

His heat became hers. Their flesh became one. She raced her hands across his back, reveling in the ripple of his muscles beneath her fingers. Moving with him, she was both amazed and thrilled at the ferocity of the building ecstasy. It raced out of control. Wave after wave of bliss crashed across her, forcing a cry from her lips.

Magnus drove harder, spurred on by her release. "*Mo chridhe!*" he growled long and low, then thrust forward with the roar of a beast unleashed. Suspended together in timeless pleasure, he sank into her embrace, melted into her, touching her heart and soul with love and a rare vulnerability.

Heartbeat pounded against heartbeat. Gasps slowed to steady breathing.

A wholeness, centeredness she had never known filled her as she held him. Such a wonderful contentment. She couldn't remember the last time she had known such serenity. "Ye have gifted me peacefulness, dear one," she whispered into his hair.

He lifted himself up and gave her a nuzzling kiss. "Ye have made me whole." His breath tickled across her as he trailed his kisses lower. "I fear I must beg yer forgiveness, though."

"Beg my forgiveness?" She combed her fingers through his hair, splaying it across his shoulder as he rested his head between her breasts. "For what do ye need forgiving?" Surely, he didn't speak of the past? She had moved that blame to fate's shoulders. The fault of all that had happened was no longer his.

Lifting his head, he smiled. "I intended our first loving to be slower—savoring each other for hours." His slight shifting with the barest shrug, a mix of confession and embarrassment, made her heart swell even more. "But I couldna help myself. I needed to possess ye and have ye possess me."

With a turn of her head on the pillow, she looked toward the window. "'Tis still early. See the slant of the moonlight on the floor. It's verra far from its zenith."

He rolled with her in his arms, settling back into the pillows with her cradled on top of him. Gently, he lifted her until she straddled him. Pressing his hand to the center of her chest, he kept it there for the longest while, a faint smile tugging at one side of his mouth. "I love the feel of yer heart through the softness of yer skin." He took her hand and placed it in the same spot on his chest. "We are matched. Feel it?"

She closed her eyes, focusing on the strong

thud against her palm. He spoke the truth. Their hearts thumped with the same steady beat. "A good omen for certain," she whispered as she leaned forward for a kiss.

"Aye, my love." He rolled with her again, resuming the ancient dance and rocking into her with a tantalizingly slow rhythm. "A damn fine omen."

Now, she understood why some called this *loving*. For that was what this was. Unexplainable joy. Excitement that squeezed your heart and knitted your soul to another's. A bliss like no other. She gave, but so did he. Both reaped pleasures of which she had never dreamed. Never had she known such a sensation of being this alive was possible. Once would never be enough. Nor would hours, days, or years spent with this man.

A lazy, fully sated smile overcame her as she collapsed atop his chest, shifting with its every rise and fall. Aye, this was how it should be between a husband and wife. For the first time in her life, she knew in her heart she no longer faced the world alone. No more did she fear the future, or what terrors life might hold. Never again. She had this. She had now. And it was enough.

ON HIS SIDE, head propped in his hand, he watched her sleep. He allowed his gaze to follow the delicious curve of her fine round rump as she lay on her stomach. The sun gave her skin the glowing luster of a pearl. Unable to resist, he leaned over and kissed the pair of dimples tucked in the small of her back, each of them nestled on either side of her spine.

With a soft snort, she wiggled deeper into the softness of the feather ticking and buried her face in the pillow.

He almost laughed out loud but contained it. She gave him such joy. He had always heard that when two souls meant to be together finally met, they would experience rare contentment. Never had he believed it. He figured it a silly legend made up by washerwomen bored with their chores. But now he knew better. The adage was true.

"Why are ye staring?" she mumbled as she cracked an eye open.

"Because I am a greedy man, m'love." He leaned over again and nibbled a trail of kisses along her shoulder and down her back. "I will never get my fill of ye."

She shifted beneath his ministrations, her sleepy groan sounding like a muffled purr. "Such a fine husband, ye are."

"And blessed with an even finer wife," he murmured as he pondered which part of her to enjoy next. Mind made up to start at the top and work his way down, he feathered nibbles along her jawline and gently pulled her closer.

With another purring sigh, her brow puckered the slightest bit. "I wish ye had waited 'til daylight to stare yer fill rather than relighting all the candles. They're too bright."

That drew a laugh that he couldn't hold back. "There's nary a candle lit in this room, my precious one." He leaned across her, cupping her luscious buttock and squeezing while he peered out the window. "I canna see the exact slant of the sun from here, but from the shadows on the floor and the hollow feeling in my wame, I would guess it to be some time after midday."

"What?" She pushed him aside and uprighted herself, squinting against the day's brilliance. "Are ye telling me we've slept away the day?"

"Aye." Clasping his hands behind his head, he rolled back into the pillows, enjoying the view of his wife's front as much as he had enjoyed her rear. Perhaps even more. "Dinna tell me ye've already forgotten how little we slept last night?"

Her pinched look softened, and she gifted him with a suggestive smile. "*Never* will I forget our wedding night." Mischief and so much more danced in her eyes. "And I shall tell our daughters to be sure to find a man willing to rub their feet, as well as other places."

With a hearty laugh, he dove forward and

pinned her underneath him. "And what shall ye tell our sons, my wife of such great wisdom?"

"That the surest way to win a lass is to rub her feet!"

Never would he get his fill of this wondrous woman. They had loved away the night. Why not love away the day? His empty wame growled in protest at being ignored. Loudly.

Brenna exploded with a belly laugh, but then her stomach growled, too. "Perhaps, we should find some food to keep up our strength, aye?" Hand to her heart, a guilty look creased her brow. "And I must see to Keigan to be sure he fared well enough last night. This is the first time he's been away from me since…"

She didn't finish, and for that, Magnus was grateful. He gave her a sound kiss, then retreated. "Aye, m'love. We have the rest of our lives together to enjoy our loving. Perhaps we best emerge from our sanctuary."

With an impish gleam in her eyes, she followed his retreat, pushing him back into the pillows as she straddled him. "I wasna trying to shoo ye away, *mo chridhe,*" she stressed with a suggestive flexing against him. "Ye ken, I'll never deny ye." Her eyes closed as she seated herself with a rocking wiggle that threatened to spill his seed before he had done right by his lady love.

He swallowed hard, struggling to maintain control. Hands encircling her waist, he bucked beneath her. "I pray ye never deny me," he groaned. "For I love ye with a fury I canna explain."

She increased the pace of her ride, holding fast to his shoulders and treating him to a delicious shudder. "I will never deny ye, my love." Her eyes flew open, and she treated him to a wicked grin. "Of course, I will thank ye to give me a wee bit of rest whenever I've just birthed one of our bairns."

"I am yer servant, m'love. Whatever ye wish is yers." And then the ability to speak left him. All he knew was sweet agony and blessed release. Brenna joined him, crying out her pleasure.

"Are ye all right, Auntie?" Keigan called from the other side of the bedchamber door. "Greer and me brought ye some food since ye and Da didna come down to break yer fast, nor show yerselves to take the midday meal." He paused, obviously waiting for an answer.

Magnus grinned and wiggled beneath her. His breathing hadn't yet settled back to normal, and neither had hers. "Are ye no' going to answer him, *mo chridhe*?" he whispered, unable to resist teasing her.

She poked him in the chest and failed at assuming a stern scowl. "Yer da and I shall be right out, my thoughtful lad. Give us a moment, aye?"

Muffled murmurings came from the other

side of the threshold. "Aye, we'll clear away the food carts whilst we wait for ye. Greer said yer both probably still naked and trying to catch yer breath after trying to make a bairn—judging by the sounds ye was making afore ye knew we were here."

"Keigan!" The young maid's horrified scolding came through the closed door loud and clear.

Brenna covered her mouth, her laughter hissing out from between her fingers. Magnus didn't try to hold back. His hearty laugh echoed throughout the room. Hell's bells, he never thought he could love life so.

"We best make haste before Keigan has poor Greer pulling every hair from her head." She jumped from the bed and hurried behind the privy screen before Magnus could snag hold of her for one last embrace.

"*Poor* Greer should be used to it. She's helped in the nursery enough times to know that bairns will repeat everything they hear."

"Be that as it may," she argued above the sounds of splashing water. "I dinna wish the girl vexed, ye ken? Ye've no idea what a rarity it is to have such fine servants as those who work here at *Tor Ruadh*. Ye must speak to Keigan. He'll sooner listen to ye than me. I've seen that in him already."

Her backhanded compliment about his word carrying more weight with the lad filled him with pride. "I'll speak to him." A groan escaped him as his feet hit the floor. He stretched and scratched all the parts of him that would much rather be back in the bed. "Ye ken my only clothing in here is my lèine, aye? I'm sure Greer's seen such before, but ye seem worried about offending the lass."

"Then ye best be moving yer things from yer room to here. These are *our* chambers now." She stepped out from behind the screen with a fresh chemise. The light from the window outlined her lovely form.

Damn, if he wouldn't love to take her back to the bed. He'd gone without food in the past and for much less pleasant reasons.

She tossed a look at the door as she stepped into her everyday skirts and donned her stays, then her bodice. "Will ye go see how Keigan fared last night whilst I finish dressing? I'm nearly ready."

"The cost is a kiss." With a mischievous grin, he tugged her into his arms before she could protest. "What say ye, wife?" he whispered so close his lips brushed across hers.

"I say make it a quick one, my love, or we'll be back in that bed and keeping our Keigan waiting."

He rewarded her with an appreciative groan and gave her a kiss he hoped made her ache for him as much as he ached for her.

"Ye're a rogue, ye know that, aye?" She gently but firmly removed herself from his embrace. "On wi' ye now."

"And now, I'll be needing yer shawl, m'lady." He grinned down at the front of his tunic, his cock like a tent pole poking out the muslin.

She threw it at him, shaking her head as he lashed it around his waist. "I warned ye!" Her scolding came off weak, and he loved her for it. She sounded happy. Contentment and relief swelled through him. Thank the gods he had made her happy.

With a flick of her hand, she shooed him toward the door. "On wi' ye now, while I tighten my laces and brush my hair."

Keigan's laughter peeled out as Magnus entered the sitting room. "Ye're wearing Auntie's shawl!"

"Just for that, my young scamp, ye can help me fetch my things today, ye ken?" He padded across the sitting room and circled the table Greer and Keigan had scooted in front of the window. A good-sized banquet met his gaze—far too much food for just himself and Brenna. Noting the size of the dome-covered platters, bowls of fruit, and pitchers of honeyed wine, Magnus turned to the red-faced maid and smiling child. "The two of ye brought in all this food? By yerselves?" He scanned the room, tossing a look at all the corners. Nary a cart, basket, or cloth sack could be seen anywhere.

"We had a wee bit of help," Greer confessed, resting a hand on Keigan's shoulder and squeezing as she spoke.

Keigan's smile widened. "We been in here a while. Ye didna notice cause ye were—"

Greer bumped Keigan with her hip, causing him to skitter sideways.

"Anyways…" Keigan continued after pulling a face at Greer. He stepped closer and lowered his voice. "Is Auntie happy? Truly happy?"

Magnus's heart swelled. "Aye, son. I believe she is."

"I'll be happier if ye grant me a hug," Brenna said as she closed the bedchamber door behind her.

Keigan dove into her arms. "I had the best time with Maxwell and Grant. Our fort stood well and good against Maisie and Effie's attacks."

"It warms my heart to hear ye did us proud, my precious one." Her eyes rounded wide as her gaze settled on the abundance of food. "Merciful heavens. Who did ye think ye were feeding?"

"Cook wanted to be sure and send plenty since ye didna eat that much last night." Greer's already rosy blush grew a shade brighter. "She said ye needed to eat well so yer first bairn would be born braw and healthy."

"Took us two full carts to bring it all up," Keigan said. He went to the table and removed a dome with a flourish. "Cook said eat until ye can eat no more, then she'll swap these out for fresh." Dragging a slice of apple through a softened cheese, he frowned. "She said ye could be here for days." With the bite held ready to pop into his mouth, he turned to Brenna. "Are ye locked in yer rooms for days after ye marry? I never heard of that afore."

Magnus almost choked on the butter-slathered bannock he'd just shoved into his mouth.

Brenna cleared her throat after a narrow-eyed glare at him that spoke volumes. "Not locked in our rooms. But often, newly wedded couples wish to have extra private time together."

"Ahh." Keigan nodded as he rounded the table, his mouth puckered in deep thought as he eyed the covered platters. "To get bairns. I guess a little brother wouldna be too much of a chore." He lifted the cover from a smaller platter, then recoiled. As he took another step back, he covered his mouth and nose, then gagged. "What is *that* supposed to be?"

A disgusting stench greased its way across the room, rising from the platter of rotting offal and maggot-covered chicken heads. Magnus strode across the room, scooped up the plate, and flung it out the window, taking care to aim the mess's landing to where it would do the least amount of damage.

"Little wench," he growled. Rage flaring hot and fast, 'twas best he didn't cut loose with all that came to mind. Insolent, ungrateful, conniving little bitch! He turned to Greer. "I want Cadha brought here. Immediately. Bring Catriona and Mrs. Fitzgerald, too."

Her rosy blush gone, Greer backed up a step. "Forgive me, but I canna fetch Cadha." With a twitch of one shoulder, she shook her head. "She's gone this verra day. Fool girl yelled at Mrs. Fitzgerald. In the kitchen. Front of everybody. Mrs. Fitzgerald took her by the ear, dragged her out, and told her to never come back. I dinna ken what Lady Catriona said about it, but she places great store in Mrs. Fitzgerald's druthers." She made a weak flip of one hand toward the door. "I can run and fetch Mrs. Fitzgerald and Lady Catriona if ye like?" With a nod at the table, she swallowed hard. "I'll tell Cook, too, so's this can all be carried off and fresh food sent. Who knows what else she did to what's here? She helped us with all of it."

"How do we know for certain Cadha did this?" Brenna asked quietly as Greer rushed from the room.

"Who else would do such a thing?" Magnus circled the table, pulling aside all the covers and tossing them to the floor. It wouldn't surprise him if something even worse waited to be discovered.

Keigan wrinkled his nose, staring in horror at the sliced apples and bowl of soft cheese. "I ate some of that. Am I gonna die?"

Brenna rushed back into the bedchamber, emerging a few moments later with a small bowl in one hand. "Drink this, then run for the chamberpot, aye? Quick now. We need to get what ye ate out of ye."

"What is that?" Magnus knew of several purges, but none safe enough for a child Keigan's size.

"A mix of wine, rowan, and some other herbs. It will work quickly."

Horrified, he blocked her way. "Rowan? And what else? Pray tell me ye didna include mistletoe." Both rowan leaves and mistletoe, in the wrong dosage, could be as deadly as any poison Cadha might have used.

"I know what I'm doing," she replied with a calmness that made him breathe easier. Kneeling in front of Keigan, she held the small wooden bowl to the boy's lips. "We dinna ken if he's been poisoned or not, but we can get it out of him to be certain." She nodded. "Just a wee sip, dear one. Ye dinna have to drink it all."

Eyes squinted against the taste, Keigan forced it down, then ran from the room. Sounds of the child retching followed soon after.

Brenna placed the bowl on the table. "I must watch him now. He willna feel well the rest of the day." She paused at the bedchamber door. Without looking back, she pulled in a deep breath and slowly blew it out. "There's enough there for yerself, as well. Since ye ate a bannock, ye best use it." Then she locked eyes with him. "I canna bear to lose ye. Not now."

CHAPTER FOURTEEN

"WE ALL KNEW she held Magnus in the highest esteem. Had a fondness for him even." Catriona scowled at the tapestry stretched on a freestanding wooden frame in front of her chair. She worked a crimson thread through a pattern of flowers dotting a field of green, then pulled it taut with a sharp tug.

"Happens often enough, ye understand," she added with a glance at Brenna. With the floss tied to suit her, she snipped it close with a tiny pair of shears. "'Tis easy enough to feel a tenderness for a person who saves ye. When someone gives ye yer first taste of mercy, they often claim a place in yer heart." Rooting through the thread basket on the table beside her, she shook her head. "But none of us realized she had grown so obsessed as to be dangerous."

"And no one knows where she might have gone?" That concerned Brenna most. It had been a fortnight since Cadha's banishment. Had the addled banshee hidden somewhere close to strike again when she got the chance?

She snapped the thread she had just knotted and frowned at the mended tear. If she ever crossed paths with Cadha again, she'd thrash her. Poor Keigan and Magnus both had retched so long and hard from the remedy for any possible poisoning that they had collapsed on the rug in front of the hearth and slept for hours. Their suffering had stoked her protective rage into an inferno. "I owe her," she said as she yanked another garment from her mending basket. "And I would give anything to repay that debt."

"No one has seen her, but I doubt she went far. I'm sure she didn't return to Glenfinnan. According to one of the other maids, the public house from which she escaped was more brothel than anything else." Catriona's mouth puckered as though she tasted something sour. "And it appears the services they offered were unseemlier than most."

"That would explain a great deal about the lass." Brenna felt for the girl, but that didn't excuse the former maid's actions. The young woman needed to be locked away before she did anyone, including herself, any harm.

The hallway door blew open. Alexander, with Graham on his heels, charged into the room.

A parchment in one hand, Alexander strode to the window and shoved both panes open wide. He leaned out over the sill, looking first to the left, then to the right. "Where is Magnus?" he asked while still hanging out the window. "The two of ye must leave *Tor Ruadh.* Immediately."

"What…what say ye?" Brenna flattened a hand to her chest in a futile attempt at calming her pounding heart.

"Why would ye say such a thing?" Catriona rose and hurried to her husband's side. "What has happened?"

Alexander, jaw clenched and hands fisted, stared at them as though struggling to choose his words. After a long moment, he held the crumpled leaflet high. "Barricourt has ordered Magnus's arrest along with any who aid him. Treason, it says. They have also charged him with the attempted murder of a British officer."

"When Magnus hears of this, it will be murder if he has his way about it." Brenna had feared there would be repercussions after Barricourt's fateful visit. She knew little about the vile man, but instinct told her his pride wouldn't ignore all that had happened that day. A Scot with the audacity to raise a weapon against him? The chieftain telling him to leave? Nay, she had known this wouldn't end well, and now here it was, come home to roost like a vicious winged demon. She wanted to drop to her knees and sob but refused to give into it. Instead, she clenched her trembling hands to her middle and steadied herself. "Magnus and Keigan are probably still in the caves. The lad's been champing at the bit to see them, so Magnus took him exploring."

Alexander blew out a heavy sigh. "The caves are probably the safest place for all of ye right now."

Catriona took the order from Alexander and read it. Her brows knotted tighter as her eyes skimmed the page. "Did they come for him today and leave this? It has been so quiet. I wouldha thought Barricourt and his men for the sort who make their presence known."

"Tom sent the warning by Alice. Said the soldiers will be here in a few hours." Alexander stormed back to the window and checked outside again. "Ye're right about the man. Barricourt has planned quite the spectacle for the arrest, and it's taking him a bit of time to prepare."

"Who are Tom and Alice?" Brenna didn't recall the names, but whoever they were, she owed them a debt of gratitude.

"Thomas Parlorn is a soldier at Fort William," Catriona explained. "A good man if ever there was one. He's sweet on Alice. She's the miller's daughter and has worked here at the keep ever since her mother died." She handed the parchment to Brenna with a sympathetic smile. "Several of the men at Fort William are good, kind souls." A despairing sigh escaped her. "Still Sassenachs, but good and kind. Lord Crestshire, God bless him, commanded with respect and honor. That man never tolerated cruelty."

"This is no time for wishful reminiscing," Graham reminded from his post beside the door. "I shall head to the caves and find Magnus and the lad." With a grim smile, he looked at Brenna. "Pack as quick as ye can and only what ye need to survive. Meet us at the entrance to the caves in the back of the stable."

"This is nay my first time running," Brenna replied. "I'll bring only what's needed."

"Does Barricourt know about Keigan?" Catriona asked as they all hurried out into the hall.

"I dinna think so." At least, Brenna prayed he didn't. She couldn't bear the thought of poor Keigan in peril.

"Then leave him here until we have a solid plan of a refuge for ye, better than the caves," Catriona said. "He'll be safer, and the two of ye can travel easier on yer own."

Brenna came to a halt, unable to believe what she had just heard. "Leave Keigan behind?"

"Aye, good sister. Ye know he'll be safer here," Catriona said with a gentle squeeze of her arm.

Alexander and Graham turned back, both frowning and fidgeting in place.

"We *must* make haste. The soldiers will be upon us soon." Graham looked at Alexander. "I best find Magnus and the lad while everything is made ready."

Alexander released him with a nod.

As much as Brenna hated it, Keigan staying safe at the keep would be the responsible thing to do. But how could she leave her dear sweet bairn behind? And for how long? Who knew where they would have to go or how long they would have to hide?

"Ye will keep him safe," she whispered, taking hold of Catriona's hand.

"As if he was my own."

A storm of emotions closed off her throat, threatening to take her to her knees. She couldn't manage words, so she gave a curt nod.

"We *must* go," Alexander gently prodded from up ahead. "Now."

It didn't take her long to gather the necessities she and Magnus would need. Running to save life and limb riddled her past. She had so hoped those days were behind her, but with Alexander's announcement, those hopes shattered.

By the time they reached the stable and made their way to the cave entrance in the back, Magnus and Graham stood talking in low tones while Keigan looked on. The poor child was wide-eyed and silent.

"Auntie!" he cried out. He charged into her, clutching her as though he would never let her go.

She held him just as tightly, memorizing every nuance of what could be the last time she ever saw him. His irresistible little boy scent, a pungent mix of damp earth and, at the moment, wet dog. The desperation in his hug squeezed her heart. His quick hitching breaths told her he was doing his best not to cry. God help her; how could she leave him behind?

"I love ye more than life itself," she choked out through the sorrow threatening to strangle her. Her teardrops broke free, tumbling down into his tangled hair.

"I dinna want ye to go," he whimpered against her, breaking her heart even more. "Please dinna leave me behind. Please take me with ye."

After a deep, shuddering breath, she knelt in front of him and took hold of his shoulders. "We will not be separated long, my precious warrior." She forced a smile she doubted he would believe. "It will be all right. Either we shall come back for ye, or we'll send word and have Evander bring ye to us. We all must be brave, aye?"

"Why can I not go? I have been in danger afore, and ye didna leave me behind."

"I didna leave ye behind before because I had no safe place to leave ye." How could she explain in so little time all she needed him to understand? She could tell by the way Graham, Alexander, and Catriona fidgeted and kept straining to see the front of the stable that time had run out.

Squeezing her dear mite's hands, she gave him the bravest smile she could muster. "No matter what happens, I love ye, yer da loves ye, and yer mama is watching over ye. No matter what, aye?" She gave him another fierce hug, then stood and forced herself to put an arm's length of space between them. "Be my courageous lad, aye? I'm ever so proud of ye, Keigan."

He didn't answer. Just stared up at her, tears streaming down his face. Then he turned and glared at Magnus for the longest time before raising his small fists and shaking them. "I hate ye both for leaving me! Ye're just like Mama!" Then he shot off down a side aisle, disappearing into the maze of horse stalls.

"Keigan!" she cried out, needing to hold him until he understood.

"Let him go, dear one," Magnus said. With another gentle tug on her arm, he pulled her closer to the cave entrance. "When he's older, he will understand."

"He didna mean his words, sister. Ye know that," Catriona said. "Dinna fash, I'll send Evander to comfort him." She lifted a trembling hand in farewell. "God bless ye and keep ye both until we see ye again."

"Stay to the caves. 'Tis safest 'til we've worked out a better plan," Alexander advised. "Ye ken well enough where the supplies are cached. Check the dragon's mouth daily. We'll leave messages there as more information comes to us."

Magnus accepted Alexander's instructions with a solemn look and a hard clasping of his forearm. He bid Graham farewell with the same silent, brotherly grip.

Brenna had no idea what Alexander meant by *the dragon's mouth*, but Magnus seemed to understand, and that was all that really mattered. With her world tumbling down around her ears, a cold numbness made it a struggle to function.

"Thank ye. For everything," she managed to say as Catriona hugged her one more time. "Please take care of my bairn 'til he's back in my arms. Tell him I love him."

"Ye know I will," Catriona said, her eyes shimmering with unshed tears. Then she turned and ran to catch up with Alexander and Graham.

"Brenna, we must go." Magnus steered her toward the dark crack in the stable wall, half-hidden by a boulder as tall as a good-sized man. "Take the torch from yon bracket. I'll carry the pitch bucket with the extra torches we'll need. It's a fair stretch of the legs to the supply cache."

She cast a last glance back through the horse stalls, wishing for one more glimpse of Keigan. Despair filled her as she saw nothing in the shadows. "What's done is done, and canna be undone," she reminded herself as she wiggled the torch free of the bracket and settled a bundle over her shoulder.

Magnus picked up the other bulging sack and the bucket. "Light our path, *mo ghràdh*. The way is narrow with no choices, so ye canna err in the direction ye choose."

Cool, clamminess of the cave engulfed her, brushing across her flesh like a troubled spirit. Hairs on her arms stood on end, making her wish she hadn't pushed her sleeves up to her elbows. It had been a warm summer's day out in the courtyard, but within the cave, it felt like dreary, wet autumn had already taken hold. The sound of dripping water echoed from somewhere up ahead. Brenna lifted the sputtering torch higher, squinting against its blinding brightness while praying the thing never went out.

"We'll stay in a fine room just past the southern storage cache," Magnus reassured. "It's none too far from the dragon's mouth and surrounded by a good-sized fissure with only a few places narrow enough to jump across. In fact, Catriona hid there for nearly a fortnight once."

While she appreciated his attempt at reassurance, something about hiding for days in the dark bowels of the earth troubled her. "What is this dragon's mouth everyone speaks of?" she asked, trying to focus on something besides the mountain swallowing her alive.

"An amazing stone formation complete with carvings by ancient ones who lived here long ago."

"And it looks like a dragon?"

"I canna do it justice with words. When we come to it, ye'll understand."

The route narrowed, but not in the steady fashion of walls slowly drawing in, but with slabs of stone jutting into the path, first at knee level, then as high as their waists and shoulders. The ceiling sloped ever lower, making Brenna feel as though she had entered a tomb and the lid was closing on her. "Is this right?" she asked, feeling like her lungs weren't getting enough air. A deep breath did little to dispel the dark weightiness crushing in from all sides.

"Aye, love. I know it's close, but this is the right path. I promise. Take heart, dear one, it opens up soon."

The acrid, oily smell of the pitch bucket made her head pound, adding to her uneasiness. She needed sunshine on her face, and a deep inhale of sweet Highland air. What she wouldn't give to be in a field of heather at this very moment. Hitching in another deep gulping breath, she forged onward, determined not to give in to her mounting panic.

"Breathe, *mo chridhe*. Focus on one step at a time and breathe. There's plenty of air in here. I swear it."

"Ye always know what I'm feeling."

"It's because ye are the other half of my soul, remember? Caves can be hard to bear. But ye've the strength to do it. Of that, I have no doubt."

His belief in her helped somewhat, but not nearly as much as when the tight passage opened out into a cavernous space with a ceiling so high, the light from the torch couldn't reach it. "Praise God Almighty." She held the torch higher and stretched her cramped muscles. Eerie formations dripped down into the light, looking like the pale knobby fingers of the dead. "Is the cache close?" While she appreciated the spaciousness of this part of the caves, the place had an unholiness about it. "Magnus?"

"Aye, love. Just a bit farther once we cross this chamber." Magnus turned toward her and guided the light from the torch to the right. "But first, look yon." With a smiling nod, he walked them closer. "Behold, the dragon."

Her breath caught at the awesomeness before her. Its mouth open and lips curled back in an eternal growl, the beast looked as though it had frozen mid-leap through the cave wall. Moving closer, the intricate detailing on the carved stone embellished with faded dyes amazed her. How could an ancient people have accomplished such an elaborate work of art this deep inside the caves? "Who did this?" she whispered.

"No one knows." Magnus stayed within the arc of the light, staring up at the creation. "We just appreciate it for the wonder that it is. It protects the back entrance to *Tor Ruadh*."

"It truly is a wonder."

Stones bounced and slid off in the distance, echoing from somewhere in another passage.

Brenna lifted the torch and stared in that direction, but only darkness waited past the glow of the flame. "Does that happen often?" She prayed it didn't. Her poor nerves were raw enough without that torture.

Magnus's furrowed brow paired with a longer than usual silence did little to dispel her fears.

"What?"

He motioned her forward. "Come. We'll rest when we reach the cache. It isna all that much farther."

When he ignored her questions, it meant there was cause for worry. "Who else might be in here?" she asked, keeping her voice barely above a whisper. Her stubbornness kicked in, keeping her in place just beneath the dragon's open maw. She wasn't moving until he gave her an answer.

"I'm sure 'tis nothing." Magnus motioned her forward. "Come."

"If ye are so certain it is nothing, why are ye

watching the shadows as though they're hiding demons?"

"I am sure it's as simple as a scurrying rat or some such animal." Resettling the bundle on his shoulder, he tilted his head to the left. "Come. We must go in that direction. See the path off to the right that's marked with the symbol chiseled above it? That leads to the cache."

His changing the subject was his polite way of refusing to answer. She had already learned that she might as well move on whenever he did that. His stubbornness matched hers. Her torch sputtered, its light getting weaker. "Should we light a fresh one? I dinna wish to lose our fire."

"Aye." Magnus touched a fresh torch to the flame, squinting as the blessed brightness flared to life. "Can ye manage them both and the bundle across yer shoulder?"

"I can manage anything I need to manage." He had no idea all she had endured, and if she had her way about it, he would never know. The dear man felt guilty enough as it was. There was no need to add any weight to his burdens. "To the cache, aye?"

The longer they hiked through the dark stone maze, the sharper her other senses became. Every scent, the slightest sound of a shifting pebble. She picked up on each of them. Whether Magnus admitted it or not, they were not alone, and it wasn't an animal. Nay, it was a more fearsome beast. It was a person.

"Are there any weapons stored in the cache?" she asked as they hiked up an incline so slippery, they had to lean against the walls to keep from losing their footing. Struggling along, she concentrated on keeping the new torch held high. She returned the spent torch to the bucket to be used for firewood later. God help her, she hated the darkness. "Are there any weapons?" she repeated louder.

"Aye, love. Swords and daggers. Maybe some lead shot." He paused as they reached a particularly tight squeeze between two shelves of stone. "Might even be a long rifle or mayhap a pistol or two, but they rust so easy, I'm doubting it. I'm none too sure about gunpowder either. It wouldna do well in this dampness." As they sidled their way along a narrow shelf bordering a dark abyss, he continued, "Why do ye ask?"

She came to a halt, unable to hold her tongue any longer. "Someone is in here besides us, and it's nay a rat or a bat, but a two-legged vermin of the most dangerous kind."

Magnus stared at her, the frustration in his eyes betraying his temptation to lie.

"Dinna lie to me. Ye know as well as I that it's the truth. Someone watches us."

He blew out a heavy breath. "From the sound of the scurrying, I'd bet my best dagger it's Cadha." Staring down into the abyss, his jaw tightened. "She has to be following our torch-light. I've seen no sign of light anywhere else."

"I have. A lantern, maybe. Or candle stub." At first, she had thought her mind played tricks on her, but now she knew better. "But tell me how Cadha knows about the caves? Does the clan not guard their secret?" If the cave system of *Tor Ruadh* was common knowledge, how could they think themselves safe from the British here?

"Many know of the caves," he hastened to explain as they continued their trek. "But only a select few know of the safe rooms and locations of all the caches. The maze of tunnels is treacherous."

"All the caches?"

"Aye. Supplies are stored in several places throughout the system." The ledge they traversed widened, once again becoming solid cave floor where they could walk abreast rather than single file. "Ye never know where ye might need to take refuge within the caves. It depends on where ye enter the mountain and if the enemy is giving chase."

Brenna quickened her pace, determined to reach the cache, and arm herself. Whether their spy was the addled maid or some other foe, they had yet to discover. She refused to meet them with only her dagger and the few throwing stones she had shoved into her pockets.

"Take care, lass." Magnus caught hold of her

and yanked her back a step. He took hold of her hand and pointed the torch downward, flooding its light across a crack in the floor wide enough to swallow a man whole. "This is the beginning of the fissure that guards the entrance to the southern cache. We can step across here, but farther around, it widens too much to do so."

She held out the torch. "Take this and lead the way. My nerves canna take anymore blind leading where I dinna have a clue I'm headed."

He hesitated, setting down the pitch bucket with a hard *thunk*. "'Tis heavy."

"I can manage it the short distance left. Now, take the torch." She still didn't know how Magnus had seen the fissure in the floor, and she hadn't, but she didn't care. Her leadership of this expedition was at an end.

"Nay, take the bundle instead. I'll keep the sparks away from the bucket. I dinna wish ye to lose yer balance." He swung the bundle off his shoulder as he accepted the torch. Holding it high and to the side, he retrieved the bucket from the floor. "I'll shine the light down so ye can see to step across, then I'll follow, aye?"

"Aye." Mouth dry as tomb dust, she adjusted the bundles on her shoulders. Heart pounding, she hopped across the split, feeling as if a monster could reach up and snatch hold of her and drag her down into the darkness at any moment. "Praise God Almighty," she uttered once both feet hit solid ground.

"Well done, dear one." Magnus followed, then shed the light on a crude set of steps created by receding slabs of stone. "At the top is the cache we seek. We'll catch our breath there, then move on to the room I had in mind and build us a fine fire."

She followed, staying close to manage the uneven layers of stone as she ascended them. One snagged toe, and she'd tumble down into the abyss. "I canna believe I allowed ye to bring Keigan into this wicked place. Never again, ye hear me? If I had known then what I know now—"

"Lads love a bit of danger in their exploring." He grinned back at her. "It's good for them, aye?" Sidling off to one side as they reached the top of the stairs, he tapped the torch along a low hanging beam. "Mind the opening here, or ye'll knock yerself silly."

As she ducked and wormed her way through the opening, she locked her jaws to keep from speaking her mind. They should've hidden in the Highlands or sought refuge higher up Ben Nevis. But nay—instead, they had burrowed into the earth like a pair of badgers setting up their den.

A squishy sensation under her right foot warned her too late. Thrown off balance by her shifting bundles, she slid across the muck, careened into a pile of broken barrels, then landed on her knees. "Mind the footing!" she shouted, floundering to rise from the heap of split wooden slats, bits of what looked like dried meat, and piles of crushed oatcakes.

"What the hell?" Magnus lit a second torch, holding them both aloft as he cast their light around the room and gingerly picked his way through the mess. "Someone's fouled every last bit of it."

"Water?"

"Gone." Magnus held up a waterskin, flat as could be and dripping. "Every bag split open with a blade."

Brenna shoved aside a broken barrel, hoping the one behind it might have been spared. Her hopes were for naught. Its bashed top revealed the small cask of flour soaked with enough pitch to light the entire cave system. "How often are the supplies checked to ensure they're safe and usable?"

"Monthly, at least." Magnus kicked aside a barrel, slowly leaking out a trail of salt as it rolled across the floor. "Graham assured me this one had just been restocked, and all was well. Said he checked it himself just days ago after the confrontation with Barricourt."

"I didna bring water nor food. Both Catriona and Alexander said we would find plenty here." Whoever had made short work of the stores had done their job well. Not a barrel, bag, nor waterskin had been left untouched. "We'll have to go back," she said, drying her hands on her skirts.

"We canna go back." Magnus pushed the keg of flour fouled with pine tar to the center of the space and lit it. He pulled up a pair of crates missing their contents and offered Brenna a seat. "Surely, the keep is crawling with soldiers by now."

A despondent weariness set in as she lowered herself to the ramshackle chair beside the fire. They could probably salvage some dried meat and oatcakes. Maybe even enough to last more than a few days. But the lack of water was a definite problem. "I heard water dripping through the tunnels. Can we not collect it?" The more she tried to think of a solution, the thirstier she felt.

"Nay." Magnus shook his head. "We tried that once, and it gave us all the skitters. Gretna thinks much of the cave water is tainted with bat shite and whatever foulness it breeds as the water stagnates."

"Then what do we do?" She was at a loss. They couldn't stay here and survive, nor could they go back. "Is there another exit close so we might go outside and find a burn? Catriona told me about several sources of water that *Tor Ruadh* uses. Surely, we could find a spring close to the caves."

"Aye, there's an exit close, but the way to it

isna easy. Few can travel it."

Brenna didn't like the look on Magnus's face, nor the way he studied her. "Ye're not leaving me here whilst ye go fetch water. Dinna even think about it." The thought of sitting in the dark, waiting for his return, made her heart pound so hard it rendered her dizzy.

"I wouldna be gone for long," he said softly, but his tone was laced with the iron of his stubbornness. The man had already made up his mind. She could see it in his eyes.

"Dinna ask this of me," she pleaded. "I beg ye."

"We have to survive. For Keigan."

He would say that. She closed her eyes and sagged forward, holding her head in her hands. Every decision they made affected Keigan, even though her dear lad had remained behind at *Tor Ruadh*. They had promised to fetch him. Reunite with him as soon as they could. If they didn't fight to survive, how could they keep the word they had given to her precious lad?

"I didna see any weapons here." Magnus spared another glance around the carnage. "But ye have yer dagger and yer stones, aye?"

"Aye," she said, without lifting her head. "One dagger and seven throwing stones. I can fend off everything but the darkness and my fears."

The warmth of his hand on her back did little

to ease her fretting. What if something happened to him? What if the treacherous trail bested him? She feared she would never feel his warmth again. "There has to be another way," she whispered, but for the life of her, she didn't know what. "How far is the next cache?"

"Too far to try without food, water, or more pitch and fresh torches."

"Let me come with ye." She straightened and looked him in the eyes.

"Nay, m'dearest love. That I canna do." He took her hand and pressed a kiss to her knuckles. "I'll not risk losing ye to the treachery of the caves. That route isna for those unused to traveling the bowels of Ben Nevis."

"But ye would leave me here wondering if I'm a wife or widow?"

"I will return. I have done it before. Many times."

She threw herself into his arms, clutching him as tightly as Keigan had held to her. "I canna bear it if ye dinna return," she confessed as she pressed her face against the sweet warmth of his neck. "Please dinna leave me. I would rather return to the keep and fight a thousand Sasse-nachs than wonder if ye're dying in the bottom of a dark pit somewhere."

He cradled her close, gently swaying to and fro, as if she were a colicky bairn. With every stroke of his fingers through her hair, she knew she had lost him. He had made up his mind.

"Please," she whispered again.

"I must go, *mo ghràdh*." He brushed a kiss across her temple. "Trust me, my dearest one. I promise I will return." Sliding a finger under her chin, he lifted her face to his. "Wait here and think of names for our bairns, aye? We canna have Keigan lonely, ye ken?"

"If ye dinna come back to me, I'll hunt ye down and haunt ye through all eternity," she threatened, meaning every word. "Ye've made me love ye. Need ye. Worry after ye. I'll be damned if ye escape me now." She reached up and touched his face. "I love ye, *m'eudail*, more than I ever thought possible. Dinna make me regret opening my heart."

He answered her threat with a hard kiss of stubborn determination. "Two days," he said. "In two days, I'll return to ye with enough water to get us to the next cache. I swear it."

"I give ye two days." She grudgingly pushed herself free and put an arm's length of space between them. "Dinna make me regret placing my trust in ye." If she didn't escape his touch, she would surely be reduced to weeping as though he had already been lowered into the grave.

"Never, my love." He slowly stood and reached for her. She weakly resisted then gave in, allowing him to gather her close once again. "Never will I make ye regret trusting me," he promised, then sealed his oath with a kiss.

CHAPTER FIFTEEN

"**D**AMMIT TO HELL and back."

Magnus gritted his teeth as he cast the torchlight up and down the heap of jagged rubble blocking his way. All that remained of the narrow passage was an opening at the top of the pile, barely large enough for a man to shimmy through—and it would have to be a small man at that. He contemplated attempting it, but common sense stopped him. It would be deadly to try such a thing with no one to help should aught go awry.

He and the MacCoinnichs had explored and mapped out most of these caves. While the maze served as a layer of extra protection for the clan, the hidden hallways of the mighty Ben Nevis were a dangerous place. They deserved the same respect and wariness given to a fearsome beast, a beast that a man never battled alone.

He lifted the light again, scanning where the jagged rocks had broken free from the wall. Landslides inside the mountain weren't all that common. New fissures often cracked across the cave floor, but the passage walls rarely collapsed. Then he spotted it. A shining mark scraped across the rock—a mark made by a chisel. An evildoer had brought on this collapse.

After one last hard look at the barrier, he decided. There was naught to do but backtrack almost eight furlongs or so and head down the only other trail that opened out close to the same area on the mountainside he hoped to access. Whoever fouled this passage might have closed off the other way, too, but he doubted it. Experience and pure gut instinct warned him this treachery held all the makings of a crude trap. Thank goodness Brenna was back at the supply cache, where it was safer. At least, he hoped she was safe. An uneasy urgency increased the speed of his stride.

He had two fresh torches ready and shoved in the back of his belt, along with the three waterskins they had mended as best they could. With his light held high, he retraced his steps. A worrisome foreboding growing stronger with every step. No way in hell could a lass as small as

Cadha have triggered that landslide. He had barely reached those chisel marks when stretched to his full height. But if not Cadha that had caused the cave-in, then who? He quickened his pace. The faster he made it outside and found water, the quicker he returned to Brenna. Then they would attempt to make it to the safety of the next cache.

More worries reared their ugly heads, filling his mind with disturbing possibilities. If they had fouled one cache, how could he be certain the others remained intact? The next stockpile he had intended to seek lay deep within the mountain's core. If they reached it and discovered it, too, had been destroyed, then the trek back out, without food, water, or more torches, would be damn nigh impossible.

He came to the split in the corridors. If he remembered correctly, the new direction narrowed so fiercely a man could scarce draw a full breath as he squeezed through parts of it. At one point, he would need to belly crawl for quite a way. It didn't matter. He had to get that water and get back to Brenna. She had looked so hopeful when she had helped him lash the mended waterskins to his belt. Three water skins.

He came to a halt and bowed his head. To get all three of the filled waterskins delivered back to her might be an impossible task. The alternate route couldn't be managed with the bulging skins thrown over his shoulders as he had planned. Tossing the thought aside with a shake of his head, he continued on. He would do what he could and then figure out the rest once reunited with his lady love. Fretting about it now did nothing but make his journey more dangerous with the distractions.

"I refuse to be bested!" He fought the cave, forging onward as quickly as he dared. When the torchlight flickered and danced as though trying to jump from the pitch-soaked rags, it made him smile. Moving air. The exit was near. He held the torch behind him and eased forward, lifting his nose and sniffing. Aye, there it was. Cool, clean air hardly tainted with the cavern's damp earthiness.

A pale glow teased its way through the darkness, like the softness of dawn peeping through curtains. He thought it might already be nightfall, considering the time it had taken them to cover the first leg of their journey. But it wasn't full-on dark yet, just well into the gloaming.

He crawled out through a narrow space between the jagged halves of a large boulder, then stretched to his full height and filled his lungs. He would tolerate the cramped confines of the caves when necessary, but that didn't mean he liked them. A gentle breeze brushed across him like a lover's caress, bidding him stay awhile and enjoy the balmy weather. But the image of

Brenna huddled close to the fire, her face taut with fear, exhaustion, and barely controlled panic urged him onward.

"Get a move on, ye selfish bastard," he scolded under his breath as he scrabbled sideways across the steep slope. He paused, squinting through the evening mist settling across the mountain like a blanket. Both nightfall and the thickening fog laughed at his torch's pitiful attempt to cast light any farther than a narrow arc. If he strayed too far from where he exited the caves, he would be hard-pressed to find the opening again until sunrise. The gurgling sound of water dancing across rocks gave him hope. The burn he had in mind didn't sound that far away. Thank the gods he remembered it from last summer.

The rough ground, washed out and littered with loose pebbles, larger stones, and thick clumps of sedge, slowed his progress. With little help from the torch, he tripped and stumbled like a drunkard. By the time he reached the precious spring, the treacherous landscape had scraped his knees and hands raw. He didn't care. All that mattered was getting water for Brenna.

After slaking his thirst, he filled the skins and held them aloft, squinting at the mended seams. Without beeswax to seal the stitchery, they had used pine tar residue scraped from the inner sides of the pitch bucket. So far, only a few drops of seepage beaded up through the dark stitches. With any luck, he'd have enough water to sate Brenna's thirst by the time he made it back. But then they would have to return to the keep for proper supplies and an alternative plan. He wouldn't risk going any deeper into the mountain with these waterskins. With the one cache fouled and possibly others as well, these caves were no longer a haven. A choice between outwitting the British or the mountain was easy. He would choose the British every time. No one outwitted Ben Nevis.

He lashed the bags together and slung them over his shoulder. The challenge of the narrow passage would be a puzzle he'd figure out when he came to it. So far, the only plan that came to mind was to wrap the skins in his lèine and either push them in front of him or drag them behind as he crawled through the tight spots. After lighting a fresh torch, he tossed the spent one to the ground and kicked dirt over the smoldering end.

Rocks crunched and shifted higher up the mountainside. Magnus dropped into a crouch and strained to see through the soft fogginess of the night. He hoped the sounds were nothing more than a beast searching for its supper. His blazing torch was a dangerous beacon, but if he extinguished it, he'd have but one left dry to make it through the caves. Hopefully, whatever made the noise couldn't see him any easier than he saw it. He held his breath and kept the fire low to the ground. Off in the distance, a fox yipped, probably a vixen teaching her kits to hunt. A powerful gust of wind drowned out all other sounds, blowing hard for a short while, then dying down, until all he heard was the gurgling spring beside him.

Still watchful, Magnus straightened to his full height and stood there, soaking in his surroundings. He might not see a bloody thing in the foggy darkness, but he could listen. Turning slowly, he caught a faint glimmering of light farther up the mountainside. What the hell was that? Too steady a glow for a torch, it separated and became three, then four, then more. They bobbed along like oversized glowworms or will-o'-the-wisps. The eerie sight sent a tingling through the hairs on the back of his neck.

A loud rumble echoed through the night. He recognized the sound of shifting ground chased by falling rocks. It came from the direction of the cave's entrance and sounded like a good chunk of the mountain had broken loose and given way. He stumbled and cursed across the godforsaken stretch of savage landscape made even more impassable by the darkness, charging back toward the entrance. Usually, he would run from a landslide, but not this time. He couldn't afford to lose that doorway back into the caves. The earth's loud heaving dwindled down into silence.

He sank ankle-deep into what moments ago had been solid ground. Floundering forward, he half-crawled up the pile of loose debris, digging aside stones and clumps of earth. Near as he could tell, this was where he had exited the tunnels. He had to find the boulder, the split in two, and reopen the space between the halves. If he didn't, it would take him a solid day, maybe more, to reach *Tor Ruadh* on foot and then hours more that he couldn't spare to get back to Brenna. The thought of her stranded so long threw him into a digging frenzy. *Damn it all to hell and back.* Apparently, his newfound contentment and happiness had angered the gods, spurring them to torture him.

"Damn ye!" Magnus pounded the ground. The shifting rocks laughed at him. He stabbed the torch into the dirt and clawed at the blockage with both hands. It hadn't been that massive of a landslide. He would find that split boulder and dig a hole wide enough to make it through. Nay, it wasn't a matter of *if* he would find the entrance, but *when.* He'd dig 'til his fingers were bare bones if that's what it took.

"Arrest the man and relieve him of his toiling. I tire of this game and have no interest whatsoever in watching this Highland badger dig his way back into his den." The order came from somewhere outside the reach of his light. The voice, a bloody Sassenach, he didn't recognize.

Before he could draw his short sword, he found himself shoved face-first into the dirt. Rough hands ripped away his weapon and secured his wrists with shackles. Since when had the damned British learned to move with such stealth? He twisted around and head-butted one man, sending the fool cursing to his knees before another kicked him so hard in the gut it left him gasping for air.

"Play this game with care, my friend," warned a familiar voice close to his head. "I'll do what I can to see you treated properly, but you make it worse if you fight them."

"Archie?" Magnus twisted his neck to see. Archibald 'Archie' Raithwaite, a rare Sassenach. Good and just. The man had been one of Lord Crestshire's closest and most trusted men. He had often accompanied the former commander of Fort William on his visits to *Tor Ruadh*, and the MacCoinnichs trusted him. Magnus thought the soldier had accompanied Crestshire to his new assignment in Barbados.

"You a friend with this traitor, Archie?" accused another soldier as he grabbed Magnus by the back of his léine and yanked him to his feet.

"I dinna have any Sassenach friends," Magnus said, saving Archie the trouble of lying. If he remembered rightly, the man couldn't tell an untruth to save his soul. It was one reason all of them trusted him so fully.

"Conversation is unnecessary." The bored voice that had given the original order gave a light cough and sniffed. "Drag him up to the horses where the lantern boys wait. We can have a good look at him then, just to be sure we have the right man. By the time we reach Fort William, Commander Barricourt will have finished his supper. This Scot can be his dessert."

"You still want us to send out the runners and give the word to smoke as many caves as we can?" asked another English heathen, who Magnus didn't recognize.

"Ye would risk yer lives in the caves just to kill a defenseless woman?" Magnus thrashed against the men as they tried to lash a rope around his shackled wrists. "Cowards! Fight me instead, ye soulless bastards!"

"Commander wouldn't wish us to endanger ourselves over the likes of a worthless whore," Archie called out as he threw what looked like a hard jab into Magnus's ribs, but it had the force of a friendly nudge.

Magnus understood and focused his energies on fighting the others, giving Archie more leeway.

"Them caves are wicked treacherous, sir," Archie continued. "We done lost two men to the pits when we spoiled their supplies. Remember?" He rumbled out a belabored grunt and grazed Magnus's jaw with his fist. "And without her stag here to lead her out, she'll save us the trouble and die all on her own. What say you, Lieutenant Cawldrake?"

Playing along with Archie's plan, Magnus struggled against him just enough for show. If he calmed too fast, the good-hearted soldier's ruse might fail. But the man's words about Brenna's fate made him even more determined to escape. He'd use the rough ground and foggy darkness to his favor.

"Fair point, Raithwaite," Cawldrake replied, sounding vaguely impressed but still quite finished with the tedious situation. "Very well, then. Let us deliver the prisoner and be done with this sorry business. I tire of it and should like to seek my supper."

Two of the soldiers yanked at the ropes tied around Magnus's wrists, dragging him up the mountainside. Determined to frustrate them into a state of carelessness, he dropped to his knees and rolled to his back, slowing their progress. Each time, he yanked the rope as hard as he could, bringing them to the ground with him. Repeatedly, they came to a halt and forced him back to his feet, each time rougher than the next. Magnus nearly laughed out loud. The fools had no idea that he toyed with them.

Lazy bastards. They should have attempted to knock him out by now and carried him to wherever they were headed. Whoever this

Cawldrake was, the man obviously had no idea how to capture a Scot or what to do with one once he had him. And how the hell had these men learned so much about *Tor Ruadh*'s cave system?

As far as Magnus knew, before this invasion, nary a single Sassenach had ever accessed the caves. Who had betrayed the MacCoinnich's? Who had given up enough information to make the English's ambush such a bloody success? He would sort that out later. None of that mattered now. He had to escape them. Brenna had to be saved from a slow death in the darkness.

He dove to the ground again and rolled hard toward Archie, knocking the man's feet out from under him. Before they dragged him away, he made as though he intended to bite the man's ear but whispered harsh and low, "Give me a key to these feckin' shackles!"

After a subtle dip of his pudgy chin, Archie acted as though he slammed his fist into Magnus's jaw but actually shoved the key into his mouth instead. "Get off me, you bloody Scot!"

Magnus bit down on the key and covered it with his lips as a yank of the rope dragged him away. He waited for the soldiers to force him to his feet, but they let him lie. He craned his neck to peer up over a small rise lit by the strange lights he had seen before. The small plateau shelved into the side of the mountain held several saddled horses. Lads with lanterns suspended from sticks surrounded them.

"We'll put him on the mare," Archie said. "Drape him across her. Never sit a Scot in a saddle," he warned. "She's sturdy enough to carry him and too slow to escape should he coax her into running."

It took Archie and three of the soldiers to accomplish the task. Magnus wasn't about to make anything easy for these bumbling fools. Blood pounded in his ears as he hung across the saddle. He stared at the ground and clenched the key between his teeth, waiting for the perfect moment. If he untied his feet from his hands and threw himself off the horse, he would make quick work of the shackles thanks to Archie. By his reckoning, they were on the west side of the mountain, so Fort William wasn't that far away. Whatever he planned to do, he needed to figure it out and get on with it. He had been inside the garrison several times when visiting Lord Crestshire. The layout of the place seemed simple enough, but he had no idea what the cells of the dungeons might be like, nor did he wish to find out.

"Forward on," Archie called out.

The small, docile horse ambled along, seeming like a child's toy compared to the warhorses of *Tor Ruadh*. The farther they moved away from the entrance to the caves, the more he tensed for his dear, sweet love, back in the darkness, waiting for his return. God forgive him for leading her into that hellish place. This was madness. He had to make his move now.

Thanks again to Archie's help, Magnus undid the loosely knotted rope from around his ankles but not from the chains binding his wrists. No matter. He would make this work. Rolling off the horse's back, he hit the ground running and jogged alongside the plodding beast. As soldiers galloped forward, he used the mare as leverage to launch his body upward and land well-placed kicks into the men. He and the MacCoinnichs had often played this game as lads, and he had been the best. Knocked from their saddles, the English bounced down the steep slope, cursing as they rolled off into the darkness.

"Get out of the way and hold the lanterns high! I'll shoot the bastard." The order came from the only soldier left other than Archie, Lieutenant Cawldrake, and the unarmed lads with the lanterns suspended on poles. All the rest had tumbled down the mountainside.

"Hold fire!" Archie countered as he headed off the mare and blocked her path. "Commander Barricourt specifically ordered the Scot to be brought in alive. You heard him, sir."

"Raithwaite is correct," Cawldrake agreed. "Do not shoot him—yet. Lash him tight enough, so he does not escape again. I weary of this heathen and am sorely tempted to accept a reprimand for bringing him in dead rather than alive."

Archie and the remaining soldier flanked Magnus.

He pulled the rough length of rope between his hands and brandished it like a heavy cat-o'-nine-tails, whipping the men with it each time they drew close. He didn't wish to hurt Archie, but if the man impeded his escape, he wouldn't hesitate to take him down as well. As they inched toward him, he sidled off the path and edged down the mountainside. Nearby, scrabbling in the darkness, warned him the soldiers he had kicked from their mounts were climbing their way back up to the path.

"Draw and fire!" Cawldrake sounded awake and interested for the first time since the debacle had started. "Wing that man or shoot him in the leg. They can carry the fool Scot to the gallows on a litter for all I care! I am done with this foolishness!"

Magnus felt sure they would not shoot him. The more distance he put between himself and the lantern boys, the harder it was for any of them to see anything.

"Take that man or suffer the consequences!" Cawldrake's voice hit a higher pitch.

Magnus chuckled. The fool redcoat sounded like he had his bollocks in a bind. Whipping the rope in an arc around himself, he shuffled down the mountainside, stinging every soldier who dared come too close. He daren't pause long enough to rid himself of the shackles. If he did, they'd fall upon him. He'd rid himself of the heavy chains later.

His heel caught the edge of a large rock and threw off his balance. He lost control of the swinging rope, the end of it popping him in the face and burning like a hot coal. Hitting the ground hard, he tucked and rolled to survive whatever punishment the slope gave. A boulder brought him to a rib-cracking stop. He scrambled around it, tucked in tight, and held his breath. Without torch or lantern to beat back the darkness this far down the incline, they would be hard-pressed to find him. All he need do was wait them out.

"I do not tolerate failure!" Cawldrake screamed. "Find that man. Find him now, I say!"

"We can't see a bloody thing, sir," one man said. "Send down the lanterns or wait 'til daybreak."

"Daybreak be better, sir," another called out. "No way will he light anything to see and give hisself away, and we got but five lantern boys left since we lost two in the caves. Them Scots are wily bastards, you know."

"I refuse to return to Fort William empty-handed," Cawldrake informed them. "You!

Lantern boys. Spread out and walk down the mountainside."

Magnus risked a glance around the boulder. He had tumbled quite a way before hitting the rock, bouncing hard every bit of the way. Never did he think he'd be thankful for an extended beating from the mountainside, but when he didn't catch sight of the lights, he was. It would take the soldiers a good while to work their way down to him.

He spit the key to the shackles into his hand, along with several pieces of a broken tooth. At least he hadn't lost the thing while tumbling down the slope. The key was worth a tooth or two. Catching up the chains and holding them tight to prevent their rattling, he unlocked the irons and slid them off. Then he withdrew his trusty *sgian dhu* out of his boot, thankful that the soldiers had missed it. The wee dagger might not be much, but it would be effective when needed. He felt better with some sort of weapon in hand.

Inching his way up the side of the boulder, he propped his arms on top and scanned the surroundings. Ben Nevis's mistiness didn't seem as dense here, but the night was cloudy, making visibility just as poor at this level. With no help from the stars, he didn't know where he was or how far to go to make it back to where he had exited the mountain and dig his way back inside.

Eventually, he would have to move. While

there was still no sign of lantern light, the troop of soldiers sounded like a herd of Highland cows stampeding down the mountain toward him. He pushed off the rock and rolled his shoulders against the ache from the land's punishment. That pain was nothing compared to his worry for Brenna.

By his best calculations, they had ridden west but a short way before he had made his escape. Near as he could tell, he had rolled straight down but wasn't sure. He would head east for a few furlongs, then climb back up the mountain as soon as it was safe to do so. No way in hell would he suffer the English to capture him again. If he could find the stream as he moved east, that would help him decipher his whereabouts and continue on.

Rocks tumbled, and a soldier growled out a curse. That hadn't been all that far away—time to move.

He took a step toward what he hoped was eastward, then the ground disappeared out from under his feet, and the mountain swallowed him.

CHAPTER SIXTEEN

BRENNA MADE ANOTHER pass around the vast storage cavern, searching for more broken barrel staves or whatever else might burn to keep the precious fire going. Sweat beaded on her forehead, even more trickled down her spine. She paid it no mind. Heat hotter than damnation was better than total darkness.

She had discovered some useable supplies and collected them to one side of the circle of firelight. The meager pile was comprised of a pair of ropes, one a bit short but still useable. The destructive marauders had somehow overlooked a double handful of oatcakes and a small sack of dried meats and fruits. Ruined supplies, she had shoved off into the shadows. Those that would burn were stacked beside the fire for fuel.

She thanked God Almighty that whoever had fouled the storage area and slashed the water bags had either been careless or in a hurry. The slab of stone beneath the waterskins' rack was covered in holes and dips that had preserved several puddles of drinkable water. At first, she had hesitated to drop on all fours and lap at the leavings like a thirsty dog. But after a careful sniff and a taste, her parched state had won out. Unfortunately, the minimal amount of water wouldn't last long.

Tired of pacing but too agitated to sit, she stood by the fire, staring down at the flames until her eyes stung with the need to blink. How long had Magnus been gone? Was he safe? Had he found water? Had the mended skins held? So many questions that wouldn't be answered until he returned—and once he did, none of those answers mattered. All she needed was her dear one back at her side. Even if fate decreed she die in this bleak darkness, she could face it, as long as her sweet love held her in his arms one more time. At least Keigan was safe with Catriona and Alexander. That bit of comfort brought her a sad smile.

"Diabhal gabh e!"

Dagger drawn, Brenna whirled about, searching for the source of the shout. Who had shouted, 'devil take it' in the old tongue? A woman for certain. Was it Cadha? The cursing had come from the right of the storage plateau where Magnus had said the fissure widened too much to cross.

Brenna went to the rim of the rock shelf and held the sputtering flames of a makeshift torch over the edge. The blackness of the void laughed at her efforts, making the light as insignificant as a spark. Another glimmer glowed several lengths down below, but it was so faint, it barely illuminated the form huddled beside it. "Cadha? Is that ye?"

"Well, who else would it be, ye stupid cow?" The lass lifted the lamp as she scowled upward, her grimy face ghostly and pale.

Brenna had half a mind to leave the sharp-tongued wench where she sat. In fact, the girl needed to think about that. "Forgive me for bothering ye, yer highness. I'll leave ye to yer privacy. After all, I'm far too stupid to pull yer sorry arse up from that ledge." She stepped back and swept the torchlight away from the void to make Cadha think she meant it.

"No! Wait!" A shuffling echoed up from the fissure, accompanied by a meek, "Hello? Are ye still up there, mistress?"

After a long enough pause to make the girl a bit more respectful, Brenna cast her light back down into the hole. "I am here. Are ye hurt?"

"I think me arm's broke, and my lamp burnt me leg when it fell down beside me." She snuffled, sounding as though she had just wiped her face on her arm. "Least it landed on the shelf and stayed put. Thought I could make the jump. Did it afore. But this time, I came up short. Held on to the edge for a bit but couldn't pull m'self out. Lucky for me, I dropped to the ledge."

"Let me get one of the ropes ye missed ruining when ye destroyed the stores." Brenna's conscience wouldn't allow her to leave the girl to die, but it didn't demand she be nice to her.

Cadha didn't comment. Brenna took that as a confession that the maid had been the one to sully the cache. She scooped up one rope, then stopped. The distance down to the rock shelf looked to be quite a stretch, and Cadha would have to wrap the rope around her slight body. Just to be sure she had enough, Brenna brought along the other rope as well.

After securing her torch in a crack in the wall, she knotted the rope, satisfied with how the loop closed up with just a tug. She lowered it over the edge. "Step into this and hitch it up under yer arms. It'll go tight as I pull ye up, but shouldna pinch ye too much since ye're just a wee thing."

Cadha did as instructed. "I canna hold the rope if'n I bring my lantern up, too," she called out. "I had it hooked to me belt, but the latch broke when I hit the wall, and it willna hold it now."

Brenna hated the thought of abandoning any

source of light. "If I lower the other rope, too, can ye tie it to the lamp somehow?" With an arm broken, one of Cadha's hands might very well be useless.

"I think I can. Send it down, and I'll try."

"I've knotted a loop in this one, too." Brenna tossed it to the girl's outstretched hand. "Tie it wherever ye think it'll hold and not catch fire, then yank tight and tell me when."

After several fumbling attempts, Cadha leaned back against the wall and waved upward. "Try it now but go slow lest the oil shifts and tips it."

Brenna eased the smoking oil lamp upward, noting the slight weight of it and wondering how long Cadha had been wandering the caves. She set it aside and dropped the extra rope beside it.

"Hurry. I dinna like the dark."

Brenna understood. She secured the rope tied to Cadha around her back and planted her feet to hold the girl's weight. Slow and steady, she pulled, feeding the rope through her hands. The lass weighed more than she looked. Brenna backed up a step and resettled her stance, bracing herself as much as she could. "Climb some if ye can," she called out, but the girl didn't answer. Brenna feared the maid had passed out from the pain of her broken arm. She inched backward, keeping the rope taut and hoping the edge of the precipice wasn't sharp enough to sever it before the girl reached safety. When the lass popped into view and clamped her forearm up over the edge, Brenna blew out a relieved huff. "Praise God!"

"Dinna drop me, ye cow!" Cadha struggled to grapple the rest of the way out of the fissure. "Ye can sing yer praises to God once I'm sitting by the fire, ye ken?" She rolled to her back, gasping to catch her breath.

"Ye're an ungrateful creature, I'll give ye that." Brenna yanked hard enough to drag the sour-faced girl well away from the pit. She untied the slip knot and jerked it from around the maid's body. "There. Get close to the fire, and I'll check yer arm."

"Dinna ye worry with it." Sullen as a spoiled child, the lass dragged herself over to the fire, hugging her wounded limb to her chest. "I'll find me a healer on my way to Fort William." She shot a narrow-eyed glare back at Brenna. "Thanks to ye, they captured him. I hope ye're happy. I heard'm say they plan to hang him." Her sullenness shifted to seething hatred. "I came back here to tell ye afore I left, so ye'd know what yer deceitfulness done to him." She snatched up a broken piece of wood and pointed it at Brenna like a knife. "Now I'll be going to Fort William, so's he can at least see me a grieving for him while he hangs."

The girl's gut-wrenching revelation knocked away Brenna's ability to stand. She dropped to her knees. "Ye lie, ye vicious girl," she choked out once she calmed enough to draw a breath. "Dinna think I willna kill ye for telling me such tales as a cruel jest."

"Why would I lie?" Cadha dared. She dismissed Brenna with a rude flip of her hand. "I'm nay the one who got him hunted down like a rabid wolf." She jabbed the stick at Brenna again. "That there sin lays at yer feet, not mine." With a scowling glance around the cavern, she shook her head. "I'm also nay the one who done all this. Them feckin' Sassenachs came through here. Lost four of their own whilst they sacked the place and didna even care about them there men."

An ugly snort exploded from her as she tossed the shard of wood into the fire.

"The redcoats destroyed the stores? All of them?" Brenna wondered if the lass spoke the truth or if the malicious babbling came from her madness.

"Aye, they did. All the necessaries I was using done been ruin't. Ever last bit." Cadha stared at her as if she thought her a dullard. "Why would I do it? I been living in these caves since old Fitzgerald kicked me out." She scooted closer to the fire. Disgust twisted her face. "That wicked old cow. I warned her 'bout that Alice whoring around with that lying redcoat, and she called me the liar. Pulled me out by my ear in front of God and ever'body." She angled around toward the fire, lifted her chin, and tapped a string of mottled bruises framing her jawline. "I even showed her proof. See here? All them MacCoinnichs trusted Alice's soldier, but this here's what that man done to me when I told him I'd be telling my Magnus about him spying to help that new Fort William officer clear them off the mountain." With a curt dip of her chin, she snatched up an oatcake and tore into it. "That Thomas Parlorn wouldha sold his soul to the devil himself if'n he thought it'd get him ahead." She laughed, spitting oatcake everywhere. "Guess he's talking to old Scratch right now. As long as his yelling lasted, probably shook every wall in Hell when he finally hit bottom."

Brenna remembered Catriona had spoken about Thomas Parlorn and Alice as though she trusted them. The picture Cadha painted said otherwise. "Ye said Magnus had been captured," she reminded, forcing the words out. "When?"

"Right 'fore I came back here to tell ye." Gingerly touching the purple knot swelling just above her wrist, Cadha frowned at the injury as she talked. "I tried my best to get to Magnus to warn him 'bout the trap the English planned to set, but I had to wait 'til I didna think the soldiers was in that part of the caves anymore." She frowned, turning her arm and studying the break from a different angle. "But they blocked my way. It took me a while to find another opening."

Easing her arm down to rest in her lap, she gave a sad shake of her head. "I came out near their horses. Saw them throw my Magnus over a mare like a sack of grain." The girl drew herself up and jabbed a finger at Brenna. "This here's all yer fault. If ye hadna made him feel all sorry for ye about yer whoring days, he wouldha never tried to jump that English dog. He and I couldha been together, like I planned."

"Enough! Just because a man saved yer life doesna mean he loved ye!" Brenna had tolerated all the insults she could stand. "Ye might think ye love him—" Both hands fisted, she charged forward, ready to fight. "But know this, ye hateful bit of scum, he is *my* husband, and if ye dinna shut yer maw, I'll be shutting it for ye!"

Cadha jerked away as though dodging a hit. "He saved me, he did, and I know'd him long before ye did," she said, but her tone had changed. She still reeked of jealousy, but her hatred had somehow waned. In its place was a hint of respect and maybe a little fear.

"Aye, that's true." Brenna stood her ground, forcing a calmer demeanor but keeping her hand on her dagger. Cadha couldn't be trusted. The girl's eyes gleamed with madness. If she wished to best the maid, she had to keep a cool head and reason with her addled mind. "Ye have known him longer." She sidled around the fire, deciding it safer to keep her back to the wall rather than the bottomless fissure. A good shove could be disastrous. "And Magnus saved ye because he has a good heart and doesna wish for anyone to suffer—not because he loved ye."

The maid frowned. Not a hateful scowl, but a studious pucker as though sorting through her thoughts. "But I love him," she argued with a disturbing calmness.

"Aye, but he doesna love ye back," Brenna said. "Unfortunately, love doesna always work as we wish it." The swelling on Cadha's arm looked worse. It needed a splint, a poultice of knitbone, and a good wrapping. Brenna nodded at the lass's wound. "Let me help ye now, aye? I'm a healer."

"Why ye acting like ye want to help me? There's no one here to see yer charity and tell ye how good ye are." The lass cradled her arm in her lap and crammed the last of the oatcake into her mouth. "My arm be fine enough healing on its own." She shrugged. "Long as I dinna fall and hit it again."

"I dinna live my life to impress anyone." Brenna fetched the bag she had filled with every remedy she could tote. Without water, she would be hard-pressed to make a poultice, but it could be done. She glanced over at the rock with the nearly depleted puddles. Nay, she couldn't risk using the last of it. "I wish we had some water."

"Water that moves be good to use," Cadha chanted as she stretched out on her side and lay staring into the fire. She yawned. "Water that's still will make ye ill," she mumbled as she pillowed her head on her uninjured arm.

"Aye, and water from a cave gives ye the skitters," Brenna added as she labored to work the knitbone into a paste by crushing the leaves without the addition of any water.

"Does not." The maid rubbed her nose as though it itched something fierce, then settled back down. "I been drinking cave water since the redcoats came, and I dinna have the skitters." She made a face and shrugged. "All's ye have to do is to be sure ye dinna drink water fouled with bat shite or something dead."

Brenna paused, trying to decide whether Cadha could be trusted. "Magnus said it was unsafe." She would leave it at that and see if the girl argued.

"He is wrong," Cadha stated as she pushed herself up to a sitting position. With a smile that gave Brenna chills, the lass tilted her head toward the rear of the cavern. "Them rocks back there, the ones that look like soft dough piled on a board? They weep, and the water gathers at their base. I drank it yesterday and day before that, too."

"Drink it again right now, and I just might believe ye." Brenna was not that naïve. Cadha might have stopped with the insults, but that didn't mean she had stopped planning ill will.

"Ha! Ye dinna trust me. Maybe ye're no' as big a fool as I thought." Wincing, the maid rose from the floor and grabbed her dented oil lamp. After taking a few steps toward the back of the cavern, she stopped and looked back. "Well? Be ye comin', cow? Ye canna verra well see me drinking the water from back there."

"If ye dinna stop calling me cow, I'll be coming up with an insulting name or two for yerself."

Cadha barked out a laugh, then pinned her with a haunted sneer. "Ye canna think of a slur I havena been called before. I promise ye that."

Something about that made Brenna's heart hurt. It reminded her of her own upbringing. She motioned for Cadha to keep moving. "On wi' ye now. Prove yer words." She didn't dare let the conniving wench think she had let down her guard.

"These rocks here." Lifting her lamp, the maid cast the light across the rocks. She had described them aptly. Colored a slick-looking milky gray, the formation did resemble soft globs of dough piled high and waiting to be punched down and kneaded. At their base, hollowed out by ages of moisture trickling down and around the pillars, was a shallow basin of water. Cadha scooped up a handful and drank it. "I know it's still, but I been drinking it." She shrugged. "I havena shite m'self dead yet."

"Since you seem to know these caves so well,

why did ye not just go outside and find a spring?" Brenna couldn't imagine choosing to drink stagnate cave condensation rather than clear, sweet spring water.

"Murdering redcoats, remember?" With a disgusted shake of her head, Cadha dried her hand on her skirts. "The mountain's crawling with them. The MacCoinnichs just dinna know it." Retrieving her lamp from the floor, she turned and headed back to the fire. "I've had enough dealings with bloody Sassenachs to last me a lifetime." She shuddered, hugging her broken arm tighter to her chest. "Cruel bastards," she added under her breath, but Brenna clearly heard it and agreed completely.

Brenna tasted the water. It wasn't good, but at least it was wet. She scooped up a handful and carried enough back to add to the knitbone paste. "After I set yer arm, we're going back to *Tor Ruadh*." She would warn Alexander about Magnus's capture and make a case for saving him from the noose—either legally or not. She didn't care. All she knew for certain was that she wasn't content to be a widow yet. "Ye'll help me find the way, aye?"

"I canna go back there," Cadha said, snorting as if Brenna had just told a poorly fashioned jest. "Fitzgerald probably set the dogs on me. Old hag hates me."

"She doesna hate ye. 'Twas all a misunderstanding. Once she sees ye were trying to protect the MacCoinnichs, I'm sure she'll welcome ye back with open arms." Brenna had to convince the girl to help her find her way back. She might make it on her own, but they could move faster with the maid's certainty of the tunnels. "Would ye not rather return to living in the keep than hiding in these caves, like a wingless bat?"

Cadha's narrow face puckered at the question. Lips pursing tighter, she looked to be weighing her options. When her shoulders relaxed and her head tilted, Brenna knew she had her. "Ye think Lady Catriona would tell Fitzgerald to let me go back to feeding the hens and gathering eggs?"

"I will vouch for ye myself."

"Why would ye do such a thing?" Angry wariness shone in the girl's weary eyes. The maid looked like a chained animal, trying to find the strength to fight off another beating.

With the poultice in one hand, Brenna held out her other. "Ye and I are not so different, I think. I've not had an easy way of it either." She nodded toward the girl's arm. "Although, I believe ye've endured more cruelties than I have. Now, give me yer arm so that we can be on our way, aye?"

Cadha stared at her for a long while. Silent. Unmoving except for the rise and fall of her chest.

"I know it's nay easy," Brenna said softly.

"But ye can trust me. I willna hurt ye." She offered a teasing smile. "Unless ye go after my husband again. And then, I will have to kill ye."

Cadha revealed a toothy smile that chased away the hatred in her eyes. She placed her wounded arm in Brenna's hand. "I guess ye're nay so bad." Her smile crooked farther to one side. "For a cow."

"I'll make ye think cow," Brenna pretended to threaten. As gently as she could, she spread the pasty green mash on the purpling knot on the girl's arm. No bone had poked through the flesh, nor did her arm show the unevenness of a severe break. But Brenna had no doubt that at least a small fracture had occurred just above the lass's wrist. With a barrel stave as a splint, she wrapped it in strips of linen she had torn from the hem of her shift. "There now. The knitbone will do its work. If I had a pot, I'd brew ye some willow bark tea for the pain."

Running her fingers along the splint, the girl shrugged. "The pain is nay so bad." She looked up with a sad smile. "I grant ye, I've had worse."

"I'm sure ye have," Brenna agreed, her heart hurting for the lass. "Do ye feel able to start the trek back?"

With a nod, Cadha stood, then lifted her sputtering oil lamp. "Need more fuel first and a new wick." She nodded toward a small pile of broken crockery. "See those? Some had goose fat.

Some had tallow. Doesna matter which ye choose. Both burn. Gather enough to fill the lamp and coat a good long strip of linen that we can shove down into the grease for a wick." She cast a disparaging glance at Brenna's faltering torch. "The lamp'll give us a steadier burn than that thing."

Lamp filled and another strip of her chemise fashioned into a wick, Brenna held her breath as she touched a flaming brand to their creation and lit it. She had used oil lamps before, but never one so crude. Cadha was right. The light burned steady and bright. Much better than her sputtering torch.

"I found a quicker way back to the keep," Cadha said as she took the lamp from Brenna. "Opens out in an old root cellar they dinna use anymore 'cause it holds water. Probably floods in the spring."

"I wonder why Magnus didna use that route if it's shorter?" Brenna wanted to trust the girl, but the fear of being trapped in the cave outweighed it. She would remain cautious until she returned to blessed sunshine.

"I had to dig my through," the maid explained as she led the way up a steep incline that wound around behind the weeping stone formation that had provided barely palatable water. "I found soft dirt blocking the tunnel instead of rocks. Seemed strange, so I dug through it for a spell. They must ha' piled it there when they built the root cellar. Magnus probably thought it still closed off or forgot about it."

The explanation made sense. Somewhat. Brenna followed close, alert to any possible trickery. She had no idea in what direction they traveled. It felt like they still climbed upward, making her wonder how the trail could end in an old root cellar behind the kitchens.

"Dinna think I'm trying to lose ye," Cadha reassured her with a glance back. She lifted the lamp higher and kept trudging. "If'n I show up at the keep without ye, there'll be no one to vouch for me like ye promised."

That made Brenna feel some better, but she still kept up her guard. "Ye said ye had to dig yer way through. Will we have to crawl into the root cellar?"

"Aye. But it's nay as close as some places ye've already squeezed through. I'll give ye the lamp when we reach it. I willna be able to hold it and crawl with just one arm." She paused and turned, shining the light so Brenna could see her solemn look. "And dinna fret. I'll still lead the way 'cause I know ye dinna trust me. Just stay close as ye can so some light reaches around me, aye?"

That Cadha could almost read her mind was more than a little disturbing. "Ye're a canny one. I'll give ye that."

"Nay." The girl shook her head and continued on, turning sideways to make it through the narrowing tunnel. "I just know how it is when ye dinna trust someone." She snorted out a laugh. "I dinna trust ye any more than ye trust me."

"Aye, well...at least we understand each other." Brenna sidled along, ducking down as the tunnel not only narrowed from side to side but dwindled in height, as well. Soon, she would be forced to drop to her knees. "Do ye need me to take the lamp now?"

"Aye." Cadha crouched low and passed it over her head. "We might as well start our crawling here."

"How far must we crawl?"

"'Til we get there."

Brenna bit her tongue to keep from snapping at the girl. Fool lass. Now was not the time for sassing. They crawled along for what seemed like forever, their tangled skirts and Cadha's splinted arm making their progress seem slow as tree sap in winter. Smoke from the lamp fouled the space, making it even harder to rein in the panic that there wasn't enough air.

"Breathe, ye cow, and dinna set my skirts afire." Cadha's scolding had a calmness and certainty Brenna envied. "I'm crawling fast as I can. Setting fire to me arse willna make me move any faster."

"What did I tell ye about calling me 'cow'?"

"If'n ye must know, I call ye 'cow' because I canna remember yer blessit name. I'll be damned if I call ye 'Mistress MacCoinnich' before ye get me hired back at the keep. I'm nay in yer employ now."

The passage grew tighter still, and the ground softened. Her knees and hands sank into the dank loaminess as though the earth could swallow them at any moment. "My name is 'Brenna,' ye wicked minx. Ye ken that as well as I do."

Cadha cackled. "Aye. I know." She halted.

"Why have ye stopped?" Brenna strained to hold the lantern higher, her back and shoulders cramped and burning from the awkward position.

"Because we have arrived, cow," the maid whispered. "Hush it now. We dinna ken who might be about nor their mood if they've been told of my...I mean 'yer' Magnus's capture. They could verra well kill us before they see who we are—or before they see who *ye* are. They dinna care about whether I live or die."

"That is about to change." Brenna gave Cadha an impatient nudge. "On wi' ye now, so we can get Magnus freed and tell Mrs. Fitzgerald ye spoke the truth." *And take a big gulp of fresh air and sunshine,* she silently added.

Upon stepping down from the tunnel, Brenna sloshed into ankle-deep water. "Saints alive!"

"I told ye it held too much water for a proper cellar. They must ha' hit a spring when they dug it." Cadha snagged hold of her sleeve and pulled her toward the wall. "Stay to the edge. It's nay as deep there."

"At least we can almost stand." She ducked her head the slightest bit as they crossed the cellar.

When they reached the door, it was hanging by one hinge. Cadha fell back and motioned Brenna forward. "Ye go first and tell'm about me. I'll hide in here until ye send for me, aye?"

If not for the wild, haunted look returning to the girl's eyes, Brenna would suspect a trap. She took hold of Cadha's hand. "Nay. We go together. Come."

The day's brilliance made her squint as they stepped outside. Brenna stretched and took in a deep breath, turning her face toward the sun peeping over the skirting wall. She didn't know what day it was, but she knew it was morning. Breaking into a run, she pulled Cadha along beside her until the girl planted both feet and yanked back just as they reached the kitchen door.

"Nay," she said. "Not through there. What if old Fitzgerald's about?"

"*Old* Fitzgerald is about." The stern announcement came from behind them.

As soon as Brenna turned, Mrs. Fitzgerald's demeanor immediately changed. "Mistress MacCoinnich! Ye've returned a'ready? Did ill befall ye and yer husband?"

"It has." Brenna nodded toward Cadha. "Magnus was captured by the English before Cadha here could warn him about Thomas Parlorn's treachery." She drew the maid closer and wrapped an arm around her thin shoulders. "She spoke the truth about Alice and Thomas's disloyalty, Mrs. Fitzgerald. The soldiers destroyed all the stores and caved in some tunnels to set up an ambush that my poor husband walked into whilst trying to find us more water."

The corner of one of the housekeeper's eyes twitched as she gave the maid a steady up and down look. "I see." With a sudden dip of her chin, the matron bustled around them, her skirts rustling with the quickness of her steps. "Come. The chieftain must hear of this."

They rushed through the pantry and kitchens. Servants jumped back out of their path, their mouths ajar and eyes wide with shock. Just as they were about to breach the archway that led into the great hall, Mrs. Fitzgerald halted and blocked the way to keep Brenna and Cadha from passing.

Brenna looked around the old woman and saw why.

Alexander sat in the chieftain's chair on the dais, and in front of him stood two English soldiers. One soldier, the officer, was red-faced and sputtering. The man's voice grew louder with every word.

"We know he is here," the officer declared. "Where else would he go once he escaped us? Upon the arrival of the rest of mine, I shall have this place searched at once!"

"Ye know verra little about Highlanders, Lieutenant Cawldrake," Alexander said. "This is the last place the man would come." He flipped a hand as though shooing away the soldier's foolishness. "He wouldna endanger his clan, ye ken?"

Brenna's heart sang. Magnus had escaped! She didn't know where he was, but at least he wasn't rotting in a cell at Fort William. Cadha squeezed her hand, as excited about the news as she was.

"Chieftain MacCoinnich speaks the truth, sir," said the other redcoat, a much calmer man, who seemed almost content with the news they had just delivered. "Highlanders protect their clans at all costs. Perhaps, we should return and do a more extensive search of where he escaped us." The soldier gave a nod as though affirming his own words. "You know how he disappeared into the mist. Perhaps, he hides in the caves? We could send in more men there."

"You are a fool, Raithwaite!" Cawldrake snapped. "We have already lost six to those godforsaken caves, and the man is still at large." He pulled at the knot of his neckcloth and worked his head as though struggling for air. "Besides, I sincerely doubt he returned to the caves. What on earth would he do for light to find his way?" With a swipe of his hand across his forehead, he unknowingly shifted his white hairpiece back a notch, revealing his bald head. "If we do not locate that traitor by the end of this day, you will be the one to apprise Commander Barricourt of our failure and suffer the consequences. I dare say, the man shall have both our heads!"

Alexander sat drumming his fingers on the arm of his chair. "While I do enjoy hearing that one of our own, a man falsely accused, mind ye, has the lot of ye chasing yer tails and worried about yer heads. I do have other business to attend to gentleman. Perhaps, ye could play out yer wee game elsewhere?"

Brenna eased through the archway, studying the soldier who had spoken as though he might possess a bit of sense. The man looked like he wanted to smile, and she could've sworn she saw him wink at Alexander. Could he possibly be an ally?

Cawldrake's face became an even darker shade of red. Brenna fully expected the man to keel over at any moment from an attack of apoplexy. "Arrogant Scots!" he fumed, foaming at the corners of his mouth like a rabid animal. "Were it up to me, I would see every last one of you shipped off to the colonies." He raised his fist and shook it. "I shall order men placed at this keep to watch for the prisoner, and every nook and cranny of those caves searched by Her Majesty's finest. We shall cover this mountain, both within and without, if it takes every able-bodied soldier at my disposal. What say you to that, sir?"

Alexander rose to his full height and stepped down off the dais. He didn't slow his stride until he stood towering over the man. "I say ye best take care, Sassenach. I dinna take threats lightly."

"I would be happy to stand watch outside the gate for a day or so, sir," Raithwaite volunteered. After a polite bow to Alexander, he continued, "that is, if Chieftain MacCoinnich would find that acceptable? And perhaps but a single unit to search the caves. With the chief's permission?"

"Outside the gate. One day. No more. Understood?" Alexander's scowl darkened. "Three soldiers may search the caves. Only if escorted by MacCoinnich guards."

Without a word, Cawldrake spun around and charged out of the hall, sputtering and cursing under his breath. "Bloody Scots. Commander Barricourt shall hear of this!"

Raithwaite leaned toward Alexander and whispered something Brenna couldn't hear. Then he rushed from the room.

As soon as the soldier exited, Brenna hurried

to Alexander. "What did that man just tell ye?"

"He thinks Magnus fell through a sinkhole higher and to the west of us. He couldn't check on his welfare because of the others." He gave her a quizzical look. "When did ye return?"

"That doesna matter," she said. "Tell me how we find Magnus?"

CHAPTER SEVENTEEN

THE IMPACT KNOCKED the wind out of him. Flat of his back, he gasped and wheezed, fearing the earth might shift and gulp him down even deeper. Once he could breathe again, he risked opening his eyes. He blinked with a slow, hard squeeze, praying he had not been rendered blind because there was no difference whether he opened or closed them. The total absence of light was suffocating. Magnus concentrated on pacing his breaths and reining in the panic threatening to take hold. To survive this black hell, he needed calm, clear thinking. He tried not to think about being buried alive.

With as little shifting of his body as possible, he checked for injuries. While he appeared to have landed on a good-sized bit of stable ground, he could just as easily be perched on the edge of a pit, bottomless or otherwise. The initial fall had felt like it lasted several lifetimes. He preferred not to repeat it. 'Twas a wonder he hadn't broken his fool neck.

Nothing hurt worse than he could endure. But his right knee, the one he had injured once before, burned as though packed in hot coals. Walking would be a chore, if possible at all. Still not moving from where he lay, he stretched out both arms, walking his fingers around himself as far as he could reach. The ledge surrounded him as far as he could touch. He rolled to a sitting position, and a stabbing pain forced a wincing groan from him. His right hip. It felt like a demon had sunk its teeth in deep and refused to let go. Shifting his weight to his left buttock, he shoved away the fist-sized rocks that had chewed his arse when he landed.

As he gingerly pulled shards out of the cheek of his arse, something bumped the back of his hand. He froze. Could he be so lucky? Sending up a prayer to any entity that might be listening, he twisted and brushed his fingers up his back to his belt. It was still there. The extra torch he had shoved into his belt. The fool British either hadn't seen it, or good old Archie had somehow concealed it so that it wasn't stripped from him when they took his weapons. May the gods bless that bloody Sassenach and whatever bit of luck that had kept the torch attached to him during the fall.

Now, if he could just strike a spark. He patted around until he found his sporran and located the steel and flint that would bring him blessed light. With his kilt hiked out of the way and the torch on the ground between his knees, he held his breath as he struck them together over the pitch-soaked rags. Sparks showered down and erupted into flames.

"Thank the gods." The light made breathing so much easier. Magnus lifted the torch and cast its glow all around. No wonder he hadn't been hurt worse than he had. The sinkhole was a narrow bottleneck that emptied out into a wide stone room. He remembered clawing at the earth on all sides as he had tumbled through the darkness. Pushing up on his uninjured leg, he steadied himself by propping against the low ceiling and leaning back against the wall. He'd be sore pressed to find anything to use as a crutch or a cane, but at least he could move by holding onto the walls.

He made another slow sweep with the torch, trying to remember if he had ever been in this part of the cave system before. If he couldn't locate any markers or anything recognizable, he was doomed. A man could wander this maze until the angel of death appeared to lead him out.

Lifting the flame, he peered up the narrow passageway that had funneled him into the mountain's core. Nothing but darkness past the reach of his torch. Perhaps he *had* fallen for several lifetimes.

Testing the strength of his throbbing leg proved to be a mistake. It buckled under the slightest bit of weight and sent him back to the floor. Cold sweat peppered across his brow and upper lip. "I will do this," he growled. After several slow, deep breaths to conquer the pain, he managed to return to a standing position with the help of the wall. He didn't think the leg was broken, just twisted something fierce. It would be slow going through the tunnels, but that was just as well. Slow also meant careful.

Stooped over, he hitched his way along the wall, searching for a way to escape the pit. He tried not to think about what would happen if this pocket of space had no exit. He worked out a rhythm, holding to the wall and swinging the torch first high, then low in search of tunnels, cracks, fissures, anywhere he might wiggle through to get to hopefully a better place rather than a worse one. As it was, he was trapped, and no one knew where he was. As far as he was concerned, things could only get better.

Before he had started this search for an opening, he had taken a stone and scratched a large cross into the wall. Not as a prayer for help. He was too stubborn for that. But to let him know where he had started. If he searched the room and came back to the cross, then he would know there was no exit. He tried not to dwell on that possibility.

Instinctively, he had started his journey by going to the left. If the void was a circle, he moved in a clockwise direction. His mother would be pleased. Deasil, or clockwise, moving with the sun, raised power and increased the odds of prosperity, while widdershins or counter-clockwise banished power. If he needed anything right now, it was power and prosperity.

His left hand slid along the wall, keeping him upright, while his right hand kept the torch swinging. Just as he swung the light downward to check the floor, he moved his hand and ran out of the wall. "Shite!"

The curse word echoed all around as he stumbled and hopped like a three-legged dog. He rounded the corner and leaned back against the side of the new tunnel that had opened up to his left. The old teachings had been right. Moving clockwise had led him to a wide passage that was tall enough he could straighten to his full height. He pulled in a deep breath and stretched, renewed hope pumping through him. A tunnel this wide in the cave system had to have been mapped. All he needed was the markings they would've left behind. Then he would know his location.

Fortified by his find, he inched along at a faster pace. The air even seemed fresher here. Could he be so lucky, or was it merely his senses feeding him false hope? Whatever the case, he would take it and use it to his advantage. Hobbling along, he noted the levelness of the passage floor, almost as if the mythical dwarves of ancient legend had chiseled his way out. He hopped along faster, tasting freedom.

Then all hope left him. A solid slab of stone ended what had turned out to not be a tunnel at all but merely an offshoot of the sinkhole. He pressed his forehead against the stone and hammered the wall with his fist, raging against the mountain's cruel jest. So much time and energy had been wasted by going down this passage. His torch wouldn't last forever. He had to find a way out before it was spent.

"Naught to be done but keep moving." For some odd reason, the act of speaking out loud soothed him. First sign of madness, perhaps? "Nay, I merely appreciate a wise voice of reason," he assured himself as he swung around and backtracked to the opening of the fickle tunnel.

Back to where he had veered to the left, he started out again, humming a tune as he swung the torch and hopped along. "Show me yer secrets, Ben Nevis. I've always treated ye well and respected yer name." His request echoed through the void, then faded into the darkness. It was followed by the skittering sound of something scrambling across the space. The noise of a startled varmint. A rat maybe?

Still steadying himself with the wall, Magnus attempted to work his way toward the sound. For an animal to be heard at this level, he couldn't be that far from an opening to the outside. He hoped it was a good-sized opening and not some crack in the earth, barely large enough for a wee mousie.

He came to another tunnel, much like the one that had cruelly made him believe he had found the way out. Should he try it or no? Staring at the new direction's darkness didn't tell him a damn thing. "In for a penny, in for a pound," he muttered as he forged ahead. Then he heard voices. Or did he? Could be cave madness setting in. He'd heard tell of that happening to others.

Moving as quietly as possible, he strained to hear more, then his heart leapt so high he smiled. At least if he was doomed to imagine voices, he couldn't think of a better one than Brenna's. "Brenna!" he called out, hoping against hope it really was her and not his own wishful thinking.

"Magnus!"

More joy and relief than he had ever known surged through him. "Stay put! I'll come to ye. These pathways are too treacherous for ye to travel alone.

"What makes ye think she's alone?" A hearty laugh that Magnus had heard many times before followed. Alexander had found Brenna, and the two of them had taken it upon themselves to find him. But why? How had they known?

Perplexed, Magnus came to a halt. What had caused Alexander to search Brenna out to save her?

"Magnus?" Alexander's voice sounded closer. "Call out again. We've come to the pit of five tunnels. We canna tell which one holds ye."

The pit of five tunnels? That told Magnus exactly where they were within the maze. "Stay put!" he shouted. "I'll come to ye." The ledge surrounding the pit was a fickle thing, treacherously narrow and crumbling in spots. He knew Brenna. She wouldn't see fit to stay put and let Alexander traverse the way. "Keep Brenna off that ledge."

"Dinna talk about me as though I'm not here," she scolded. "Are ye hurt? We were told ye fell prey to a sinkhole."

"A mite banged up, my love," he said, feeling better with every painful hop forward. "I'm finer than fine now that I'm but a moment away from having ye back in my arms." He hitched along the path, hurrying into a swinging gait. Lights flickered up ahead. Three. Maybe more. He didn't care how many as long as one of them belonged to Brenna.

Just as he reached where the tunnel opened into the cavernous concourse with the pit surrounded by the other passageways, the stone beneath his feet crumbled away.

"Magnus!" Brenna's scream shattered the darkness.

His torch spun down into the darkness until it disappeared. Fingers clamped on a thin lip of stone. Body flattened against the rock face. He scrambled for a toe hold. Excruciating pain shot through his right leg as he hooked the toe of his boot onto a whisper of a ledge. Aches and pains could just be damned. He had not come this close to reuniting with his lady love to fail now. With his left boot toe wedged in a vertical crack, he couldn't climb upward, but at least he couldn't fall farther, either.

"He's gone." Brenna's sobs filled the space. "My heart...my soul...he's gone." Her keening wail tore through the tunnels like a wraith rising from the grave.

"Brenna!" It was hard to shout without losing his hold. "Alexander! Over here!"

"He lives! I heard him just over there. Hurry!" shouted a voice he never expected to hear accompanying his wife and the man he considered a brother. 'Twas that wench, Cadha. What in the devil's name was she doing with them?

"I am here!" he called out again, hopes rising as the darkness above him fell away to the soft flickering of torchlight.

"So you are," drawled Commander Barricourt as he none too gently settled his boot on top of Magnus's fingers. "Before you die, you should be commended, Master de Gray. I rarely take such a personal interest in the retrieval of escaped prisoners." The boot pressed harder, slowly crushing his fingers and threatening his hold. Barricourt sniffed, then rumbled out a wicked chuckle. "Such a perfect outcome. Her Majesty and the entirety of England thank you for saving them the trouble and expense of imprisonment and hanging. Your tomb here is ready-made."

"Bastards!" Alexander roared from across the way. "The conniving whoresons followed us, Magnus. Hang tight. I'll kill them with my bare hands and have ye out of there in no time."

"I very much doubt that," Barricourt laughed. "While Cawldrake might appear useless, he is a fine shot." The tip of his boot twisted as though the man turned. "The chief, shoot him now, Cawldrake."

"Nay!" Raithwaite's voice rang out loud and clear. "A shot in here could cause a cave-in for certain."

"I see." Cawldrake hissed out a frustrated huff. "Well, no matter. If the chief moves while I'm toying with this fool, shoot him. I am willing to risk it."

"Leave my husband alone!" Brenna screamed from the other side of the fissure. Magnus wished he could turn and see his precious dear one, but he didn't dare. He would lose his hold for certain.

The boot ground harder atop the fingers of his left hand, twisting with more pressure. "Madam," Barricourt rudely snorted, "and I do use that term with as much disrespect as possible, my little whore. Your husband has been found wanting and is set to descend into his grave forthwith. Any last words for him to take with him?"

"If she doesna have anything to say, I do!" screeched Cadha.

Barricourt exploded with a shrieking cry as he tumbled over Magnus, then disappeared down into the darkness. His screams grew faint, then went silent.

"Commander!" Cawldrake shouted. "Commander!"

Only silence answered.

Magnus struggled to improve his hold, his crushed fingers numb. He had to get up on that ledge. Fast.

"You have killed the commander and made me look the fool!" Cawldrake roared.

"Aye, I killed the man, but ye didna need my help to look the fool." Cadha laughed. "Ye had that task well in hand all by yerself."

Pulling himself up as much as his waning

strength allowed, Magnus peeped over the ledge. Wee Cadha faced off Second Lieutenant Cawldrake, as though ready to battle the man. How had the slip of a girl made it past him to shove the commander over the edge?

"I shall snap your neck with my own hands!" the lieutenant shouted, tossing his pistol aside.

Cadha crouched a bit, swaying from side to side like an adder about to strike. "Come at me, if ye dare."

"Dinna ye touch her!" Brenna warned. "Cadha, lay on the floor and hug the wall, Alexander's coming!"

"Raithwaite, you will stop that man whilst I deal with this bit of rubbish," Cawldrake ordered as he dove for the girl.

Raithwaite jumped for the lieutenant just as the officer caught hold of Cadha. "Leave her be, sir! Leave go of her, I say!"

"Never!" Cawldrake roared.

"Then die with me!" Cadha cackled, lunging backward. She wrapped her arms around his neck while at the same time kicking off the wall and swinging the two of them toward the abyss. Her valiant efforts were rewarded. Cawldrake lost his balance and fell with her into the gaping maw of the pit.

"God bless her and keep her," Raithwaite whispered as he knelt on the edge and stared down into the darkness.

"A little help, Sassenach?" Magnus grunted, his tenuous grip about to fail. As much as his heart ached at Cadha's precious sacrifice, he didn't wish for her to have died in vain.

Both Raithwaite and Alexander took hold of his wrists and pulled, giving him the needed support to climb up onto the ledge. He'd never been so thankful to stretch out across cold, hard rock in his life.

"Thank God Almighty, ye're safe." Brenna crouched at his head, raining kisses on his face and in his hair. "I feared ye dead," she wept as she pulled him into her arms and hugged him to her breast. "I've ne'er been so afraid in my life," she whispered.

Magnus rolled to sit and scooped her into his lap as he leaned back against the cavern wall. He crushed her to his chest, closing his eyes as he breathed her in and held her. "I thank God for ye, m'love." And he meant it. For it had to have been Divine Providence alone that had kept him hanging on that ledge. "Thank God Almighty."

"What say we hie to the keep?" Alexander asked, crouching down beside them. "Can ye walk?"

"I shall be more than happy to help if not," Raithwaite volunteered. "But before we emerge from the caverns, I'm none too sure the keep is the safest place for Master de Gray. Especially not with both the commander and Lieutenant

Cawldrake dead."

"What about yerself, man?" Magnus asked. "Will ye be safe as the sole survivor?"

"I do have an idea," Raithwaite mused with a cocked brow, then his smile beamed brighter than the torchlight. "I truly believe it will work."

"HERE LIES MAGNUS de Gray and his beloved wife Brenna Maxwell de Gray," Brenna read aloud. "It feels strange to visit yer own grave and read the inscription on the headstone."

"Now, now *Renna MacCoinnich*," Magnus said as he hugged her close and brushed a kiss to her cheek. "Magnus and Brenna were dear friends whom we shall never forget, aye?"

"Aye, *Jedidiah MacCoinnich*." She smiled, praying that Archibald Raithwaite's plan worked. From now on, all would know her and Magnus as Jedidiah and Renna MacCoinnich, long-time residents of *Tor Ruadh*. Their old selves had fallen to their deaths in the caverns of Ben Nevis, along with Commander Barricourt, Second Lieutenant George Cawldrake, and poor, misunderstood Cadha. Her gaze fell to the bundle of flowers she held. "I brought these for Cadha. We should pray for her, aye?"

"Aye," Magnus agreed with a quiet reverence, shifting his stance and situating his cane to firmer ground. He couldn't bear the same position for longer than a few moments. His injuries forbade it.

Brenna bent and placed the bough of vibrant pink heather and ivy at the base of Cadha's tombstone.

"It's a shame we didna ken her surname." Brenna kissed two fingers, then pressed them to the marker located beside their own. "I pray the poor lass has, at last, found peace."

"I do, as well." Magnus frowned down at the maid's grave with a sad shake of his head. "From all I gathered about her, she never knew peace in life."

Brenna rose, her heart aching for the troubled girl. Aye, the maid had been a thorn in her side, but toward the end, she felt sure they had developed something akin to friendship. She returned to Magnus's side, walking on his right since he held his cane on his left. "Do ye think Raithwaite will be able to convince them we died?"

"I will consider nothing to the contrary." He gave her a smile, but she wasn't fooled. Concern tightened the corners of his mouth.

They strolled through the peaceful kirkyard, taking advantage of one of the last days of balmy sunshine before bitter winds brought frost to paint the Highlands with the vibrant colors of fall.

If Raithwaite's report, filed for the next commander's review, didn't conceal them, then passage on one of Duncan MacCoinnich's smuggling ships would have to be booked before the seasonal storms made it impossible to reach his island and take up residence with him, his wife, Tilda, and their children.

Magnus flinched, then grunted, his knuckles whitening on the handle of his cane.

"We've walked too much. Yer leg will never heal if ye dinna rest it." She and Gretna had hurt his pride as well as his arse by digging out several shards of stone embedded deep in his right buttock. His right knee, badly wrenched and swollen to twice its normal size, received herbal wraps daily. He would heal, but it would take time, and Brenna feared he might be left with a permanent limp. She turned them toward a secluded bench beside the low wall separating the chapel garden from the rest of the keep. "What say we sit here a while, aye?"

"Ye treat me like a sickly bairn." His growling sounded like a wounded beast, but Brenna heard the relief in his tone.

"And I'll tell Keigan that a ride this afternoon is out of the question." The child would be disappointed, but it would be an excellent lesson in compassion and consideration. "He and the lads can hunt with Merlin instead, aye?" Keigan enjoyed working with the falcon almost as much as he loved riding.

Magnus huffed out a disgusted snort as he lowered himself to the bench. He rested both hands atop the cane planted between his feet and rocked forward and back like a sulking child. "I dinna wish the lad to think me weak." He cut a dark glare in her direction. "It isna fitting, ye ken?"

"Weak? How many times has he made ye repeat yer story of all ye endured in the caves?" She resettled her skirts and met his dark scowl with a stern frown of her own. "Ye're a hero to the lad. Ye heard him retelling yer tales to the other children. He doesna think ye weak." After an unladylike snort, she added, "And I havena heard a peep from the rotten wee scamp about my adventures or all I endured!" She flicked a hand and laughed. "'Tis obvious—only his father's bravery matters!"

"Which reminds me." Magnus sat straighter on the bench and slowly shook his head. "Ye never told me how Cadha came to know so much about the caves. The way ye talked about how she led ye back to the keep made it sound as though the lass knew the maze better than any of us."

Memories of how their odd friendship came to be made Brenna smile. "While I bound her broken arm, she told me she had learned the caves to impress ye. Said that just after ye brought her to *Tor Ruadh,* she heard ye had helped Alexander and Graham map out the tunnels." Her smile faded, wiped away by the hurt in her heart as Cadha's words replayed through her mind. "She said she had no friends, so whenever she finished her duties, she learned the caves to impress ye." Scooting closer, she looped her arm through his and rested her cheek on his shoulder. "She loved ye true, *mo ghràdh.* In her own sad, twisted way."

"Poor lass." Magnus squeezed her hand and pressed a kiss to the top of her head. "I wish Alexander had made the both of ye stay behind whilst he came and looked for me." A gruff sigh left him. "Then she would be alive, and perhaps we couldha freed her from her addled mind and helped her find happiness of her own." He squeezed her hand again. "And if the caves had claimed ye. too, I wouldha released my hold on that ledge and joined ye in death." Shifting on the bench, he wrapped his arm around her shoulders and lifted her face to his. "Ye are my heart, my soul, my all. I canna imagine life without ye."

"And that is exactly why I came with Alexander, my dearest love." She reached up and caressed his cheek, his day's stubble scratching her palm in the best sort of way. "I couldna bear to stay behind and wonder. No one couldha kept me from ye."

"Ye are a verra stubborn woman," he whispered, bending closer.

"Aye. That I am." Time for talk was over. She closed the space between them and kissed the man she loved more than life itself, the man she had once hated but now couldn't imagine a life without. "I love ye," she whispered against his mouth. *"Mo chridhe, m'anam, mo chuid."*

"My heart, my soul, my all," he repeated, throwing the cane to the ground and pulling her into a proper embrace. "And I thank God Almighty for putting ye in my life."

A giggle escaped her, bubbling up between them. "Father William would love to hear ye say that," she said as she tightened her arms around his neck.

With a wicked glint in his eyes, he shifted them around on the backless bench and rolled her off into the softness of the thick ivy between the bench and garden wall. Settling himself atop her, he nuzzled kisses along her throat and jawline. "I shall be sure and repeat it to him when he's christening the bairn we start here in the kirkyard."

"Magnus, we canna do this here!" she scolded in a harsh whisper. "'Tis blasphemy!" She gave him a meaningless push, knowing she had no intention of refusing him. "What if someone sees? And yer hip! What about yer hip and knee?"

"Exercise heals a man's ailments." His warm breath tickled the sensitive skin behind her ear in a way she couldn't resist. "And if anyone sees—they'll know that Jedidiah MacCoinnich loves his wife and canna keep his hands off her." He paused in his nibbling, lifted his head, and gave her a look that made her ache for him even more. "I love ye, *mo ghràdh*, and need ye with a fury."

"'Tis a good thing, my love—for I love ye and need ye just the same."

EPILOGUE

MacCoinnich Chapel
Ben Nevis, Scotland
One Year Later...

"I BELIEVE YE swore to repeat something to me on this blessed day," Father William announced with a superior air.

Magnus cut his eyes over at his cherished lady love. "Ye told him?"

"Of course, I told him," Brenna said, then pressed a tender kiss to the velvety head of their two-week-old son. For the moment, their precious wee bairn slept while bundled in his loving mother's arms. She gave him a wicked smile that made him love her even more. "It was yer oath, remember?"

There was no getting around it. She had snared him well and good with his own words. He didn't know if they had conceived the wee one in the kirkyard that day, but he had promised, and a promise was a promise. Wrapping his left arm around Brenna and his right around Keigan, he hugged his beloved family closer. 'Twas a wonder his heart didn't burst with all the happiness it held. He threw out his chest and spoke loud enough for all gathered for the christening to hear, "I thank God Almighty for bringing this wondrous woman into my life." After a hard swallow to bridle more emotions than he had ever known, he continued, "I am truly blessed. Two healthy sons and a woman I love so much it frightens me. What more could a man ask for?"

Father William beamed at him with a proud smile. "Well said, my son, well said." He held out both hands. "And now, let us welcome this precious child into the house of God."

Magnus tensed. He didn't like anyone other than himself, Brenna, or Keigan holding the babe. He was a mite selfish and protective when it came to his family, and proud to be so.

As soon as Brenna passed the little one to Father William, the baby's bright blue eyes popped open. His tiny forehead wrinkled into a furious scowl, and his face turned red.

Magnus didn't attempt to suppress a smile. He knew what was coming. His new son had a ferocious temper and a squall loud enough to be heard across the Highlands.

"There now, my fine wee one," the holy man said as he settled the squirming babe in the crook of his arm. He scooped up a palmful of holy water, then looked first at Magnus and then Brenna. "The name?"

"Gray Tamhas Maxwell MacCoinnich," Brenna supplied.

The babe kicked and wriggled, fighting his swaddled blankets as he grunted and growled his displeasure.

"He's about to cut loose," Keigan warned. "Ye best hurry so's ye can hand him back and cover yer ears."

"Now, now," Father William swayed from side to side and cooed. "This isna my first christening. I'm good with the bairns. They all love me."

Little Gray chose that moment to argue the fact with an ear-splitting shriek.

The holy man cleared his throat, leaned closer to the baptismal, and wet the child's head. "I baptize thee, Gray Tamhas Maxwell MacCo-innich in the name of the Father, the Son, and the Holy Ghost."

The tiny babe shrieked with rage, squirming and fighting as though the priest had tried to drown him. All those gathered in the chapel laughed and cheered.

"Ye've still got the touch, Father!" Alexander called out from the front pew where he sat surrounded by his family. Catriona elbowed him and fixed him with a stern look.

"Why do ye always pinch them?" Graham shouted, then flinched and grabbed his arm. Mercy lifted her chin, her sightless gaze fixed straight ahead. "Shame on you, saying such a thing in church. Speak of pinching again. I dare you."

Brenna scooped the squalling mite out of Father William's arms and cuddled him to her breast. She crooned and hummed a tuneless song to soothe the furious wee beastie.

Magnus couldn't be prouder nor more content. Two sons, both canny and fierce and braw. A woman who not only stole his heart but also healed his soul. Life couldn't be better.

"I *am* thankful," he said as he hugged his lady love close and smiled down at his yowling son. The babe squeezed his finger without lessening his wails.

"And I, as well." Although weariness shone in her smile, love and contentment sparkled in her eyes. "I love ye, my own."

"I love ye, too, my all."

From the Author

Dear Reader,

And so, the Highland Heroes series comes to an end. The romantic tales of the seven warriors bound by blade and blood.

I hope you've enjoyed meeting the men and women who shaped Clan MacCoinnich and returned it to its glory. I like to think they thrived in their homes at Ben Nevis, Edinburgh, Castle Greyloch, and a hidden island in the Caribbean, then eventually emigrated, fully escaping the final Jacobite uprising and the bloody period in Scotland's history that followed.

In my mind, some MacCoinnichs and their descendants ended up in North Carolina, some in Nova Scotia, and, of course, Duncan's branch populated the Archipelago of El Perdido (fictitious name for a cluster of small islands around Barbados). Wherever they settled, they cherished each other, living and loving their happily ever afters they fought so hard to win.

Thank you for taking the time to get to know my beloved Highland Heroes.

All my best,
Maeve

About the Author

"No one has the power to shatter your dreams unless you give it to them." That's Maeve Greyson's mantra. She and her husband of almost forty years traveled around the world while in the U.S. Air Force. Now, they're settled in rural Kentucky where Maeve writes about her beloved Highlanders and the fearless women who tame them. When she's not plotting her next romantic Scottish tale, she can be found herding cats, grandchildren, and her husband—not necessarily in that order.

SOCIAL MEDIA LINKS:
Website: maevegreyson.com
Facebook Page: AuthorMaeveGreyson
Facebook Group: Maeve's Corner
facebook.com/groups/MaevesCorner
Twitter: @maevegreyson
Instagram: @maevegreyson
Amazon Author Page: amazon.com/Maeve-Greyson/e/B004PE9T9U
BookBub: bookbub.com/authors/maeve-greyson